DARKEST NIGHT

KYLA STONE

PUBLISHING
Paper Moon
Est. 2000
PRESS
Company

Darkest Night

This book is a work of fiction. Any references to historical events, real people, or real places are used fictitiously. Other names, characters, places, and events are products of the author's imagination, and any resemblances to actual events or places or persons, living or dead, is entirely coincidental.

Printed in the United States of America

Cover design by Christian Bentulan

Book formatting by Vellum

First Printed in 2019

ISBN: 978-1-945410-43-7

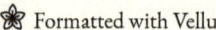 Formatted with Vellum

For my family, because you guys are everything that matters to me in the whole world. I love you.

1
DAKOTA

T he dull gray light drained all the color out of the world.

The rain had finally stopped, but the morning brought a gloomy haze—like the sky itself was in mourning.

Dakota Sloane walked among the corpses. A dark sucking energy surrounded her, the black hole of her grief threatening to pull her under. If she let it out, it might undo her. She pushed it down somewhere deep.

Not now. Not yet.

The humid air clung damply to her skin. Bullfrogs croaked. Cicadas trilled.

Along the shoreline, a tall white bird with a bald black head entered the water—a wood stork. Long black legs, bright pink feet. It swept its bill back and forth in the water, trawling for fish.

And the flies. Hundreds of them buzzed around the bodies.

She was searching for Reuben: Maddox's cousin, the Prophet's son. In her panicked search last night, she'd only been looking for one face.

But Reuben wasn't here, either. Maybe once he and Maddox had kidnapped Eden, they'd decided to cut their losses and flee, abandoning their remaining men to death.

Whatever noble titles they anointed themselves with, in the end, they were still despicable cowards.

She wiped her aching eyes with the back of her arm and kept moving. She had tried to sleep for a few hours last night, but it was pointless. Julio had managed to sleep, but Logan had remained awake beside her, alert and vigilant.

When the sky had lightened from pitch black to indigo, Logan had finally collapsed into a restless slumber, and Dakota had risen to take in the extent of the damage. Maybe she just needed some time to think.

The stench of blood and excrement stung her nostrils. They would have to take care of these bodies, and soon. Maybe burn them. Or roll them into the swamp and let the gators have them.

So many dead. So many young, wasted lives.

Who would these men have been if they hadn't been raised in fear and hatred? If their vulnerable brains hadn't been steeped in superstition and twisted ideology from the moment they were born?

If neither of them had been sucked into the Prophet's vortex of evil, who would she have been? Who would Maddox have been? If Eden, Sister Rosemarie, and the other innocents like little Ruth had never been tangled in the Prophet's web of lies and deceit?

The endless *what-ifs* were pointless. She had no control over the beginning of it all. The only question now was whether she could end it.

The shed doors still hung open, the single bulb shining with dim yellow light. Dakota couldn't bear to look inside—at the shelves full of Ezra's precious stash, all the things he'd so carefully stored away to save them. At the blood staining the floor.

A radio spat static.

She jerked to attention, adrenaline shooting through her veins. Instinctively, she tugged her pistol from her holster and held it in the low ready position, scanning the clearing, searching the shadows deep in the trees.

The static came again.

It hadn't come from out there. It was close by.

More crackling. She tilted her head, following the noise.

She crept to the first body, fallen next to one of the cisterns not five yards from the shed. She nudged it with her toe. The radio attached to the dead body's belt crackled.

She bent, picked it up with her left hand, and dialed up the volume. She pushed the push-to-talk button for a moment but didn't speak.

She knew deep in her gut who it was. Let him go first.

The radio spat and crackled. "Dakota Sloane, is that you?"

"Go to hell, Maddox."

He chuckled dryly. "You always were a scintillating conversationalist."

"You killed Park."

"He got in the way."

"You killed Ezra."

"He had something I wanted."

"No!" Anger bubbled up, obliterating her grief. "I did! You should've come after me instead!"

"Trust me, I wanted to. Eden convinced me otherwise. You should thank her. I'll pass it along."

"Why are you doing this?" She clutched the radio so hard her fingers ached. "Jacob hated you. Your father despises you. Eden is the one who loves you. And you kidnapped her, killed her friends, and took her back to the monster who wants to enslave her!"

"I saved her!" he shouted. "I'm saving her soul."

"You're too smart to spout that crap. Or to believe it."

"I know what's best for her. I know what's best for you." He was quiet for a moment. "You love me, Dakota. You *need* me."

"I hate you," she forced out. "I hate you with every fiber of my being."

He laughed darkly. "You wish you did. But let's be honest. You don't. You can't. There's too much between us."

She swallowed the lump in her throat. "I do hate you."

"I wish I could hate you, too. I wish I could. But for some damn reason, I can't. Do you know that? Can you understand? I think you do. I think you know exactly what that feels like."

She did know. Because once upon a time, Maddox was all she had. He was the lifeline that kept her sane in the sadistic, insane world of the River Grass Compound, where a girl could be beaten and branded just for reading.

In that place, she'd been weak, small, and invisible.

Only Maddox saw her. Only Maddox made her grim existence bearable with his cynical attitude, sarcastic jokes, and that sly, mocking grin of his.

Out on the boat, exploring the Glades, they'd escaped the harsh rules and restrictions shoved down their throats, the constant threat of violence, the shame and humiliation disguised as religion.

She had loved him for it.

Then he changed. To gain the approval of his father, he'd turned on her. Turned into whatever he was now. Cruel, ruthless, and vengeful.

She hated him. She did. And yet, there was still that thread of the past that connected them, a slender but indestructible filament that she couldn't sever, no matter how much she wished she could.

"You and I aren't that different."

"We're nothing alike," she spat into the mouthpiece, wanting to crush it into pieces, imagining it was Maddox's windpipe instead of a stupid radio. "You're insane."

"You only wish that I was insane. You hate that you understand me better than you understand yourself."

She did hate it. She hated it even more that he was right. "Your father abused you. He forced you to abuse me, taught you it was good."

He hesitated. "You clearly don't understand the concept of mercy."

The scars on her back burned like they were on fire. "What they did to us wasn't mercy. It was torture. Once upon a time, you knew that."

"You sound bitter, Dakota. Are you bitter that you lost to me?"

"I haven't lost yet."

"No?" He gave a mirthless laugh. "It sure looks that way from here."

"You can still do the right thing, Maddox," she said. "You can still turn this around. Let her go."

"I won't." The arrogant confidence in his voice faltered—for just a second, just a little, but it was there. She felt it as much as heard it. "I don't have a choice."

"You clearly don't understand the concept of choice."

He snorted. "I always did like that about you. You were the only one in the whole damn compound with the guts to speak your mind."

She turned back toward the shed, forced herself to stare through the opened doors to the dark stain in the center of the cement floor, the blood almost black in the light.

She'd thought if she gave everything, it would be enough. It wasn't.

Park was dead. Ezra was dead. Eden was gone.

Nothing would bring Ezra back. She'd failed him. She'd thought she was strong enough, tough enough to defeat whatever came at them.

How wrong she was.

She trembled with anger, with sorrow, with a pain so deep it was endless. She could fall forever and ever and never strike the bottom of her grief.

But the anger was there, too. A fierce, smoldering rage.

She wasn't finished yet. She wasn't dead. She thought she'd given everything, but she was wrong about that, too.

There was always more. As long as she was alive, as long as

she still had breath in her lungs and blood in her veins, there was more she could give.

A great flock of birds flew beneath the low scudding clouds shrouding the bruised sky. They were fleeing ahead of the hurricane. They were the smart ones.

She watched them soar arrow-straight, cawing hoarsely to each other, until they vanished over the horizon.

The early morning air was wet and suffocating. Her footsteps squelched in the mud as she turned away from the shed and headed back toward the cabin.

She was done with this. Done with him. Done with this manipulative cat-and-mouse game he wanted to play.

She didn't want to play. She wanted to burn everything to the ground.

Dakota raised the radio to her lips one final time. "I am coming for you, Maddox. I'm going to kill your father. I'm going to kill the Prophet. And then, I'm going to kill you."

After Logan awoke an hour later, he and Dakota and Julio slumped at the kitchen table, staring listlessly at each other until Julio insisted that they needed to eat something. They were all drawn and haggard from the previous night's events.

They forced themselves to down a few granola bars and electrolyte drinks from Ezra's pantry, though no one had an appetite. Dakota felt the energy slowly returning to her exhausted limbs. The calories did them all good, but no amount of food could fix a broken heart.

"How are you feeling, Dakota?" Julio asked.

Her gaze slowly focused on Julio, his kind face, his features tight with apprehension and sorrow. His eyes were puffy and bloodshot. Globs of dark red stained his filthy shirt. Dried blood clung to his ear and neck.

She sucked in her breath. In the shock of Ezra's death, she'd forgotten about everything else. Her mind was still numb and fuzzy, her thoughts filled with cotton.

She couldn't forget about the living. They needed her, too. They needed each other now.

"We have to take care of that ear," she said.

"I'm fine—"

"No, you aren't. It could get infected. We can't wait any longer."

Julio grimaced. "You're as bad as Shay."

"I'll take that as a compliment." She pulled gauze, iodine, and antibiotic ointment out of one of the upper cupboards. Three bullet holes had punctured the door, the wood splintered, flakes of paint fluttering to the counter.

She froze, staring unblinking at the holes. The thunderous roaring of gunshots and an awful, endless scream echoed in her mind. Her heart thudded in her chest, her ears ringing.

In an instant, she was right back in the middle of the battle, the fear and anxiety clutching at her, lost in the moment-by-moment fight for survival.

If only she'd refused to allow Eden to flee to the shed. If only she'd checked on them earlier. If only she'd drilled Maddox in the skull with a bullet when Park tried so desperately to offer her a distraction.

She'd failed. She'd failed Park, Eden, and Ezra.

The *what-ifs* were paralyzing. If she focused on those destructive thoughts, she'd never leave Ezra's cabin again. She forced herself to snap out of it, to move.

Her hands trembled as she brought the supplies back to Julio. She examined the wound after she'd irrigated it with clean water, like Shay had taught them.

She wished for the hundredth time that Shay was here. That Ezra was still alive.

"Mother Mary and Joseph," Julio muttered, wincing. "It hurts."

"At least it's not bleeding anymore. I think you can escape stitches, but it's gonna leave a wonky scar."

He gave her a pained smile. "Scars are sexy, or so I've been told."

It was Julio who swept up the cabin and scrubbed it down, filling several industrial-sized garbage bags with debris, shards of glass, splinters of wood, and shell casings. He wouldn't let Dakota help.

When she tried to argue, he sent her outside to take care of the bodies. It was an ugly job, but she'd rather dispose of a thousand corpses than try to pick up the pieces of her shattered home.

Somehow, Julio knew that.

Logan joined her. They worked in near silence. They didn't speak. They didn't need to.

Nearly choking against the fetid stench, she and Logan confiscated almost two dozen M4 carbines, as many pistols and tactical knives, and plenty of spare ammo from the dead Shepherds.

They collected NV goggles, tactical vests with bulletproof plates, and radios with headsets. The Shepherds had switched to a different frequency, but they could use the earpieces with their own communication gear.

"We should strip their ACUs," Logan said. "The headshots still have uniforms in good shape. You never know when we might need them."

"Good idea."

"Look for the ones who haven't soiled themselves. Some of these guys are pretty ripe."

After they'd finished gathering everything they wanted from the bodies, they piled the weapons and gear in two wheelbarrows and hauled it back to the cabin, taking a few trips.

Next, they disposed of the corpses. Dressed in garden gloves, N95 masks, and ponchos from Ezra's stash, Logan and Dakota rolled each body into a tarp, wrapped them up, and used the wheelbarrows and ropes to cart them out to the dock.

They didn't want to leave the corpses in the shallow water so close to Ezra's property, so they took the bodies out in the fishing boat, three or four at a time, and dumped them near a gator hole. The work was back-breaking, disgusting, and reeked worse than anything she'd ever smelled.

Afterward, they each took a long shower. The generator and solar panels only created so much hot water, so Logan insisted Dakota go first.

She stood in Ezra's small white shower stall and washed off the grime, soot, and speckles and streaks of Ezra's blood. She scrubbed every inch of her flesh with a rough kitchen sponge, rubbing until her skin turned bright red. It felt like the foul particles still clung to her skin.

Her fingernails were long and jagged, a few of them broken. Blood curved in little half-moons beneath her nails. She seized the slippery bar of soap and raked it across her fingertips again and again, but it wasn't enough.

She still wasn't clean. Maybe she'd never be clean again.

3
DAKOTA

There wasn't a funeral. Julio offered, but he wasn't a priest, and Ezra wouldn't have wanted a religious ceremony anyway.

Logan found stacks of dry firewood in one of the outbuildings, along with long sections of a cypress tree Ezra was planning to chop for firewood later. But later never came.

She swallowed back the tightness in her throat and used the wheelbarrow to lug the wood down to the picnic table beneath the live oak tree. Dakota picked a spot on the opposite side, near the tree but within sight of the water and the tall, rustling sawgrass spreading as far as the eye could see.

It was as good a spot as anywhere.

Together, she and Logan stacked the wood, alternating their orientation layer by layer until it reached a height of around three feet. They added smaller branches, twigs, and other kindling to the center.

Once the pyre was ready, they trudged back to the house for the body.

"Dakota," Julio said, too gently. Like he thought she was too fragile for this. "Are you sure you want to—"

She brushed him off. She needed to do this. All of it. "I'm fine."

Logan's mouth was a grim line, but he didn't say anything. He took the head and shoulders, Dakota the feet. They carried him, still carefully wrapped in the blanket. Julio shuffled behind them, carrying a jerrycan full of gasoline.

Ezra seemed lighter somehow in death. She'd expected his body to be incredibly heavy, an enormous burden, but it wasn't. The sturdy, broad-shouldered, larger-than-life man took up so much more space in her memories.

Now, he was fragile, insubstantial, already slipping away. How long until he faded from her memories, too?

She made herself stop thinking. The pain and grief were there, crouching behind the iron wall of her will. She couldn't let herself keep feeling it.

Not now. Not until this was over. Not until she'd ended it.

Logan helped her position the body in the center of the pyre. She took the jerrycan and poured on the gasoline. The clear liquid soaked into the blanket—some ancient dusky blue thing Ezra had probably had forever, since long before his wife died. The gasoline splashed across the wood, dripping down, slowly drenching each piece.

The harsh stench of the gas filled her nostrils and stung her eyes. She took a few steps back, set down the empty jerrycan. Julio handed her a box of matches. He put his hand on her shoulder. His expression was strained, his pallor ashen, dark circles beneath his eyes.

She nodded. Lit the match, watched the fire waver for a moment. She stared at it blindly as the tiny flame burned the matchstick black, eating the wood until it reached her fingers.

Pain seared her fingertips. She dropped the match. She ground it out in the grass with her boot heel.

Logan and Julio stood on either side of her. No one spoke.

She lit another match. Then a third, each time letting it burn down to her fingers.

The Everglades were eerily silent. No crickets trilling, no frogs singing to each other. No birds twittering and chirping.

Above the sea of sawgrass, the sky was gray as a shroud.

Pressure built behind her eyes, her throat too tight to breathe properly, to swallow. An aching numbness started in her belly and spread into her chest, her arms, her legs.

She held the fourth match, unlit, between her fingers.

This had to mean something. There had to be a purpose to all this death and suffering. In Park's death. In *Ezra*'s death. She couldn't bear it if this was all meaningless, the universe's idea of a sick joke.

She refused to believe it was meaningless.

Pain meant nothing. The anguish wrenching her heart into pieces meant nothing.

Only action meant something.

She had to get Eden back. If she couldn't, then Ezra died for nothing. Then they all suffered and lost *for nothing*.

And that was unacceptable.

Dakota struck the fourth match.

She tossed it on the pyre and watched the flames leap to life, smoke pouring into the sky.

4

LOGAN

Once the pyre was blazing, Julio turned to Logan. "I noticed a couple of the solar panels aren't working. I think a few bullets did some damage. I'm gonna go up on the roof and see if I can repair them."

Logan nodded. He watched Julio trudge back toward the cabin, his shoulders hunched, head down. He glanced back toward Dakota. She gazed intently at the crackling fire, her back stiff, her hands balled into fists at her sides, her eyes glassy.

His heart ached to see her so anguished, but he couldn't do a damn thing about it. It seemed wrong somehow to stay here. It felt like he was invading her privacy, intruding on her sorrow. She needed to grieve in peace. "I'll go, too."

"No!" She sucked in a ragged breath. "I mean, I'd like you to stay. If you want to."

"I want to."

They stood side by side, less than a foot apart. He felt her presence vibrating through every inch of him. The heat from the flames warmed his face and arms. Together, they watched Ezra's body burn.

"Dakota, I'm truly sorry. I—I failed him."

"You did your best."

He stared at the fire. He could still hear the thunder of gunfire, could feel the dust roiling all around him, splinters flying as bullets roared past his head. The muscles in his neck, back, and shoulders were sore from the constant tension.

His nerves were on a hair-trigger, his finger curling instinctively, robotically, like he was still squeezing the trigger, over and over. "If I could do it over again, I would. I could've saved him. If I was faster. If I'd taken a second to aim more accurately..."

So many mistakes. How easily things could've ended differently. But tunnel vision was real. In the heat of battle, the mind was focused on nothing but survival. Kill or be killed.

It was easy to pick apart every decision afterward, when things were calm and orderly again, when you weren't in the grip of gut-wrenching panic and blinding terror.

But it didn't matter how many times he reminded himself; the guilt and self-recrimination wouldn't fade.

"You did everything you could. I know that." She clenched her jaw. "What matters now is what happens next."

She returned her attention to the pyre. Several long minutes passed, silent but for the crackle and pop of the flames.

The fire danced higher and higher, its orange, shimmering tongues singeing the branches of the live oak. Swaths of Spanish moss crinkled black and disintegrated into ash.

"Ezra was a difficult man to love," she said softly. "He never made things easy. But he was there when no one else was. He saved us. Eden would've died without him. Probably, we both would've. He saved us, in more ways than one."

"I know how much he meant to you."

She turned to face him. Her eyes were wide and shiny, her mouth quivering. They stood there looking at each other, the foot of space between them pulsing with electricity.

She leaned in, rested her hands on his forearms, spread her fingers over his tattoos. She ran her fingertips lightly over his barbed-wire Latin inscription, sending jolts of electricity through every inch of him.

He wrapped his arms around her and pulled her close. She stiffened. He felt her heart thudding like a wild thing against his chest.

For a terrible moment, he thought she would pull away. That no matter what they'd been through together, she still wouldn't let him in.

The tension in her body released. She slumped against him; her cheek pressed against his chest, shaking with silent sobs.

Grief was a world unto itself. It came slowly and then all at once, pummeling you again and again, receding for a time—only to surprise you with a tidal wave that knocked you right back on your ass.

He'd fight a hundred Shepherd thugs bare-handed if it would spare her this. Ezra wasn't important to Logan, but he was to Dakota. And for that, he grieved with her, felt her pain throbbing inside his own chest.

He couldn't do a damn thing for her but this, so he did it as well as he could. "I'm right here. I'm here."

She wept, releasing her grief, sorrow, and loss into the world. He simply held her.

5
EDEN

E den was home again. She didn't want to be.

Last night, she'd watched in horror as the Shepherds marched on the cabin. She'd watched Maddox whirl, lift the gun, and shoot Park in the head. Then bullets exploded all around her.

Park was dead. The Shepherds had shot Ezra in the chest. She'd crouched beside him, helpless and terrified, as the blood leaked from his body with every ragged gasp and shallow beat of his heart.

When she'd heard Maddox's voice outside the safety of the shed, she'd known what she had to do. If she stayed inside that shed, Ezra would bleed out and die right in front of her.

Maddox would continue killing the people she loved, and he wouldn't stop until he had Eden.

Huddled in the shed, weeping as she clutched Ezra's hand, she had made a choice. No one else would die because of her.

She didn't know for sure whether Maddox would uphold his end of the bargain. But she had nothing else, no other bargaining chips, no power or authority to do a thing to protect her friends.

Only this.

Her heart hammering in her throat, she'd said a prayer. Then she opened the door to whatever fate awaited her.

She still didn't know whether Ezra had made it, whether her surrender had given Dakota and Haasi the precious minutes to save him, if it was even possible. Maybe she would never know. She prayed it was worth it.

Maddox had brought her directly to their family cabin where her father, Solomon Cage, waited. At first, he seemed delighted, pulling her into his arms and stroking her matted curls. He pushed her back by her shoulders and took a good hard look at her.

His eyes narrowed in alarm when he saw the thick, wormy scar arcing across her throat. "What is this?"

Her cheeks burned with embarrassment and shame. Instinctively, she covered the ugly scar with her hands. She barely heard Maddox and her father as they argued, her father's voice rising in indignation and anger, Maddox shouting right back.

"After three years trapped among the perverse and wicked heathens of Miami, you're lucky she's even alive," Maddox snapped. "She's still pure. Isn't that what you wanted?"

That finally softened him. He ordered her bathed, scrubbed, and brushed to within an inch of her life. Her stepmother, Sister Hannah, barely spoke or even looked at her.

Sister Hannah had never shown her love or affection—her long absence hadn't changed that. If anything, the woman watched her with barely restrained distaste and a hostile wariness, as if she expected a demon to pop out of Eden at any moment.

Eden dressed in the familiar long, itchy skirt and a white short-sleeved blouse that buttoned up to the base of her throat. Her stepmother brushed her curls with hard, tugging strokes until they were smooth and golden, and left them loose around her shoulders.

When her father returned, he handed her a wide blue satin

ribbon. "Wrap that around your neck and cover that repulsive thing."

She obeyed, her hands trembling.

Her father glared at her, his eyes flashing. "Maddox tells me you're mute?"

She kept her head bowed, her eyes stinging. Three years ago, she would've been a blubbering mess. Now, she refused to let him see her cry.

"Are you stupid, too?"

"Maybe it'll work out better," Maddox said coyly from behind her. "She can't whine and complain like the other wives, now can she?"

Her father snorted. "Maybe so. Maybe God has offered us a blessing in disguise."

She bit her lip. *Don't cry. Don't cry.*

Her father gripped her jaw with one hand and tilted her chin up, examining her like he might examine his livestock for defects. "At least she still has her looks. You're lucky that the Prophet is so compassionate and understanding. He could've rejected you. He could've banished our family because of this."

She waited stiffly for him to be done with her. She wanted to wriggle away from his shrewd, piercing gaze, but she couldn't. His hand still gripped her jaw so hard she felt his nails digging into her cheeks.

"Don't you see how important you are? You were set aside as a child. You were chosen. You represent the remnant, the holy church of God, perfect and unblemished." His gaze dropped to the blue ribbon around her neck. His mouth tightened in revulsion. "That girl—we should never have taken her in. A devil in our very midst. She is the harlot Jezebel. Was. It doesn't matter now. We have you back. You are the bride, prophecy fulfilled. And the greatest honor for our family."

What do you mean, 'was'? Eden signed. *Is Dakota okay? What happened to her?*

But of course, they couldn't understand her. No one bothered to try.

Her father must have seen something he didn't like in her eyes. He released her chin, but seized her hand, and squeezed until her bones felt like they might crack.

A raw, hoarse gasp tore from her lungs. She bit her lip to keep the tears at bay.

"You may have engaged in heretical behavior out there, daughter of mine." He leaned in so close she felt his breath on her cheeks, caught the faint scent of the lemony lye soap her stepmother made from scratch. "Anything you did was the fault of that Jezebel who stole you from us. But you've returned to the fold. Blasphemy in any form shall not be tolerated. Whatever you do, do not shame this family!"

She nodded frantically, just wanting the grinding pain to stop. Her gaze slid from her father's face to Maddox. But if she expected help from her brother, she wasn't going to find it.

Maddox only smiled, his eyes cold and distant. "When is the wedding, Father?"

Her father released her hand and wiped his palm on his pantleg. "Today."

She stumbled back, clutching her aching fingers to her chest. A wave of dizziness lurched through her.

Did she hear correctly? Today? Already? She should've had at least a few days to prepare herself for what lay ahead. She wasn't ready.

"The Prophet announced the service this morning. It'll happen after the regular worship service in only a few hours. There's no time to waste. Everyone is required to attend." He turned to Maddox, the displeasure in his expression unchanged. "As for you, Maddox, you'll be honored as the Prophet's new Chosen."

Maddox bowed his head, his smile widening.

Her father strode toward the door. Before he opened it, he

paused. "We have a lot of work to do. I expect each of you to do your part. The storm the Prophet prophesied—it's coming."

6

EDEN

Eden waited in quiet panic, her whole body thrumming with foreboding. Maddox stood beside her and watched with sly amusement. They were the only ones in the elders' room, the back room located behind the sanctuary in the chapel.

The elder's room was small, simply furnished with a few chairs and a narrow cabinet with a Bible laid open on the top shelf. A painting of the Prophet, his face glowing with God's holy favor, hung above it. Neatly folded white robes sat on the lower shelves, along with a couple of totes to stash a person's regular clothes.

One of the robes was for her; the other, for Maddox. They would both be presented at the service less than an hour from now. They were supposed to be preparing themselves in prayer and supplication.

But Eden couldn't pray. She was far too anxious.

Maddox patted Eden's shoulder. "You were brave, Eden. Honestly, I didn't think you were capable of it. I'm impressed."

She shrank back from him.

He clucked his tongue in disapproval. "We're on the same side now. There's no need to be afraid of me. We're going to work together, you and me. You do your duty to please the

Prophet while I work my way into his good graces. You heard our father. You're our family's ticket."

She shook her head. She didn't want to be her family's ticket. And she certainly didn't want to be anything to the Prophet. Just the thought made her dizzy with trepidation.

"Everything is going to be fine now." Maddox's smile didn't reach his eyes. His face was gaunt, his skin red and peeling, fading blisters pocking his thin hard lips. Even still, he was roughly handsome, his body lean and rangy as a mountain lion, his every movement radiating strength, power—and danger.

I will do what I promised, she signed. *What about Dakota?*

He scowled and pointed at the small spiralbound notebook and stubby pencil in her hands. "Use your words."

She stabbed the pencil into the paper, nearly tearing it in her haste. *You promised not to hurt Dakota. You promised me.*

He cocked his brows. "Have I ever not been a man of my word? I'm many things, sweet sister, but a liar isn't one of them."

Eden wasn't sure she agreed. Her stomach twisted with apprehension. *Tell me the truth.*

He leaned forward, his eyes intense and glassy with fever. "I'm about to become one of the Chosen, God's own soldier. I am nothing if not honorable. And merciful."

Dakota is safe? She underlined the word *safe* and held the notebook up.

"She is, but you can't tell our father that. I told him she was dead. It's the only way to keep him from attacking them again. Do you understand?"

She nodded tightly, slightly relieved but not enough. *What about Reuben?*

"Don't worry about him. When I sent him with you, I told him I'd go back and finish them. But those pain-in-the-ass Collier brothers showed up. Reuben believes the threat is eliminated, that's all that matters. For now."

She raised her eyebrows.

Maddox's smile turned sly. "I'm not naïve enough to believe

that Dakota will abide by our little agreement. She's far less noble than I am, far more conniving. She accused me of playing games. Well, the game continues, and she'll play it whether she wants to or not."

Eden studied his face, searching for clues. He was boasting, preening, cocky and overconfident as usual. There was a flicker of something else in his eyes, a shadow behind the arrogant smile.

She wasn't naïve enough to believe he'd spared Dakota solely because Eden demanded it in their exchange. She'd been desperate for a way out, any way out—but now that she was here, now that the panic and terror had subsided from a thunderous roar to a low disquieting hum, she could think more clearly.

Maddox wanted revenge. He wanted more than just to get Eden back—he wanted Dakota's head on a pike, and all their friends dead.

That shadow flickered behind his eyes again.

The realization hit her like a shock of ice-cold water. It seemed impossible. But it was true.

Maddox was afraid. He feared Dakota.

Dakota wasn't the helpless girl he'd known before the outside world toughened her up, before Ezra taught her to fight, to shoot, to kill.

Eden saw it playing out in his head. The battle had been fierce and more difficult than he'd anticipated. Half of his men were killed before they'd gotten close to breaching the cabin.

Her brother had never cared much for playing by the rules. The fact that others were dying on his command wouldn't even faze him. He saw an opportunity to snatch Eden without risk to himself, and he took it.

But if he returned and admitted the job wasn't finished, the Prophet would send more men to end it. Wave after wave, until it was finished. Dakota would be dead, but at the same time,

Maddox would prove his own inadequacy, earning the eternal disdain of both their father and the Prophet.

Instead, he'd lied. Did that mean it was finally over? Would Dakota let this fragile truce stand?

Eden closed her eyes. For Dakota's sake, she hoped she would. All Eden wanted to do was end the fighting and the death. Eden wanted her to be happy, to live her life, to be safe. She wanted it more than anything else. Why couldn't Dakota see that?

"She'll come for you," Maddox said, "but when she does, it'll be too late."

Eden's eyes snapped open. Dread chewed at her insides; every nerve was strung taut. She started to sign, then sighed in frustration and lifted her notebook. *Why?*

Maddox smirked. "They didn't tell you, did they? Poor Eden. Always in the dark."

WHY????

"The Prophet is taking you away to one of his hideouts to put you with the other wives or something. I don't know for sure. This one isn't safe anymore for a wife of the Prophet. Better say your goodbyes now, Eden."

Her heart stopped beating. *When?*

Maddox gave her a pitying look. "Tomorrow. At dawn."

7
MADDOX

Maddox shifted uncomfortably on the hard wooden seat. He was supposed to stay in the elder's room until summoned. He'd undressed as directed, removing everything but his underwear—his tunic and slacks, his belt, his radio, and his knife and pistol—before donning a pure white robe.

Anticipation and nausea roiled in his gut. He ignored it.

Eden had already been called to the pulpit. The ceremony would be simple yet elegant, a holy rite more than a marriage. She wasn't a girl anymore but a divine symbol of the church itself.

He'd traded a protracted battle for Eden that would have cost more time and more lives for revenge. He'd told his father and the Prophet that everyone else was dead, including the old man.

He'd accomplished everything he'd set out to do—well, almost everything. It was good enough. He'd done far more than Jacob ever had. His brother had been all talk, no action.

He imagined the approval shining in his father's eyes. The moment it would all be worth it.

One of the Chosen—Aaron Hill—stuck his head in the room. "It's time."

Maddox rose, smoothed his pure white robe, and headed for the door. Standing tall, he walked up the three steps to the wooden stage and took his place next to the Prophet himself.

His sister, now the Prophet's bride, stepped back so he could have this moment in the spotlight. Eden understood the momentousness of this occasion. Of course, she did.

He tried to catch her eye to show his gratitude, but she kept her head down, her hands folded demurely in front of her stomach.

The Prophet beamed at him, eyes shining. "Here on this most auspicious day, we are blessed beyond measure, for God has chosen another soldier for His army. Maddox Cage, son of Solomon Cage. Come, my son, rise and take your place at my side!"

A chorus of hearty *amens* sounded from the pews.

Every seat was filled. Dozens crammed into the back and stood in the side aisles. The Prophet had commanded the attendance of every soul, from infants and children to husbands and wives to the Chosen Shepherds. All told, almost one hundred and fifty people were present.

It would've been more with the twenty-six Shepherds Dakota and her people had slain over the last week. Maddox gritted his teeth and forced a placid smile. Now wasn't the time to think about that.

Sister Hannah, his stepmother, sat beside his father, her lips pursed and eyes narrowed like she was sucking on a lemon. The woman was never happy. Today was no different.

He was sure the only joy she felt at Eden's return was the satisfaction of her family's influence cemented and strengthened. His greedy father wasn't any better.

Maddox looked away from them. He wouldn't let his family ruin this honor. Today was *his* day, the day he'd longed for, bled and fought and suffered for.

He'd walked through the literal hell of Miami, endured

misery and destruction, burnt flesh and radiation sickness—all for this.

To become a Chosen. To finally become one of *them*.

There was no way in hell he'd let anyone steal that from him.

A woman appeared from a wooden door on the opposite side of the sanctuary. She walked across the front aisle beside the dais, her head bowed in meek reverence, a wooden bowl filled with a crimson liquid held gently in both hands.

She mounted the steps and stood before the Prophet, waiting. The Prophet dipped his finger in the fresh blood and turned to Maddox. "With the blood of the lamb, we mark you as Chosen of Christ Jesus Himself, hand-selected to carry out His divine will, no matter the cost or sacrifice. For as Paul said, we willingly die daily to this world in order to gain divine immortality."

"I willingly die," Maddox said, repeating the holy rites.

"Maddox Cage, son of Solomon Cage, do you accept this most holy honor?"

"I accept the blood."

The Prophet swiped the blood across Maddox's forehead. It was still warm, the lamb freshly slaughtered. Blood dripped into his eyebrows as he took the Prophet's hand and kissed it.

The congregation roared their approval.

It was done. Maddox had finally earned his place. He'd walked through Hell and passed every test demanded of him.

He was just as good as Jacob now. He was *better*.

Maddox looked down at his father expectantly, his chest swelling with pride and satisfaction.

Solomon Cage wasn't even looking at his son. He was leaning forward, whispering urgently to one of the men sitting in the pew in front of him. He sat back, put his arm around his wife's shoulder, and gazed up at the platform, a broad smile on his face.

His eyes were on Eden and the Prophet. Not Maddox.

Something collapsed inside his chest.

Maddox's heart thudded against his ribs. His palms were damp. The drying blood prickled his skin. Anger throbbed with his pulse.

To hell with his father. He didn't need his approval anymore. He was his own man. A Chosen among the chosen.

At the edge of the dais, Aaron gestured at him. Numbly, mechanically, Maddox obeyed, moving to the left, still on the dais but no longer in the spotlight. His moment to shine was already over.

The woman took her bowl of blood and left the sanctuary. The Prophet motioned for Eden, who stepped forward and took her place beside him.

He waited to be transformed, for it all to *mean* something.

It didn't come.

8

MADDOX

M addox remained on the dais but shunted off to the side. His arms hung rigid at his sides. His hands curled into fists. A bitter, gut-wrenching disappointment churned in his belly, but his stony expression gave nothing away.

The Prophet raised his arms, smiling indulgently. "My children, I have called you here today for a very important reason. God has given my precious bride to me as a token, as a sign of His grace for all of us, for the new world that we are creating. Even her name bespeaks of her most critical role. She is our symbol, for just as I have chosen her, so God has chosen us!"

A chorus of "Amens" from the crowd. Their eyes were glassy as they gazed up at the Prophet, adoring him, worshiping him.

"As the Children of Israel didn't step foot in the promised land until they'd vanquished every enemy of God, so we have been called to destroy our enemies. That time is at hand! Just as in the days of Sodom and Gomorrah, God has called His chosen to rain fire down upon our enemies!"

His voice was resonant and powerful, almost hypnotic. "America is God's country. America is His shining flag of truth. But it has become corrupted and evil, bloated and fat with laziness and gluttony.

"But do not weep for America, my children! God has called us to tear it down so we can begin anew! For America has fallen to its knees, but God Himself will pull her to her feet and set her on the righteous path of The Way. She will be stronger than ever, and with God's blessing, America will become a shining beacon of wealth, prosperity, and justice to the entire world! No threat will stand against our country once we take our places at God's right hand!"

The Prophet's eyes burned with fevered zeal. "My people, Shepherds of Mercy, we have done it! Even as I speak, our glory is at hand! America is our Sodom, the United States our Gomorrah! We have destroyed the wicked cities, just as God commanded us. As Revelation eighteen commands, Babylon has fallen!"

Beside Maddox, Eden stiffened.

"Miami is burning. Los Angeles is burning. New York City is burning!"

The people gazed up at the Prophet, mouths hanging open in astonishment, eyes wide. A few women glanced at each other, confused, maybe a little apprehensive. The children just stared. The names of the cities meant nothing to them; they'd never left the compound in their lives.

Maddox glanced down at his sister. She looked as stunned as the rest of them. The tendons in her neck stood out. Her face went pale as she twisted handfuls of her white gown in her fists.

She hadn't known.

"New Orleans. Houston. Norfolk. Atlanta!"

"Amen!" someone shouted from the crowd.

"Washington D.C., the hotbed of corruption and evil, is burning!"

Cheers, hallelujahs, and cries of "Blessings!" and "Praise God!" rose all around him.

For the Lord shall execute judgment by fire...

Maddox stared straight ahead, his vision going blurry. Fragments of memories crashed through his mind. The immense cloud as it boiled above downtown Miami, monstrous and raging, a violent orange-red mass blotting out the sky itself.

The blackened steel skeletons of the skyscrapers, warped and bent, jutting into the sky like broken teeth. Block after block of destroyed buildings, twisted wrecks of mangled girders, and jagged mounds of rubble.

The thick, ashy air clogging his throat, the singed stench clotting his nostrils. The fine, sand-like particles swirling from the darkened sky like poisonous snow. The survivors staggering through the haze like ghosts, filmed in ash and soot, their skin peeling off their bones.

And the bodies. Bodies broken and crushed and charred, missing legs or arms, pulverized beneath fallen roofs and crushed cars. Bodies vaporized instantly, leaving behind only their sooty shadows. Bodies charred where they stood, like coal statues. Bodies burnt and ravaged beyond recognition—no longer human.

He shook his head, forcing himself back to the present. Everything seemed dull and distant. His ears were ringing. Everything he'd sacrificed. Everything he'd endured.

He stared at the people before him and saw only corpses.

Their bodies blackened from head to foot, skin melted, hair completely burnt off, their clothes rags. Their faces were frozen rictuses of agony—white bulging eyes, mouths gaping like cavernous pits.

This was the hellfire the Prophet had wrought. These were the dead left behind in Miami, in New York City, in every other targeted city. The ghosts of the dead had followed him here. Haunting him. Hunting him.

His veins went ice-cold. He closed his eyes, opened them, blinked rapidly.

The terrible images faded. The people were just people, still alive, fragile creatures of mere flesh, bone, and blood.

"We destroyed their ports!" the Prophet shouted, his voice rising above the tumult. "We destroyed their skyscrapers, their monuments to sin. We tore down their polluted cities and poisoned their air!"

More cheers. Men, women, and children raised their hands and swayed their arms in the air. Tears tracked down the cheeks of some of them—not tears of sorrow, but tears of jubilation.

Gone were the startled looks, the apprehension. Whatever they'd initially felt upon hearing of the destruction of their fellow countrymen had been eradicated by the Prophet's powerful, mesmerizing words.

"The destruction of the wicked makes the soil fertile for the planting of the New Eden!" the Prophet roared. "Now is the time of testing! Now you will prove your final allegiance to God. The battle is not yet won. The storm is coming! The black clouds are already forming upon the horizon. The wicked are coming for you, body and soul! Behold, they are already at the doorstep!"

The Prophet paused to mop his brow, that fervent, fevered passion in his face as he gripped the pulpit, features rigid and drenched in sweat, eyes bulging. "Sacrifices will be required! Just as our Savior sacrificed his very life, just as the martyrs of the early church gladly laid down their lives as gifts of purest offerings to prove their devotion. God shall call for the same from you, his Chosen!"

"We're ready!" a woman cried. "Jesus, take us now!"

"God has sent me a precious gift. A vision of our glorious future! You shall all be rewarded for your faithfulness. Every man, woman, and child. The glory of God will reveal Himself to us soon, as he promised! Hallelujah!"

"Hallelujah!" The people lifted their faces in adoration and worship, their expressions ecstatic, exultant. They shouted in delight, singing jubilant hymns, their eyes shining, skin almost glowing, so transcendent was their joy.

Maddox stared down at them. Jealousy burned in his gut. How simple they were. How easily swayed. How pure their devotion.

They were unwavering in their conviction, absolute in their faith. He saw no flicker of doubt or disbelief, no uncertainty, unease, or confusion.

They suffered none of his own cynicism, knew nothing of the qualms, misgivings, and suspicion that plagued him.

They weren't haunted by the charred and mangled bodies of the dead.

He hated them for it.

This was supposed to be his moment. He was finally Chosen. Selected by God for his tremendous demonstration of faith, his purity of purpose. He was clothed in white, the blood of the lamb smeared across his brow.

Uncontaminated. Untainted. A mighty, virtuous soldier in God's own army, standing at the right hand of the Prophet himself.

Where was the glory? The elation, the bliss of pure, unadulterated belief? Where was his rapture into paradise?

They felt it. These sheep so blindly allegiant to their master, such ignorant simpletons. Why did they get to receive the blessing of faith while he remained in the dark, isolated, as much an outsider now as he ever was?

Sharp bitterness welled on his tongue. Where was his? Hadn't he wanted it badly enough? Hadn't he suffered through hell itself to get here, to earn his place?

He felt none of their exaltation.

All he felt was an aching, hollow emptiness.

9
EDEN

E den sat in the chair in the elders' room, her hands clasped in her lap to keep them from shaking.

She was still wearing the crisp robe, white and unmarked, unblemished and unwrinkled. The blindingly white fabric hurt her eyes.

The service was finally over.

The Prophet, her father, and several Shepherds were still talking in the Sanctuary, making plans, discussing the hurricane preparations but also something else, probably the Prophet's plans to leave with her in the morning.

They'd left her alone in here to change and to wait. Maybe, if she was lucky, they'd forget about her for a little while so she could be alone with her frantic thoughts.

If only they'd forget about her forever.

She was numb all over. The room was spinning. She could barely recall the ceremony. A whirling, dizzying cacophony of noise and lights and faces, so many faces.

She hadn't needed to do anything but stand there, everyone watching her, singing their sacred hymns, arms raised and swaying in exultant celebration.

No one cared that she didn't speak, that she didn't say "I do."

Everything blurred together. Everything but one terrible thing—she was married. She was a wife. Bride of the holy Prophet, chosen and blessed by God Himself.

She didn't feel blessed. She felt sick, nausea churning in her gut. She wasn't just a fifteen-year-old girl married to a fanatical cult leader—she was trapped in a nest of sadistic terrorists.

The Shepherds did it. They detonated the nuclear bombs.

She'd heard it with her own ears. When she'd glanced at Maddox up on the dais in stunned disbelief, the look on his face —pride and triumph mixed with guilt—told her everything she needed to know.

It was true.

Icy fingers skittered up her spine. Sour acid burned the back of her throat. She clamped her mouth shut. If she vomited in the hallowed chapel, even back here in this little room, there'd be hell to pay.

Almost against her will, her gaze drifted up the opposite wall to the painting of the Prophet. It was a head-and-shoulders portrait, the paint strokes elegant, detailed, and realistic—but for the angelic glow that emanated from the man, like the archangel Gabriel himself had opened Heaven to shine blessings upon his head.

The Prophet was charming, charismatic, and handsome. His long, wavy corn-yellow hair fell loose around his narrow face. His tanned skin was creased with laugh lines; a kind, paternal smile on his lips. His gaze was benevolent, like he wanted nothing more than to care for you and keep you safe.

She stared at his image until her eyes blurred. He didn't look like a dangerous mass murderer. But then, he didn't look like the sort of person who would order his followers to be beaten and tortured in a mercy room, either.

But he had done those things, all of them. The Prophet and the Shepherds of Mercy had committed these atrocities, including her own father. She felt the truth of it down to her very bones.

What was she supposed to do now? What would Dakota do?

Her heart squeezed with a physical ache. She missed Dakota more than anything, so much she could barely breathe. Dakota had always protected her. Eden had tried to protect her this time.

Little good it did.

What had the Prophet said? She closed her eyes for a moment, her brow scrunching. She forced her rapid breathing to calm, willed her frantic thoughts to slow down so she could *think*.

Her marriage had been a symbol of God's church in the New Earth, the New America. But to build their pure, perfect New America, they had to destroy the America that existed now.

They'd already dealt the country thirteen devastating blows. America was on her knees, struggling and desperate, but she wasn't defeated yet. The American people weren't defeated.

Neither was she.

Eden opened her eyes. She looked at the Bible lying open on the top shelf of the cabinet. She wasn't allowed to read freely here. She wasn't even allowed to pick up that Bible and see for herself what it said.

Maybe that's how the Prophet got away with claiming God spoke to him. If no one could read what God actually said, who would know the difference?

Her gaze lowered to the shelves beneath the Bible, to the two totes on the bottom shelf. The first one contained her own clothes. Not *her* clothes, but the rough, itchy skirt and blouse that the meek and obedient women of the compound wore to show their piety.

She was supposed to change out of her blindingly white robe and put them back on. Would she spend the rest of her life confined in those awful rags? She hoped not. She hated them. She wished she had a lighter so she could burn the clothes right here and now.

The second tote snagged her eye. It was filled with Maddox's clothes that he'd exchanged for his own white robe. Something small and black poked out of the tote.

Before she could think better of it, Eden rose quickly and pressed her ear against the wooden door. The faint murmur of voices. Maddox was still out in the sanctuary.

Her heartbeat thudded in her ears. Her mouth went dry. Slowly, she padded across the room, careful so her footsteps didn't creak. Five steps. Six steps. Seven.

She knelt, pushing her robe out of the way, and pulled out the tote. Everything was there—Maddox's gray tunic, khaki pants, belt, holster, pistol, knife. And his handheld radio.

She picked up the radio with numb fingers, pushed the tote back into place, and backtracked to her chair. She sat down, crossed her legs, settled her hands in her lap. Took a breath, exhaled, and stared down at the radio.

Before the service, Maddox had called Dakota on this radio. She'd watched him do it. He'd moved out of her hearing, but not before she heard Dakota's voice.

Maybe it was still tuned to the same frequency. Maybe Eden could talk to Dakota *right now*.

Her heart surged in her chest. Just as quickly, fear clamped down. If they caught her...

No. She had to risk it. Tomorrow, she'd be long gone. Lost forever.

She wasn't worried about herself—or at least, she wasn't only worried for herself.

The Shepherds were terrorists. Their bombs had killed over a million people. They'd murdered her beloved foster parents, Jorge and Gabriella Ross, two people she'd adored with all her heart.

She couldn't let that go. She refused.

Her finger hovered over the *talk* button.

She froze. The realization struck her like a slap in the face. In her agitated state, she'd completely forgotten. She couldn't *talk*.

And she couldn't use sign language or write over the stupid radio.

Despair flooded through her veins. She opened her mouth in a soundless moan, furious at herself and her own weaknesses. She was just a helpless, stupid girl, unable to protect herself or anyone else. She couldn't even *warn* the people she loved. She was useless.

As she adjusted her grip on the radio, her finger grazed the small red CW—continuous wave—button.

She sucked in a sharp breath. *Thank you, Ezra. Thank you.* She could communicate after all.

Here goes nothing. Or just maybe, everything.

10

DAKOTA

Dakota whipped around in her seat. "What was that?"

From the counter behind them, the handheld radio crackled again. It was the Shepherd's radio she'd confiscated from the body outside the shed. The radio Maddox had called her on.

She stared at it—a viper that might strike at any moment.

Julio's expression tensed. "Is that Maddox?"

"Why didn't you destroy the damn thing when you had a chance?" Logan asked.

"I don't know." She really didn't. Something—an instinct, a gut feeling—had made her keep it.

It wasn't because she wanted to speak to Maddox again. There wasn't any use trying to talk sense into him or beg him for mercy—real mercy. He wouldn't know mercy if it slapped him in the face.

Whatever they may have shared in the past didn't matter. The love and affection she'd once felt for him, the person he used to be—none of it mattered.

There was only one way their story ended.

She shoved back her chair and stood slowly, dread and apprehension flooding through her veins.

"What are you doing?" Julio asked. "Don't pick it up, Dakota. He only wants to hurt you. It's not going to help anything."

That same strange, disquieting feeling niggled at her gut again. She couldn't ignore it.

Logan and Julio watched her, unmoving. They were sitting at the kitchen table. Two freshly loaded M4s hung from the straps on either side of Logan's chair. His Glock 43 rested on the table beside him. A dozen magazines were spread across the table next to a few boxes of ammo. They were methodically loading each magazine, snapping in the rounds one by one.

Heart thumping, she picked up the radio and pressed the mic. "Who is this?"

No answer.

"Tell me who you are, right now."

Nothing.

"If this is Maddox Cage, then you can go straight to—"

A high-pitched beeping sound filled the room.

Dakota shot a confused look at Logan.

"It's a code!" Julio shoved back his chair so hard it tipped over and clattered to the floor. He spun around, searching wildly. He strode to the end table beside the sofa, picked up Eden's drawing pad, and rifled through it until he found the page he wanted. He held it up. "She's using the CW frequency. That's Morse code."

"Holy hell!" Logan dropped the half-filled magazine to the table. "Does that mean...?"

Dakota's lungs constricted. She could barely speak around the lump in her throat. "It's Eden." She pressed the PTT button. "Eden, is that you?"

Another garble of beeping with a mix of short and long pauses.

It was Eden. It had to be. Eden was the only one who couldn't communicate with words. She was the only one who would think to use a non-verbal code.

Dakota pressed the radio to her chest, her eyes suddenly wet. Her scared, meek little sister had managed to steal one of the Shepherd's radios right out from under their noses. Because of Ezra's survival instincts and foresight, Eden could communicate with them.

Julio returned to the table, ripped out the pages depicting the Morse code alphabet Eden had drawn, and set them down in the center of the table. He pulled several fresh pieces of paper from the middle of the pad and handed them to Logan along with a pencil Eden had tucked inside the spiral.

"Tell her to repeat her message. We'll write it down and repeat it back to her."

"Wait," Logan said. "Didn't Ezra give her a code name? Have her say it, just to verify that it's really her. You said yourself that Maddox is cunning."

Dakota nodded tightly. She asked Eden for her code name.

It took several tries, mistakes, and restarts, but they finally got the first message.

"R-O-S-E," Julio spelled out. "Rose."

Logan looked at her. "That's the call sign she chose, isn't it?"

Her throat was so tight with nerves and emotion, Dakota couldn't speak. She nodded.

"I-M-S-A-F-E-I-S-E-Z-R-A-O-K-A-Y," Julio spelled out. "I'm safe. Is Ezra okay?"

"I'm so sorry, Eden, but Ezra is..." She squeezed her eyes shut, fighting back a fresh wave of sorrow. "Ezra didn't make it."

Silence on the radio.

"We're coming to get you, okay?" She sucked in a ragged breath and forced herself to keep going. "I need you to be brave until then. I'm not going to let them have you. Tell me where you're staying. We'll come as soon as we have a plan. A few days, maybe. I'm not sure."

Right now, her plan was to break in and murder every Shepherd she could find. Emotionally satisfying, but not exactly a working ploy. She needed something better, and soon.

After a moment, the beeping started up again, slow and halting.

When they'd figured it out, Julio repeated her words in a stricken voice. "Too late. Married Prophet today."

Logan swore. "That scumbag didn't waste any time, did he?"

Anger surged through her. Her blood rushed to her head. She was going to strangle the Prophet with her bare hands. She clenched the radio. "Did he touch you? Did he hurt you?"

More beeps.

"No," Julio answered.

Dakota sagged against the counter in relief. "Do whatever it takes to keep him from hurting you, Eden. We're coming. As soon as we can."

Eden relayed her message.

"No time," Julio translated.

Dakota's breath hitched in her chest. "What do you mean?"

A symphony of beeps followed.

"He's leaving tomorrow at dawn. Taking me too."

Dakota and Logan exchanged strained glances.

"What is she talking about?" Logan asked.

She took her finger off the button. "He's taking her out of the River Grass Compound. He has another place, out west I think, where he has a big house and some of his other wives. He could have multiple compounds, I don't know. I don't know about anything outside the compound." Panic twisted her gut. "Once he takes her, she's in the wind. We'll never find her."

"Ask her when she's leaving," Julio said, his voice tense but even.

Dakota asked. Eden didn't know.

"How many armed men at the compound?" Logan asked.

Eden answered again that she wasn't sure. There was a pause before she answered: 100 or 120.

"Okay." Dakota thought hard, her mind scrambling. They might not get another chance to communicate. "We'll figure something out. I promise, okay?"

"Okay," Julio read.

"I love you, Eden," Dakota whispered. "With all my heart."

The radio beeped some more.

Julio stared down at the words he'd just written. He glanced at the Morse alphabet again, then looked up at Dakota in confusion. "She said, 'Shepherds did it.' What does she mean?"

"What did the Shepherds do?" Dakota asked, pressing the mic.

Eden beeped her response. The radio crackled and went silent.

"Eden?"

Nothing.

She bit her lip. She hoped none of the Shepherds had walked in on Eden. She hoped Eden was just being smart and making sure no one discovered her. She didn't even want to think about what might happen if Maddox or the Prophet found her with a radio.

She set her radio down on the table and pressed her hand against her stomach, willing herself to calm down. She couldn't panic, couldn't let her stress and worry over Eden's welfare cloud her judgment.

"What did she say?" Logan asked. "What did the Shepherds do?"

Julio fingered his gold cross, his face stricken. "They detonated the bombs."

11

LOGAN

L ogan, Dakota, and Julio stared at each other in shock. For several long moments, no one spoke.

The fan in the corner whirred. The ceiling fan creaked as it turned. Outside, the wind picked up, the trees rustling loud enough to be heard inside the cabin.

"Is it true?" Julio asked finally.

Dakota shrugged helplessly. "I don't know. I mean, they always had plenty of heavy-duty weapons. The Prophet was obsessed with his war against the devil—you know it better as the government. He was always preaching about raining fire down on Sodom and Gomorrah."

"How?" Julio asked, incredulous. "Is it even possible? How could they get ahold of nuclear weapons here?"

"Could they have smuggled in nuclear material and made bombs there? I mean, I guess it's possible. There were areas the women couldn't go. Military-type buildings. That place is full of secrets. And it's out in the middle of millions of acres of swampland. As good a place as any to hide, if you're homegrown terrorists."

"Could she be mistaken?" Julio asked.

"I believe her," Logan said quietly.

Dakota shot him a startled look, her eyes widening. Slowly, she nodded. "Eden is...you know her. She's not a liar. She doesn't make stuff up, and she's not dramatic. It's possible she's mistaken, but what could she have seen or heard to make her believe the Shepherds did this? A religious cult making nuclear bombs. It sounds crazy. It's unbelievable."

"Except that it happened," Logan said. "Thirteen nuclear bombs destroyed thirteen cities on American soil. Someone did it. Why is it more believable that fanatics living in caves in the Middle East could pull this off, but fanatics living here couldn't? I think American terrorists would be even more dangerous—more educated, with better resources."

They all looked at each other, letting that sink in.

"Even if it's true, that doesn't change the fact that they have Eden." Dakota's hands were trembling, but her back was straight, her shoulders stiff. "These people are even more dangerous than anyone thought. We have to get her out of there."

Logan sucked in his breath. "This is a massive undertaking. Say he takes her at dawn tomorrow. It's ten a.m. now. That means we have less than twenty hours. That's not enough time. We don't even have a plan! We don't know their defenses or even how many hostiles we're up against—"

"I know!" Dakota's voice cracked. "I know, okay. I know it's insane. It sounds impossible."

Logan shook his head in resignation. He knew her too well. None of that mattered, when it came down to it. When her sister's life was on the line.

Deep down he knew that if he were in the same situation, he wouldn't hesitate to move heaven and earth to save Dakota. He'd walk through hell to reach her. No matter how insurmountable the odds. "But you're still going."

"I'm still going." Her hands curled into fists. She stared down at them before lifting her head to meet Logan's gaze. Her eyes were tortured. "I don't expect anything from you. After everything you did last night, both of you, asking anything else is too much."

"But—" Julio sputtered.

"I'll do it alone. I know the compound. I know how to sneak in. I can do it."

"And let you hog all the glory?" Logan snorted. "Nice try."

She looked at him, confused.

She was ready to battle Maddox Cage single-handedly if she had to. She was ready and willing to go to war alone against a hundred armed and dangerous men within a secured and guarded compound.

She had balls of steel, he had to give her that much. More than most men. He admired her for her grit, her strength, and her courage. But it was more than admiration.

He wouldn't just go through hell to save her; he'd follow her down there.

Dakota was willing to sacrifice herself for Eden. Logan would gladly sacrifice himself for both of them. This wasn't just about Dakota anymore. He cared for Eden. He wanted to save her, too.

More than that, he needed to do this for himself.

An image of Tomás flashed in his mind—the little boy's tousled black curls, delicate face, and those huge black eyes always beseeching, blaming, accusing. Logan knew what he'd done, what he was accountable for.

But the cancerous shame that ate away at his soul for so many years no longer controlled him. The Latin phrase he'd tattooed on his arm was no longer a condemnation but a vow: *et facti sunt ne unum.*

Lest you become one.

He cracked his scarred knuckles. Violence was in him. There was no denying it. But he would never become that monster again. He'd never kill or harm an innocent. But it wasn't enough simply to *not* do something.

Dakota had told him to do enough good that someday it

might tilt the scales against the bad. He didn't know about that, but there was no harm in trying.

Everything we do matters. It has to. Otherwise, nothing matters.

"I'm going with you."

She opened her mouth, about to protest, then pressed her lips together. A range of emotions crossed her face at once— gratitude, concern, fear, acceptance. She reached out and touched his hand. "If you're sure."

"I'm sure."

The faintest smile curved her lips. "Okay."

"Even if we save Eden, what about the rest of the Shepherds?" Julio asked. "Won't they just attack us again? And if they're the ones behind the bombs? What then?"

"We're not just going to rescue Eden." Dakota spread her hands, pressed her palms against the solid wood of the table. "It's time to take the battle to them. I'm going to kill Maddox, and then I'm going to kill the Prophet. It's time to end them, once and for all."

Logan crossed his arms over his chest. "I'm with you one hundred percent, Dakota. You know I am."

She looked at him, her eyes on fire. "But?"

He didn't want to contradict her. He wanted to go to war with her, to fight side by side, to destroy everyone who'd ever hurt her or any of the innocents in that horrible place.

But they couldn't let their emotions get the best of them. That was a good way to get yourself pointlessly killed.

He shook his head. "This is too much. Rescuing Eden and killing Maddox, the Prophet, and all his soldiers? How many Shepherds are we up against? What weapons do they have? How strong are their defenses?"

Dakota didn't say anything.

"There are too many of them for the two of us, Dakota. I'll take low odds and bet on us any day. You know that. I've done it.

We've done it. But this...if we try to do this alone, we'll only get ourselves killed, and probably Eden as well."

Dakota pressed her lips together. He saw it in her face—she knew it, too.

"We need help," Julio said.

"From who?" Dakota asked. "There's no 911, no police. Not around here, not anymore. There's no one else. We're on our own."

"No, we're not." Julio pulled the satphone out of his pocket and placed it on the table. "We have Hawthorne."

Dakota gave a small nod, her eyes wary. She still wasn't used to asking for help or trusting people, but she was coming around.

They both were.

Logan leaned across the table, grabbed the phone, and held it out to Dakota. "Make the call."

12

SHAY

"I don't want to go," Shay Harris said.

She stood beside the Greyhound bus, holding the small backpack that held a couple of changes of ill-fitting donated clothes, essential toiletries in travel sizes, and little else. It was everything she called her own.

The bus was one of several dozen parked along the tarmac outside Miami International Airport. The airport had served as the Emergency Operations Center for greater Miami for almost a month. Now, everyone was evacuating before the hurricane hit sometime tomorrow morning.

Shay was the last of the medical personnel to leave. Hundreds of wounded and radiation victims had already been medevacked over the last few days to the FEMA camp south of Orlando near Kissimmee.

Trey Hawthorne rubbed his smooth, bald head with his free hand and sighed. With his other hand, he cupped Shay's elbow and held her close. "I don't want you to go, either. I pretty much hate the thought of you lost in some huge displaced persons camp with no law and order, no one to keep you safe..."

Shay stiffened. "Well, I can protect myself, you know."

Hawthorne shook his head, mortified. "Oh, no. That's not

what I meant at all. I know you can take care of yourself. You're a capable, grown woman. Clearly. I am, ahem, definitely aware of that detail..." His voice trailed off.

She stepped back and crossed her arms, craning her neck to glare up at him. She wasn't short at 5'10", but her new boyfriend boasted a height of 6'5". *Boyfriend.* She liked that term.

He shuffled his feet in embarrassment. "Yeah, I royally screwed that up."

He gave her that sheepish grin that she adored. In his late twenties, Hawthorne was lanky and tall, his skin a warm chestnut brown, his jawline lean and chiseled beneath a trim beard. He was handsome, smart, skilled—and a bit goofy.

"I just want you safe," he said.

"You're lucky you're cute." She stepped closer and nuzzled against his chest. She breathed in the crisp scent of his aftershave, which he'd gotten who knew where. Most people were barely bathing, and yet he'd made it a priority to smell nice.

"Aftershave? Seriously?"

"Hey, it's not the apocalypse yet. There's no reason to smell like a barnyard, even if you've been rolling in crap."

"Saving the world, one sweet-smelling man at a time?"

"You've got it. Surprising as it is, shaving and cologne products are not a priority for the hungry masses looting grocery stores."

"I'm shocked."

He gave her a repentant grin. "Forgive me?"

"I forgive you. And I'll be okay. The National Guard is there to keep the peace. I'll be spending most of my time volunteering in the medical ward, anyway."

The wind whipped her hair into her eyes. She took off her purple, square-framed glasses and cleaned them on her frayed, well-worn Nirvana T-shirt.

Hawthorne's ATF-emblazoned jacket flapped as a strong gust tore across the tarmac. Someone's hat blew off and tumbled past, bright red against the flat gray of the sky. Electrons surged in the air, raising the tiny hairs on her arms.

They weren't kidding about the approaching hurricane.

Behind them, a long line of at least a hundred people waited to board the buses. A soldier dressed in ACUs stood at the door to check ID tags and driver's licenses against the manifest list on her tablet.

"Time to go," the soldier barked at them.

Hawthorne thrust something into her hand—a package of spearmint gum. "Call me when you get there. I'm still finishing up some reports. They're shipping me out late tonight on a chopper."

The Joint Field Office had assigned Hawthorne to wait it out in Tallahassee before returning to Miami to inspect the hurricane's damage and continue recovery efforts. He was ATF, but in the aftermath of the terrorist attacks, he'd been assigned the duty of Preliminary Damage Assessment Coordinator for the Miami EOC. He assessed and reported infrastructure damage, civil unrest activity, and analyzed community needs.

The emergency medical teams and most of the civilian volunteers wouldn't be returning. They'd remain at the FEMA camp—nicknamed Camp Disney for its proximity to the famed theme park—for the foreseeable future.

Hawthorne kissed her, long and full, until her stomach fluttered and every inch of her skin tingled. She'd give up coffee and gum for a year if it meant she could have just a little more time with him. With the chaos and destruction all around them, he was her anchor, a harbor in a storm that seemed like it might never end.

"I'll quit my job," he said when he'd pulled away. He ran his hands over her hair, smoothing her wild, unruly spirals against the wind, and cupped her jaw in his hands. "They're not paying me for all this overtime anyway. I can come with you and wait in your bunk every day until you come back. That'll work, right?"

"I think you'd be bored out of your mind."

"Maybe," he conceded. "Probably."

"Definitely. Besides, you're wired to help people. So am I. That's what we're doing. I'm nursing the wounded, and you're restoring law and order to make this country a safe place again. We're doing what we're supposed to do."

He sighed ruefully. "You're right—again."

She wrapped her arms around his lean torso encased in his flak jacket and holstered weapons. "I heard somewhere that absence makes the heart grow fonder."

"My heart doesn't need to grow fonder," he murmured into her hair.

Her own heart beat a little harder. She already missed him, and he wasn't even gone yet.

Shay's satphone buzzed in her pocket. Only a few people had her number—her mother, Hawthorne, and Julio, Dakota, and Logan.

She stepped out of Hawthorne's embrace so she could use her hands, pulled it out, and hit the talk button. "Hello?"

"Shay, it's Julio. It's important."

13
SHAY

"What's wrong?" Apprehension flickered inside Shay. The last few times she'd tried to call to warn them about the hurricane, no one had answered. "Is everyone okay?"

Julio's voice was strained. He didn't sound like his usual gentle, affable self. In only a few terse, clipped sentences, Julio told her about the attack on the cabin. Park and Ezra were dead. And a crazy religious paramilitary cult had kidnapped Eden.

The words hit her like physical blows. Sorrow tangled in her gut. Park was kind and funny. How could he be dead? Sweet Eden was gone? She'd never met Ezra, but she grieved for Dakota. She must be heartbroken.

Her eyes stung. Tears slid down her cheek. She gripped the phone tighter. "Oh, Julio. I'm so sorry. What can I do?"

"Pray for us, and for Eden," Julio said. "But there's more."

Shay felt dizzy. "There's a hurricane. You have to get out of there."

"Not that." He sighed into the phone. "Is Hawthorne there? Can you put him on the line?"

Shay motioned to Hawthorne. They moved away from the buses and lines. The soldier shot them a look. "We're leaving in five. You better be on this bus."

"She will," Hawthorne assured her.

When they'd found a private corner, Shay put Julio on speaker. She and Hawthorne hunched over the phone, using their bodies to shield against the wind.

They listened in silence as Julio filled them in. Shay's eyes widened in disbelief.

With every word Julio spoke, dread spooled tighter and tighter.

Shay took several deep, steadying breaths. It couldn't be true. Americans killing other Americans? Trying to destroy their own country? It seemed inconceivable. But of course, it wasn't.

"Send reinforcements," Julio said. "Send the FBI, ATF—the whole army if you have to."

Beside her, Hawthorne had gone very still. "You said they call themselves the Shepherds? Their compound is called River Grass, right? We know about them. Religious fanatics, to be sure. They believe their Prophet speaks to God. They keep to themselves, do everything the hard way like the Amish, only they use electricity. Hate women. The usual cult."

"That's them," Julio said.

"If I remember correctly, we received a few troubling reports about them a few years ago, but we couldn't verify anything. They don't recruit, at least around here. We tried to send a man in, but we couldn't infiltrate them. They're out in the middle of a million acres of bug and gator-infested swampland no one wants. They weren't a priority."

"Maybe you should make them a priority now."

Silence on the phone. A shuffling sound, and then Dakota's voice: "You don't understand. The Shepherds are violent. They have automatic weapons. They've been planning the demise of the U.S. government for two decades. They're dangerous."

"Even if what you say is true—and I do believe you—that doesn't change anything. Listen, these types of people, they're insane. Their leaders are charismatic charlatans. They must keep their followers under their thumb.

"So they make grand claims exaggerating their own power and influence. Do you know how many reports the Joint Field Office has already received accusing various persons, organizations, and governments? Thousands. We've already gathered hundreds of straight-up confessions, mostly from lunatics or hate-groups or pathological attention-seekers.

"I'm not downplaying their potential threat. Every few years, a cult rears its ugly head—David Koresh and the Branch Davidians. Heaven's Gate. The People's Temple. The FBI estimates there's roughly ten thousand actively maintained websites and web forums that support terrorist activities. Eighty percent of these sites are located on U.S.-based servers. And then there are the lone wolf terrorists—Ted Kaczynski, Omar Mateen, Stephen Paddock."

"Can you imagine the horrific destruction Tim McVeigh would've wrought if he had access to nukes?" Dakota asked darkly. "You don't have to imagine it. It just happened."

"There are literally thousands of cults in America. Some more dangerous than others. But that doesn't mean they're anywhere near capable of acquiring nuclear material."

Shay wanted to agree with him. She wanted to dismiss the idea immediately as preposterous. It was easier to think that the culprits were Middle Eastern terrorists from Iran or Iraq—not Americans attempting to destroy their own country, decimating thirteen cities and incinerating hundreds of thousands of innocent men, women, and children.

But she couldn't allow herself to bury her head in the sand of denial just for her own comfort. Hatred was alive and well in her country. It was a festering cancer, a toxic mold that spread in the darkness, hidden and unseen, rooting itself in the hearts and minds of the broken and disenfranchised.

It was possible. Of course, it was.

She put her hand on Hawthorne's arm. "Can't you send out an investigative team anyway? Just to be sure?"

Hawthorne shook his head in helpless frustration. "We're

stretched razor-thin as it is, operating at less than thirty percent of operational capacity. We're investigating hundreds of leads already, fighting back the remnants of the Blood Outlaws and other gangs, working through the rubble to retrieve and identify bodies, and decontaminating an entire city, one brick and blade of grass at a time. And that's only here in Miami."

"Surely there's something you can do," Shay said.

"With this hurricane and the evacuations...maybe in a few days, after the storm passes. I can talk to my superiors and send someone out there to check it out."

"That's not nearly enough," Dakota said in a scathing voice.

"I'm sorry." Hawthorne hung his head. He truly looked miserable, like it was killing him not to help, the same as it was killing Shay. "But without more—evidence, an eyewitness who laid eyes on it, an inside source—I'm not sure I can do a damn thing right now."

Silence on the phone.

The soldier at the bus shouted something at them. Everyone else was already loaded. She was the last one.

It was time to go.

"What if we get it?" Dakota asked. "What if we can get some evidence?"

"Don't do anything stupid."

"Answer the question," Dakota said.

Hawthorne set his jaw. "Get me something I can use, and I'll personally lead the best ATF, FBI, and Homeland agents on the planet to raze that compound to the ground."

14
EDEN

E den stood at the window, looking out at the compound. The sky was a steely gray. A mass of low scudding storm clouds approached in the distance.

She was inside the Prophet's house. For some reason, she thought she'd go to her father and stepmother's house after the ceremony.

But she didn't belong to them anymore. She belonged to the Prophet.

After about an hour, two of the sisters brought lunches of sandwiches, carrots, and salad on stacked trays. Eden had barely touched hers. She had no appetite. Her stomach roiled with nerves. Sour sweat prickled her temples and the back of her neck. She was still shaky and light-headed from the shock of the ceremony.

The Prophet, her father, and his inner circle were somewhere in the restricted area. The rest of the Shepherds were busy shoring up the compound for the approaching storm. She was alone but for the two guards, one stationed outside the door to the Prophet's house, one inhaling his lunch in the kitchen.

When he'd come to retrieve her from the elders' room, the Prophet had given her a chaste kiss on the forehead, his lips dry like dead leaves. "This is an incredibly busy—and momentous—day, but I won't forget about you my bride, I promise. I will see you tonight."

He'd told her the guards were for her own protection, but that was a bald-faced lie.

The only thing they were protecting her from was her own escape.

She felt the shape of the radio under her skirt. She'd had no choice but to tuck the radio in the front waistband of her underwear, inside her skirt. Thank goodness the fabric was heavy and full. She kept her hands folded over her lower belly for better concealment.

She'd almost put the radio back in the tote before Maddox returned. But if she lost it, she'd have no way to communicate with Dakota. It was no small feat for a girl to get her hands on a radio.

The pistol and knife had tempted her, too, but Maddox was particular about his weapons. If one went missing, he'd hunt for it.

If his radio went missing, he'd just go grab another one from the comm shack. That was her hope, anyway. Maybe it was a foolish plan born of desperation, but it was all she had.

So far, Maddox hadn't said anything. Maybe she'd get lucky.

Dakota had promised she was coming. Dakota would get help.

But Eden couldn't just sit around and wait to be rescued. Because even if rescue came, it wouldn't be before tonight, when the Prophet...

Her mind stopped there.

She had to get out of here before then. She had to.

Do it afraid.

Her stomach constricted, wild and fluttering. Fear throbbed through her, ice slicking her veins.

Do it afraid.

She needed to be as strong and courageous like Dakota,

clever and clearheaded like Julio, as bold and unflinching as Logan. Just thinking about them, she felt somehow closer to her friends. Even though it felt like it, she wasn't alone.

She willed herself to focus, to think through the fear. To make a plan.

First thing—she couldn't stay here. There were too many guards and Shepherds milling about everywhere. The Prophet's own house was one of the most dangerous places to be trapped. If Dakota and Logan tried to break her out of here, they'd likely be spotted and caught.

Eden didn't want to contemplate what would happen then. She had to make sure that didn't happen. She scanned the compound, searching for someplace safer to wait, someplace she could convince the guards to take her...

Another wave of dizziness washed over her. She still felt sick.

An idea came to her. She searched the compound again, her gaze settling on a small building across the clearing, set apart from the hustle and bustle of the rest of the grounds.

That just might work...

She turned and studied the house. The guard was out of sight in the kitchen. The living area was large with a wooden plank floor and walls painted white, lace curtains hanging over the windows, and a beige sofa with a coffee table and end table only a few feet from her.

A grand piano stood in the opposite corner. Along the far wall hung a large metal cross, a small, neat desk beneath it holding a Bible, a satellite phone, and a radio.

Her pulse thudded in her head, her throat. She steeled herself. It was time to be brave.

She took a few faltering steps and pressed her hand against an end table for balance. A beautiful, antique ivory lamp sat atop a lace doily on the end table.

She shifted her weight and bumped her hand against the edge of the lamp. It jostled, but didn't tip. She leaned over, left hand pressed over her stomach, and inhaled several deep, gasping breaths. With her right hand, she pushed the lamp over the edge.

It fell with a crash. Several pieces broke off and skittered across the wooden floor.

The Shepherd in the kitchen raced into the living room, hands on his weapon. He stared at her, eyebrows raised in concern. "What happened?"

She shivered, her whole body trembling, still clutching her stomach. She gave him a desperate look, scrunching her brows and opening her mouth, gulping in air like she couldn't get enough oxygen.

"Are you okay?"

She took one shuffling, trembling step toward him, one hand reaching out, grasping at empty air. Her legs wobbled beneath her. She collapsed.

To make it believable, she kept herself from throwing out her hands to shield herself from the fall. She landed hard on her back. A flash of pain struck her tailbone, radiated up her spine, and flared at the base of her skull. Her eyelids fluttered.

"Hey!" the Shepherd shouted. He knelt over her. "Hey, Sister!"

The front door slammed open.

"What's wrong?" the other guard asked.

"The Prophet's wife is down! She's sick or something. I don't know—"

"What're you standing around for, you moron? Get her to the infirmary."

She kept her body limp as one of the men gathered her up and carried her in his arms. She managed to fold both hands over the radio, keeping it safe.

The guard hurried her outside into the humid air. The hot wind whipped her skirt and flung strands of hair into her eyes.

Eden forced herself to snuff out the tiny grin creeping across her face.

15
DAKOTA

"No way." Dakota leaned back in her seat and crossed her arms.

Her whole body trembled with anger—and fear. "No way can we ask Eden to look for evidence of a dangerous cult's terrorist activities. If they catch her, they'll torture her. Or worse. It won't matter whose daughter she is or what God she's promised to. The only mercy the Shepherds dole out is with burning brands and razor-tipped whips. If you're lucky."

Julio and Logan exchanged wary glances.

"I'll go myself. I'll find whatever evidence Hawthorne needs."

"You can't do it all!" Logan threw up his hands. "You can't."

"We don't have the time," Julio said. "Not with the hurricane bearing down on us and the Prophet planning to take Eden at dawn."

She blew out a frustrated breath. She wanted to kick something hard. Preferably, a Shepherd. She wished they had kept one alive so she could strangle him to death with her bare hands, so she could watch the terror and panic in his eyes while she crushed the life out of him.

As if Logan could hear her murderous thoughts, he put a

hand on her shoulder and squeezed. "I'm not sure we have a choice."

"Of course we have a choice!" Her mind spun, frantically searching for an idea, any idea, where she could do the dirty work herself and save Eden. "You don't understand what they'll do to her..."

"This is bigger than us," Julio said gently. "I do understand your pain, Dakota. But this is about more than just Eden. It's about more than us and the women and children in the compound. A million innocent people are dead. Millions more are dying of radiation poisoning as we speak. Our entire country is devastated. Our nation is in mourning. Almost everyone has lost someone they love."

"I know! I was there."

Julio rubbed his temples, his expression strained. He looked like he hated the words even as he spoke them. "If the Shepherds did this, if they're behind the worst terrorist attack in history, we have to act. We have to. But we can't do it ourselves. We need help. And to get that help, Eden may have to do something dangerous, just like we would if we were in her place."

"It's a risk," Logan said softly, "but one we have to take."

She closed her eyes. She didn't want to give in. Every fiber of her being screamed at her to protect Eden. At all costs. At any price.

"Not Eden. Anyone but her. She's just a teenager. She's already suffered enough."

"Eden is stronger than you give her credit for," Logan said. "Trust her."

"Logan is right." Julio leaned forward. He touched the gold cross at his neck. "Have faith, Dakota. I can't speak for God, but maybe this is what she's supposed to do. That's why she's there."

Dakota remembered their conversation, remembered the unrelenting heat, the shovel blistering her palms as they scooped dirt into sandbag after sandbag. She nodded slowly. "We all have a purpose."

"Believe in something bigger than yourself." He smiled at her. It was rueful and sad and hopeful, all at the same time. "Maybe this is your purpose, to stop the Shepherds. And maybe it's Eden's, too. Maybe the terrible things you endured were to prepare you for this—both of you. You're the only ones who can."

Outside, the wind rattled around the corners of the cabin. The sky was still dark and gloomy, even though it wasn't even noon yet.

The sweltering humidity had given way to a cold front. It wasn't refreshing, but chilly. Dakota shivered like a ghost had just walked over her grave.

Have faith, Julio said. What if he was right? What if there was a reason for all of this that she couldn't see? *Everything we do matters, or nothing matters.*

There had to be a purpose, a meaning to life. This was hers. And that was Eden's.

She had to believe it.

Even if it meant she had to let go.

"Maybe you're right." She sighed heavily and stared at the satphone sitting in the center of the table until her eyes blurred. "But I can't contact her. Someone else might answer. Or hear the radio and find her out. She has to call us."

Wordlessly, Logan pushed three empty magazines toward her along with half a box of 5.56 ammunition. He understood her. He knew she needed to be useful. A useful distraction was even better.

Besides, they had to be prepared for anything, including a shootout. They wouldn't be caught with their pants down.

She gave him a grateful smile and got to work snapping in round after round. Logan and Julio took their own piles. The steady *click, click, click* filled the small cabin.

Dakota settled in for the longest wait of her life.

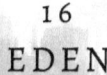

16

EDEN

The guard dumped Eden on the infirmary bed. She kept her eyes closed, her face tense with pain. It wasn't difficult. The pain from the fall and her nauseous stomach made it easy.

Her body shuddered and trembled. She rolled onto her side in a fetal position, shaking and gasping.

"What now?" the first guard said nervously. "Should I call the Prophet?"

"No," the other guard said. "He's too busy. Let the Sisters take care of it. That's what they're here for. Where's Sister Rosemarie?"

"No idea."

"Well, go find her! I'll wait here."

Two pairs of footsteps stomped across the floor. A door opened and closed. Then, silence.

Cautiously, Eden opened one eye.

The room was empty.

The medical clinic was a large, simple building with a wooden floor, low ceiling, and windows on three walls. A row of cabinets was set against the fourth wall beside a small fridge running on a generator that housed antibiotics and other medications.

A medical cart with a stainless-steel countertop stood in the middle of the room. Baskets, tubs, and containers filled with scalpels, trauma shears, rolls of gauze, and other supplies were clustered on the lower shelves.

The guard's head and torso were visible through the window, standing several yards from the door. He was leaning comfortably against the trunk of a live oak tree, his head back, weapon slung carelessly over his shoulder.

Victory thrummed through her. She'd done it! The Shepherds had barely checked her. Now, all she had to do was manage to stay here through tonight. Plus, with the guard outside, she could call Dakota again.

She was desperate to hear her sister's voice, to be reminded that there was a world waiting for her outside this insidious place. Plus, Dakota needed to know where exactly she was located inside the compound.

She flipped onto her other side, so she faced the wall with the cabinets opposite the door. Her back still ached, but she ignored it. Her heart pounding, she stuck her hand beneath the waistband of her skirt and pulled out the handheld.

Using the CW frequency, she keyed in her code name. Dakota picked up right away.

"Where are you? Is it safe to talk?"

She closed her eyes, concentrating hard to bring back everything Ezra had taught her last week. She'd sketched the Morse code alphabet a dozen times in her drawing pad to help her remember. In her mind's eye, she saw a neat series of dots and dashes.

I: two dots. N: dash, dot.

Slowly, painstakingly, she keyed in the letters.

After a minute of silence while they decoded her message, Dakota exhaled sharply through the speaker. "Infirmary. Okay, good. That's smart, Eden. Stay sick, okay? That'll work." She paused. "Eden. I—I have to ask you something important."

Eden waited.

"We called Hawthorne. He wants to help catch the Shepherds, but he needs evidence. An eyewitness. It can't just be what you heard, okay? That's not enough. Do you—have you seen evidence?"

Eden stopped breathing. She closed her eyes. She sent the message: N-O-T Y-E-T. *Not yet.*

"If you could find something...see it with your own eyes. To make sure. Do you think you can do that?"

The fear was back, crouching over her, its cold shadow sending terror slithering up her spine. It was one thing to fake sickness and deceive a few guards. Quite another to sneak around the compound searching for evidence of terrorist activity.

If they caught her...an image of the mercy room flashed through her mind. She shuddered at the thought. Her heart hammered weakly inside the cage of her ribs. Her mouth was dry, her palms damp.

She couldn't do this. It was asking too much.

The night they'd reached Ezra's cabin, Dakota had told her she had to do hard things even if she was afraid. She was afraid now.

She wanted to run and hide. She wanted to curl up in her old bed at her foster parents' house, bury herself beneath the covers while Gabriella sang her back to sleep, and pretend this was all just a bad dream she could wake up from.

But she couldn't. This was real. All of this was real.

Back in Miami, at the checkpoint controlled by the Blood Outlaws, Julio had almost died for her. She had frozen, allowed herself to be rendered useless by fear.

She couldn't let that fear keep winning. It put good people in danger.

She wasn't a warrior like Dakota and Logan, couldn't fix

stuff and handle a car like Julio, wasn't a prepper like Ezra. She was still figuring out what she was—an artist, maybe.

But what good was an artist in the middle of a devastating catastrophe? Her drawings couldn't save anyone.

She didn't want to be a burden.

That's exactly how she'd felt for years—the troubled, weird, useless mute girl. She longed to be useful, to prove she was worth it—that all of Dakota's dedication, loyalty, and sacrifice weren't misplaced.

And more than anything, more than her fear, Eden didn't want to disappoint Dakota.

She could do this. She had to do this. To prove to Dakota that she could. To prove it to herself, too. She wasn't a burden. She wasn't just someone else's responsibility, a helpless child to be saved and rescued, over and over.

Dakota trusted her. Dakota depended on her. They all did.

She pressed the CW button and keyed in the code for each letter. *Yes.*

"Eden, be careful. If it's too dangerous, don't do it. We'll find another way, okay?"

But there wasn't another way. Eden was already inside. She knew this place like the back of her hand. Maybe Dakota could get here in time to rescue Eden, but not to stop the Shepherds. By the time Hawthorne came, the Prophet might be long gone.

It was up to Eden to do this, no one else.

"I'll come for you, no matter what," Dakota said, her voice cracking. "I'll never leave you. Never, ever."

Never, ever, Eden repeated in her mind.

"Whatever you do, don't trust anyone. Don't trust anyone except—"

The infirmary door banged open.

Before Eden could move, rapid footsteps strode into the room. "Just what do you think you're doing?"

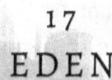

17

EDEN

Eden went completely still, but not before she quickly turned off the radio. She faced the wall, her cheeks and throat burning hot, her heart galloping in her chest a million miles a minute.

"Turn around," ordered a stern voice.

It'd been three years since she last heard it, but Eden instantly recognized the deep, raspy voice. Sister Rosemarie. A firm, practical Sister. Never cruel or unkind, like her stepmother.

But she was still a Sister. She was one of *them.*

If Sister Rosemarie caught her with the radio...she didn't have time to consider the consequences, to hum and haw over what to do. She had to act.

Shaking to hide her movements, she lifted her skirt, shoved the radio into the waistband, and loosened her blouse over it. There was still a slight bulge, but she couldn't do anything about it.

"I'm waiting," Sister Rosemarie said.

Eden forced herself into a sitting position and turned to face the Sister. A sour, sickening heat flushed through her. Her stomach was so twisted with anxiety, she could probably throw up on command.

It wasn't nearly as hard as she thought it would be to fake illness. Every minute that passed, she felt worse and worse.

I'm sick, she signed, even though she knew Sister Rosemarie couldn't understand her. *I feel like I'm going to die.*

The Sister's terse, suspicious expression didn't soften. A plump woman in her sixties, Sister Rosemarie had a kind but no-nonsense face, her weathered skin scored with fine wrinkles, her blue eyes sharp with intelligence—and impatience. "Stand up. Let me see you."

Eden stiffened. She couldn't recall ever disobeying a direct order from an adult. Every fiber of her being begged her to move, to acquiesce so she wouldn't be punished or disappoint anyone.

Instead, she imagined her bones turning to water and collapsed back on the bed, her head nearly striking the headboard. She gave a ragged sigh and clutched at her stomach again.

It worked with the guards; maybe it'd work on the Sister, too.

"I heard voices." Sister Rosemarie crossed her arms over her ample bosom. Her gaze drifted to the ribbon still tied around Eden's throat to cover the scar. "They told me you couldn't talk."

Eden squeezed her eyes shut. At least the ribbon hid the throbbing pulse at her neck. Could she pretend to pass out again, too? Would a person with medical experience buy it? She had no clue, but it was her only option.

She heard Sister Rosemarie's footfalls as she stalked closer, right up to the edge of the bed. What was she doing? Could she see the radio? Was she plotting who to tell first? Or maybe she'd just drag Eden to the mercy room herself.

Her closed eyes made everything worse. The not knowing. Dread and apprehension clawed up her throat. Cold sweat prickled her forehead.

"You can't fool me," Sister Rosemarie said in a low,

dangerous voice. "You aren't nearly as helpless as you appear to be. Stand up. Now."

Eden obeyed. She opened her eyes but kept her gaze down, too terrified to meet the Sister's gaze in case she accidentally gave something away. Sister Rosemarie had laser eyes like that. She'd always known when a kid had broken the rules just by looking at them.

She clambered off the bed and stood beside it, her hands folded over her pelvis. She stared meekly down at her feet.

Sister Rosemarie thrust out her hand. "Give it to me."

Eden's heart stopped. She swallowed hard. What was she supposed to do now? She needed Dakota. She needed Ezra and Logan and Julio. They would know what to do.

But they weren't here.

"The consequences will be worse the longer you wait, girl. I don't have all day."

She didn't have a choice. With a defeated sigh, she lifted the fabric of her shirt and withdrew the radio. She placed it in Sister Rosemarie's hand.

Sister Rosemarie didn't say anything. She didn't make a sound, only stared hard at Eden, like she was penetrating her very soul.

"Look at me, Eden," she said finally, an edge in her voice.

Eden looked at her.

"Why do you have this?"

If she said Maddox gave it to her, the woman would know she was lying. *I found it*, she signed. *I was just playing around. I didn't mean any harm.*

Sister Rosemarie frowned. She hurried across the room, the confiscated radio still in her hand but held low at her side as if she were also hiding it from view. She shoved open a couple of drawers in the wooden cabinet set against the far wall and returned with a yellow memo pad and a pencil.

Her brow wrinkled as she gazed at Eden, that sharp percep-tiveness in her eyes making Eden incredibly uncomfortable. She held out the pad and pencil. "Try again. And Eden, I need you to tell me the truth. The absolute truth. Do you understand?"

Eden took them and stared down at the pad, her eyes blurring. The pencil hovered over the yellow paper. She hesitated. This felt like a test. A test with questions she'd never seen before and had no idea what the answers were supposed to be.

A memory struck her. She saw Sister Rosemarie in her mind's eye, bent over the bed with the stainless-steel cart beside her. Gauze, medical tape, and antibiotics littered the cart, along with a little container of soothing ointment.

In the bed, Dakota moaned and writhed in agony. The room smelled of medicine, but also the awful, singed stench of burnt flesh. Sister Rosemarie was there, her head bent as she applied ointment to the wounds and asked Eden for more gauze, tears trickling down her weathered cheeks.

She'd wiped them away quickly, but Eden saw them.

Sister Rosemarie cared about her and Dakota. She had always cared. How many times had Eden helped Sister Rosemarie tend to her sister? A dozen? More? The woman had never been anything but compassionate and gentle.

But then, there were many kind, compassionate people here. They were also blind followers of the Prophet who would do anything he told them to do. Absolutely anything.

"Eden," Sister Rosemarie said softly. "Why do you have the radio?"

Dakota had told her not to trust anyone. But the truth was, Eden couldn't do this alone. She needed help. Either this was her chance to get that help, or it all ended right here.

Eden closed her eyes, took a breath, and opened them. She wrote the words with care and precision as if they might be her last. Maybe they would be.

She held up the notepad. *I stole it from Maddox. I wanted to hear Dakota's voice.*

Sister Rosemarie stared at the words. She didn't move. Her expression didn't change. "Why?"

Because...this is a bad place.

Sister Rosemarie sucked in a sharp breath through her teeth.

She took the radio in both hands and moved back to the cabinet. She bent, opened a drawer full of fresh linens, and tucked the radio between the towels. She closed the drawer with her hip and turned back to Eden. "We need to talk."

18
EDEN

"Sit," Sister Rosemarie said.

Obediently, Eden sat on the edge of the bed.

Sister Rosemarie remained standing in front of Eden, her body between the bed and the window, blocking the guard's view in case he decided to wake up and peer inside. "I wish I could say it was good to see you, child. I wish I could say that I missed you. But to be perfectly honest, once you left, I prayed daily that I'd never see your lovely face again."

Eden just stared at her.

The stern lines in the woman's face softened. Her eyes glistened. "I'm so sorry about Dakota. The world is a darker place without her in it. The young man I tended to with the dog bite —he told me you were the only one who made it out of the firefight."

Eden tried not to show it in her face. She didn't do a very good job.

Sister Rosemarie's eyes narrowed. "What?"

Eden shook her head. She didn't write anything down. She was afraid, afraid of what might happen if she told the truth. There was too much at stake.

Sister Rosemarie nodded to herself. "You don't trust me. I

understand that. If I were you, I would have a hard time trusting, too. Dakota was the same way. I saw you that night. You had blood all over you, Dakota's shirt tied around your throat. You were barely conscious. You probably don't remember, but I do."

She reached out and let her fingers graze the blue ribbon. Eden tried not to flinch. "I helped you and Dakota get out. I gave her the key to the gate and to the boathouse so she could get the keys to the airboat. I gave her some of my savings to give her a head start. Did Dakota ever tell you that?"

Eden shook her head warily. Dakota hadn't told her the full truth of that night until a few days ago. Eden still didn't have every detail clear in her mind, but she knew enough.

"That makes trusting each other a little harder, I suppose, but I hope not impossible. I want to help you, Eden. I know the Prophet is taking you somewhere tomorrow. I know he's planning something big, something bigger than they've done before. I don't have a good feeling about it. I've been sick with worry for days, but that's neither here nor there."

Sister Rosemarie sighed and rubbed her forehead with the back of her arm. "If you go with him, I have a feeling I'll never see you again, and not in a good way. If Dakota were still alive, I know she would want me to do whatever I could to help you."

Eden wrote a single word on her notepad. She underlined it three times. *WHY?*

Sister Rosemarie smiled. "I suppose I deserve that. You're afraid. Can I tell you a secret? I'm afraid, too."

Eden realized with a jolt that this was as much of a risk for Sister Rosemarie as it was for her. Eden could go straight to her father, to Maddox, or to the Prophet and tell them Sister Rosemarie committed blasphemy. They would beat her to within an inch of her life. Or worse.

Sometimes, a named heretic had disappeared from the compound. One day there, the next day gone. No one ever asked too many questions.

You didn't cross the Prophet without serious consequences.

Tell me why, she wrote.

Sister Rosemarie nodded to herself. "You're right. You deserve an explanation. Let me tell you my story. Then you can decide what you would like to do. I will respect your decision either way. I give you my word."

Eden simply stared at her.

"This place wasn't always a bad place. I want you to understand that. I had a rough past, much like Dakota. I had a family in name, but...suffice it to say, they weren't good people. I turned to smoking, drugs, alcohol, drifting from boyfriend to boyfriend, destroying my body little by little from the inside out. Life was cheap and brutal and meaningless. I was lost, in every sense of the word.

"Then one day in my early twenties, I stepped into a Catholic church. I fell in love with the candles and incense, their rituals and traditions, the promise of redemption, of a complete and total do-over. It was an intoxicating idea, dedicating my whole self to someone who mattered—God Himself.

"But over the next few years, I became disillusioned. I couldn't explain it, but I still felt this emptiness. I was still hungry, still searching.

"And then about twenty-five years ago, I met a traveling preacher named Henry Worthington. He was so fervent, so devoted to God and to this idea of a New Eden here on Earth: a place we could escape the cruelty, destruction, and evil of the world while we eagerly awaited the Lord's return.

"I fell completely under the spell of his dream. I was still hungry for meaning, for *something*, so I followed him to this place. There were maybe thirty other devout followers here at that time. We didn't have electricity. We were like the Amish. It was a simple life, filled with worship and prayer services, warm fellowship, and hours of hard, physical labor in an inhospitable land. But I was happy. I thought I'd finally found peace.

"There was another man who had arrived shortly before I did. I don't know where Henry found him. He called himself

Norman back then. No last name. Just Norman. You know him now as the Prophet."

Eden raised her eyebrows in surprise.

"If anyone used that name now, they'd likely be whipped to death," Sister Rosemarie said ruefully. "Remember that. Even back then he was far more charismatic than the founder, Henry. More powerful and controlling. After several months, he started giving Bible studies, preaching things a little differently than what we were used to. He said he had visions, that God Himself spoke to him. People flocked to Norman. He just...drew people. He knew the right words to say. Well, you know."

Eden nodded. She knew. She felt the same hypnotic pull whenever she was in the same room as him, that same fervent desire for his approval whenever his penetrating gaze fell upon her.

"One day, Henry just disappeared. Norman said he'd gone out to recruit more followers of The Way. We never saw him again. After that, Norman took charge. No one questioned him. Solomon Cage became his righthand man. They began calling themselves brothers. They handpicked strong, fit young men to become their inner circle and their security, calling them part of God's army.

"We were the remnant, the Prophet told us. God's chosen to usher in a new age of righteousness. It was easy to believe that we really were special. It's intoxicating, isn't it? That's what we all truly want in the deepest parts of ourselves—to belong, to be loved, to have a purpose, to *be* someone.

"The Prophet offered that. And we ate it up, hook, line, and sinker. The other things came gradually. The Prophet's absolute control. The separation of the women, the rules and restrictions. The mercy room. Until one day I woke up and realized the things I used to believe were no longer true. That I had ended up so far from where I'd started that I didn't even recognize myself anymore. I had journeyed so far and sacrificed so much, only to lose myself again."

Why did you stay? Eden wrote.

"Please understand, it was a slow process. How he slowly militarized everything. How women became the servants. How the outside world transformed into the enemy. Change didn't happen overnight."

She rubbed tiredly at her face, as if dredging up all these old, painful memories had drained her energy. "Once my eyes were opened to what this place had become, I knew I had a choice. I could save myself and attempt to run. Of course, without a car, I had miles of hostile wilderness and swampland to navigate. Maybe I could've made it, but with every passing year, it seemed more and more impossible."

And your other choice?

"I chose to stay to be a light in a place of darkness, to protect the other fragile lights around me and keep them from going out."

Did it work? But Eden already knew the answer to that.

"I thought I was doing the right thing. I really did. If I stayed, I could counteract the cruelty with kindness. I could offer grace in a merciless land. I could show the children that the brutal, hateful God of vengeance the Prophet and their parents believed in wasn't the only way.

"But I didn't know...I didn't know how truly depraved the Shepherds had become. The bombs they say they dropped on all those cities..." She ran her hands over her stricken face. Her mouth was a thin flat line of anger, remorse, and shame. "Religion is twisted to justify atrocities all the time. It's only one of the myriad ways the morally-bankrupt use to prey upon the innocent. They use politics, the government, business, power. They wear the guise of sheep, but they are wolves."

How can you tell? How do you know who is good and who is bad?

Sister Rosemarie turned and glanced at the window—the Shepherd was still leaning against the tree, his body angled away from them, his head tilted back against the trunk like he was dozing.

She bent down so she was eye-level with Eden and cupped her hands around Eden's cheeks. "There is good and evil in everyone, in every single heart. Usually the ones who believe they are the most good are the ones who harbor the most evil.

"If you hear nothing else, hear this: God's love never changes. God *is* love. Love is the gift that God gave to humanity. Real love cannot be twisted into evil. Shame, fear, and power are the devil's tools. Love never destroys. It only builds. Love never controls. It does not coerce. Love believes in choice above all else. For without free will, there is no love. That is its very nature. That is how you know."

Is that why you saved us?

"It's the reason for everything I've done for the last twenty years, child." She shook her head wearily. "In the end, I'm afraid I've failed completely."

Eden made her decision. She scribbled hastily on her notepad. *Dakota is alive.*

Sister Rosemarie stiffened. She took a faltering step backward. She covered her mouth with her hands, like she couldn't believe it was true. "But they said—"

Maddox lied. Dakota is alive. She's coming to get me. And I need your help.

Sister Rosemarie blinked away tears, but they leaked down her cheeks anyway. Her eyes were shining. "You have it, child. Anything you need. Anything."

19
EDEN

E den watched as Sister Rosemarie hurried to her wall of cabinets. She squatted, opened one of the bottom drawers and pulled it all the way out, off its runners. Grunting, she reached deep inside, all the way to her shoulder, fumbling around for a moment before repositioning the drawer and sliding it into place.

"Ah, here we go." She glanced out the window, made sure she was positioned to hide what she was doing, and held out her prize. "The keys to the kingdom."

They were literal keys, almost two dozen of them, attached to a rusty keyring with pieces of duct tape still stuck to the ring. Sister Rosemarie must have taped the keys in the very back behind the drawer so it wouldn't be discovered.

Eden had spent the last several minutes telling Sister Rosemarie everything—including Dakota's request for visual proof of the Shepherd's complicity in the bombings. She'd filled up almost twenty of the small pages, writing so much and so fast, her hand was cramping.

The guard had come in to check on Eden, but she'd seen him heading for the door. She had laid down quickly, shoving the used papers underneath her torso. With a deft movement, Sister

Rosemarie had slipped the keys into her skirt pocket as she turned and berated the Shepherd for disturbing the healing sleep of the Prophet's wife. "I know you don't want to be the one to tell the Prophet his bride is still ill on her wedding night?"

His face had gone crimson, and he'd scurried out as fast as he'd entered. He remained camped outside the door.

Eden asked, *What do the keys open?*

Sister Rosemarie's smile was so broad it nearly split her face in two. "Almost every building in this entire complex."

Eden's eyebrows shot to her hairline. *How?*

"Fifteen years of waiting and watching—and a bit of thievery. I hoped it would pay off someday."

They never caught you?

She winked at Eden. The new light in her eyes made her appear a decade younger. "One of the few benefits of men believing women are weak and stupid. They tend to underestimate us."

She flipped up two of the keys. "This one will open the armory in the restricted area. And this one is for the communications building."

Eden's eyes widened, impressed.

Sister Rosemarie chuckled. "I know what you're thinking. How in the world did I get this? I've had it for five years now. I bribed one of the Shepherds, Aaron Hill. You remember Ruth? He's her big brother. I'd just saved his life from a water moccasin bite on his shin. Thank goodness the Prophet allows me to keep antivenom here. Aaron was grateful enough that he bent the rules just a little.

"I always thought I would sneak in there someday and find a way to communicate with the outside world. Tell the FBI or ATF or whoever would listen what goes on here. Of course, I didn't know about the bombs. I didn't know..."

Her voice trailed off, and her eyes went dim for a moment. She looked like she was dredging up all her regrets, mistakes, and what-ifs all at once.

Eden put her hand on Sister Rosemarie's arm. She didn't blame her for any of this. She wrote: *Can Aaron be trusted?*

"He's not cruel like some of the others, but he's a true believer. He'd follow the Prophet to the grave if that's what the Prophet asked of him. Most of these people, they're just so lost, so desperate to be found, and the Prophet manipulates and controls and deceives them until they don't know down from up anymore. Or wrong from right. I'm afraid we're on our own."

Eden nodded soberly. She'd feared as much.

"I can get you out of the compound with these keys, Eden. We can keep you in here until it gets dark. I have no idea how to get through that maze of mangrove swamp like Dakota did, but I can get you to the road. We can use the radio to call her and have her ready to meet you and take you far, far away from here. Not back to the cabin. You'll have to run. But I can get you out."

I have to get the evidence, Eden wrote.

She gazed steadily at Eden, her eyes so intense Eden wanted to look away. But she didn't. The fear was back again, clawing up her throat, churning in her belly. The anxiety and dread of what awaited her...

"You don't have to do this. You can save yourself."

The Shepherds must be stopped. We have to stop them. She underlined *we* and thrust the pad at Sister Rosemarie.

"Then let me do it. I'll go."

Eden spent her whole life meek and afraid. She'd only escaped the Shepherds because other people had risked their lives for hers. Her whole life, everyone else had done the hard labor, made the difficult decisions, faced the danger.

She could lay here, safe for the moment, and let Sister Rosemarie put herself in peril.

Or she could step up and be brave.

She got to choose. That was love, wasn't it? The freedom to choose, to be who you wanted to be, who you needed to be. There were always costs and consequences, some steeper than others.

Maybe she wouldn't make it out of this place alive. Maybe she would die here. But some things were worth more than your own life. Family. Love. Doing the right thing.

Dakota had taught her that.

This was her right thing.

Fear dug its claws into her chest. It was hard to breathe. But she did it anyway. She took the pencil. *I have to stop them.*

Whatever Sister Rosemarie had been looking for in Eden's eyes, she must have found it. She cleared her throat and wiped her eyes briskly. "If you can get into the restricted area, one of those buildings will have evidence. They hid the bombs here. I remember the day they came in with all those vans. They told the rest of us it was a resupply run. They bugged out in the middle of the night so no one would see anything. But there were rumors. The Prophet told us the time was at hand. I should have known..."

She shook her head again. "Are you ready?"

Nausea still swirled in her stomach, but she nodded.

"You come straight back here. We'll contact your sister and figure out a way to get you out." Sister Rosemarie glanced out the window at the guard again. "We're going to have to get rid of him. I need to check on Gregory Puckett anyway to see if his bite wound is infected. That dog really did a number on his arm. He needs intensive surgery, but..." She gave a helpless shrug. "This is the Prophet's way. His people can always be replaced."

She glanced out the window again. "Puckett is in the Shepherds' barracks. I can't go in without an escort. I'll get this guard to take me there. You pretend to sleep. I'll tell him I gave you some heavy-duty medication to help you rest and keep you from vomiting tonight." Her mouth tightened. "Do you know how to get to the restricted area?"

Eden nodded.

"Right now, almost everyone is on duty preparing for the storm that's coming—boarding up windows, securing supplies, taking care of the animals. Even the Chosen are helping. We can use that to our benefit. If there was ever a time you could get in, it's now."

She turned and walked to the window. The guard was still dozing beneath the tree. "The restricted area has its own guard. And another layer of chain link fencing. I'm not sure how to get past that."

Eden tapped the bedpost to get her attention. *Aren't there bolt cutters in the sheds?* she wrote.

"Yes, I think there is. Good idea. We need to hurry. Whatever the Prophet has planned for tonight...you need to be gone before then."

Eden's stomach lurched. She pushed that thought down deep, somewhere the fear couldn't touch. If she let herself think about it too much, the terror would paralyze her.

She wadded the used yellow squares into a ball and gave them to Sister Rosemarie to get rid of. Her hands were trembling. She tried to hide them in her skirt, but Sister Rosemarie saw it.

"Do you remember what I used to say to Dakota after they took her to the mercy room?"

Eden did remember. Dakota had told her the same thing more than once. She counted with her fingers, then inhaled a deep breath.

Sister Rosemarie smiled. "One, two, three. Breathe. That's how you get through the hard stuff, when the fear or the pain gets too much. That's how you endure."

Eden nodded. She stood, squared her shoulders. *One, two, three. Breathe.*

"God be with you." Sister Rosemarie squeezed her shoulder. "Make it count, child."

2 0
EDEN

E den hadn't wandered the compound grounds in three years, but she still remembered every inch of it. The parts she'd been allowed into, anyway.

But it was the restricted area she needed now. She knew from Maddox and Jacob's stories that the Shepherds had built a tactical training ground to prepare for Armageddon. She'd grown up with the *rat-a-tat* of gunfire as familiar as birdsong and the buzz of mosquitoes.

There was an armory and a communications building, and a few others that her brothers were forbidden from speaking about. Those were the buildings she needed to find.

The wind whipped stray tendrils of hair into her face. Even with the breeze, the air was still sweltering. Sticky sweat dripped down her neck and collected at the small of her back. The heat was so oppressive, it felt like a furnace blazing from the inside out.

She adjusted the basket in her arms to push her hair behind her ears. Clean white towels and several boxes of gauze covered the bolt cutters Sister Rosemarie had retrieved for her from the janitorial storage shed behind the family cabins.

Sister Rosemarie had given her the basket as a ruse. "If

anyone stops you, tell them you're bringing me fresh supplies for Gregory Puckett. Everyone knows about the dog attack. They'll let you go."

So far, the only people to notice Eden either congratulated her or bowed their heads reverently and continued with their tasks. It was eerie. Mostly, no one even noticed her.

As Sister Rosemarie had said, everyone was busy preparing for the storm. There was something off about it all, and in a place like the compound, that was saying something.

She pushed the uneasy thoughts from her mind. She had enough on her plate right now.

If all went to plan, she'd be gone by tonight.

Instead of taking the path beside the water, she gave it a wide berth and circled back behind the men's barracks and the family cabins. A large swath of dense cypress, live oak, and slash pine forest separated the restricted area from the living quarters.

If she went directly south through the woods, she should run into the fence somewhere along the perimeter—hopefully far enough from the guard at the entrance to be noticed.

At the edge of the woods, she hesitated. Until this moment, she hadn't done anything unusual or wrong. She swung around, trying her best to look nonchalant, and casually took in her surroundings. She almost started whistling, but that was just dumb.

A few hundred yards away, a handful of Shepherds were busy boarding up the men's barracks' windows, but none of them were looking her way.

The bathrooms and solar-heated showers were near the family cabins. The compound had toilets that worked on a septic system using the river water, powered through solar and gas generators.

Another hundred yards behind them, a few children helped their mothers collect the rows of clothing drying on the clothes-lines strung between the trees.

No one was paying attention. She took a breath and slipped

into the woods, brushing past saw palmettos and ferns, the Spanish moss hanging like beards from the thick oak branches twisting above her head.

The wind sighed through the trees. Branches creaked. Leaves whooshed and rattled against each other. Without the sun, the shadows were deep and quivering, like dark shapes slinking here and there, lurking in the dark spaces, just waiting to pounce.

She shook the silly thoughts from her head. The only predators she needed to worry about were the human kind.

The air smelled dank and musky. The muck and layers of rotting vegetation sucked at her shoes. Thorns and twigs pulled at her skirt, scratching her shins as she moved slowly and cautiously, trying to make as little noise as possible. Even her breathing seemed loud.

Something glinted through the trees. She crept closer, her heart in her throat. She reached the high chain-link fence, stared for a moment at the foreboding razor wire circling the top. Luckily, she didn't need to climb.

She could just make out the green-painted buildings through the trees, and only because she knew they were there. She waited for several moments, straining her ears for any sounds other than the forest, searching for any movement.

Nothing. No Shepherds in sight. She knelt, set the basket on the ground, and pulled out the bolt cutters. It was harder than she thought to cut through each metal chain as she slowly worked her way up from the base in a semi-circle shape.

When the hole was large enough, she put the bolt cutter back in the bottom of the basket, covered it with towels, and pushed the basket ahead of her. She squeezed in after it.

One of the jagged prongs scraped her shoulder blade. A stinging pain raked her back. She hissed but didn't stop.

And then she was through.

She climbed to her feet and grabbed the basket. She was tempted to leave it behind, but she might need it for cover later. She kept moving.

Slowly, one building after another appeared through the thick screen of waving branches and fluttering leaves. The first one bristled with wires and antennas. The murmur of voices floated from the opened front door. The windows were already boarded up.

That one must be the communications building. Probably okay to skip it. She kept to the trees and gave it a wide berth.

Several minutes later, she came to another building, this one without any windows at all. She waited but heard no voices. She moved stealthily to the door and tried the handle. Locked. She set down the basket and pulled the keys from her pocket.

Some were old and rusted; others looked brand new. Sister Rosemarie had shown her the correct ones, but in her anxiety, Eden had forgotten. Hands shaking, she tried them one by one.

The sixth key worked. The doorknob turned, and the door opened with a creak she was sure could be heard for miles. The hairs on the back of her neck stood on end. It felt like she had a giant target on her back.

She slipped into the darkened room, blinking so her eyes could adjust. The tang of oil and something metallic filled her nostrils.

Floor-to-ceiling shelves of ammo and handguns covered each wall, along with large corkboards to hang rifles and shotguns of all kinds and sizes. Some of the weapons she'd never even seen before.

Eden searched the room quickly, but didn't see anything resembling a bomb. She backtracked, shutting and locking the door behind her.

A few big military vehicles were parked beside the next building. After straining for any sounds, she crept closer. It wasn't locked. It was just a clubhouse type building, with a small electric fridge, a few card tables, a ping pong table, a hammock in the corner.

She walked deeper into the woods. She could barely see the

sky through the canopy of leaves above her. So far, she'd found nothing.

Dread coiled in her stomach. What if it wasn't here? What if whatever evidence existed had already been destroyed? The Shepherds would get away with the worst terrorist attack in human history.

All those people who'd died. All their loved ones in mourning.

No. She'd promised she'd find something. It had to be here.

She kept walking. The perimeter fence was ten yards beyond her, marking the boundary of the restricted area. She could go no further.

She stopped, spun in a slow circle, scanning everything.

And then she saw it. Nestled between several huge live oaks to her left stood one last building. Windowless, it was built of concrete and painted green like the others, solar panels affixed to the roof.

This one was it. It had to be.

The forest was quiet but for the breeze. She barely heard any insects. The birds were eerily silent. She crept along the far side of the building closest to the fence and hid the basket behind a clump of bushes, just in case.

She returned to the door and tried the first several keys. Nothing. Still nothing with the tenth, eleventh, and twelfth key.

One left.

She squeezed her eyes shut. If this didn't work, she had no way to get inside the building. There was nowhere else to look.

She inserted the key in the lock. Turned it, slowly, slowly. *Click.*

The door unlocked. She pushed it open and stepped inside.

21
EDEN

E den blinked. The light was still on. The air smelled sharply of chemicals. Her mouth tasted weird, faintly metallic.

Her lungs constricted like all the air was sucked out of the room. She saw everything all at once.

Her eyes kept jumping from object to object, unable to land on any one thing for more than a few seconds. The workbenches filled with high-tech equipment she didn't know the names of. The dosimeter and Geiger counter on the desk. The corkboard on the wall papered with maps, research articles, and schematics.

A few large, weird-looking crates were stacked next to a large metal shelf packed with metal pieces in strange shapes, wires snaking over it. A couple of yellow contamination suits hung on one wall.

But it was the thing in the center of the room that filled her with cold terror.

She took a stumbling step backward. Every cell in her body screamed at her to run, to flee, to get as far from this terrible place as she possibly could.

She pressed her fist to her mouth, fighting back the crazed, panicky sobs threatening to overwhelm her. Her thoughts fractured into jagged pieces. Everything started somersaulting, flipping upside down.

This was more than evidence. This was more than proof.

The Shepherds had built another bomb.

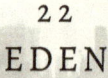

22
EDEN

E den's brain couldn't process the information. *No, no, no!* Another nuclear bomb?

It couldn't be. It wasn't possible. Couldn't be possible.

She closed her eyes. In an instant, she was back in her foster home, trapped in that bathroom, completely alone and terrified as the brilliant white light flared down the hallway, the deafening thunder of the blast trembling the whole house, followed by the darkness so thick and absolute that she hadn't been able to see her own hands in front of her face.

The horrors of the attacks came flooding back. The blinding terror, the destruction, the death. Her foster parents would never come home again. Millions of people would never go home again.

How could anyone do this? How could the people she knew —her father, her brother—how could they be a part of such horror?

But it was true. It was all true. They'd incinerated thirteen cities. Brought a country to its knees and devastated the world.

And they weren't going to stop. It wasn't enough. They wanted more destruction. More blood. More death. How could—

A sudden noise shook Eden from her stunned stupor.

Voices. Gravel crunching beneath boots. People were coming. They were headed straight for her.

She twisted around, frantically searching for a hiding spot. She could hide under a desk, behind the trash can in the corner, or between a wide metal shelf and the wall. But if whoever it was stayed more than a few minutes, they'd likely find her...

She whirled and moved for the closed door.

The voices grew louder.

No time to run.

She scurried for the righthand corner, the metal shelf against the wall to her right, the large, industrial-sized garbage can to her left. She squeezed in behind the garbage can, her butt on the cement floor, knees up, hands wrapped around her legs to keep them pressed against her torso.

She shifted the can slightly, wincing at the soft scraping sound, moving it a few inches until it sat directly in front of her, blocking her body from the view of anyone standing in the doorway across the room.

They'd have to come right up to the desk to see her. Which very well might happen.

The basket. It was still outside. Thank goodness she'd taken the extra few seconds to hide it around the corner. The only way they'd see it was if they walked all the way to the fence.

Her mouth was dry, parched like she hadn't had a drink in days. Her heart hammered against her ribs. Her head pulsed with fear. *Go away. Please, just go away.*

But they didn't go away. The murmur of voices rose until she could make out the words.

"God did not choose you for this purpose for you to make excuses!" a man said. She recognized the warm, melodic voice of the Prophet. Only his voice wasn't melodic now, but sharp and impatient.

"No excuses," a second man said. He spoke with a thick accent that sounded Eastern European, like the movies she'd watched with Nazi or foreign mobsters. Harsh, back-of-the-throat, and phlegmy, though his English was precise. "It is ready to go, just as we planned."

"Pack up only what's needed," the Prophet said. "Leave the rest."

"Leave the rest?"

"We don't need it anymore."

"But...what if it's found?"

"That's the point, isn't it, Franco?" the Prophet said, amusement in his voice. "They need their breadcrumbs laid out for them."

"Yes," the second man said, sounding as confused as Eden was. "I suppose it is so."

"It will all come to light very soon. You do not have long to wait, my friend. Our glory is at hand."

The other man chuckled nervously. "Then to God be the glory."

"Of course." The Prophet cleared his throat. "The chopper will arrive in a few hours. See that the asset is on board with everything needed to complete the final mission."

"I will see to it personally, comrade," the man with the accent said. "I need a few men."

"You have them. I'll have Solomon send some over."

"And a vehicle for transport to the chopper."

"Get it now. The hurricane will arrive a few hours after dawn, but winds could get nasty before then. We may need to leave at a moment's notice."

"I will bring it around."

"If only we had ten thousand loyal soldiers such as yourself," said the Prophet. "The entire world would kneel at our feet."

"They already will," the second man said.

The Prophet laughed—a deep, hearty, joyous laugh. "The match is lit. We have only to toss it to burn our enemies to the ground, brother."

"It will be a glorious sight to see."

"You are right about that," the Prophet said. "Blessings be upon you."

"And you."

More crunching on gravel. Footsteps leading away from the building.

Eden didn't breathe. Her tailbone hurt. Her muscles cramped from the tension, but she didn't dare move. Not until it was safe.

As if this world would ever be safe again.

23
EDEN

E den waited. Her ears strained for any noise that didn't belong. Trees creaked and rustled in the wind. A skitter of dry leaves across the grass. Nothing else. *Please, please be gone.*

She stayed put a few minutes more. Still nothing.

Cautiously, she pushed the garbage can a few inches. It scraped across the concrete. She winced, waiting for a shadow to fall over her, a shout of alarm.

Nothing.

They were gone.

She didn't have time to think about what she'd heard. She needed to get out of there before the man with the accent returned with the transport vehicle and more Shepherds.

She shoved the garbage can out of the way and stood, her knees creaking in protest. Once she'd put the can back in its place, she hurried to the door and peeked around the corner.

The men were out of sight. For now.

She retrieved the basket with shaking hands and ran. She stumbled through the woods, trying desperately to be as quiet as she could but too afraid to slow down. She barely felt the thorns clawing at her legs and skirt, the twigs catching in her hair, the mud sloshing her shoes.

What felt like an eternity later, she reached the men's barracks and broke through the tree line. She forced herself to slow to a walk, craning her neck to check if anyone had noticed her.

Everyone was still busy. The sounds of hammering filled the air. The wind shook the trees. She started for the infirmary and then halted, her pulse thudding in her throat.

She could just make out the medical clinic across the wide clearing. Two people stood outside in front of the door. Sister Rosemarie—and Eden's father. Hopefully the Sister was making up an excuse for why her father couldn't check on her. Hopefully, he believed it.

At any rate, she couldn't go there now. She glanced around again. Most people were concentrated at the cabins, the gardens and barns, and the cafeteria. No one was down at the water's edge or within a hundred yards of the boathouse.

She needed to contact Dakota immediately. Nothing was more important. A hot, sickly wave of dizziness flushed through her. Her knees wobbled. If she got caught...

It didn't matter. She didn't have a choice. *Do it afraid.*

Eden steadied herself, strolling with forced calm, skirting the trees so she could duck back into the woods if she needed to. When she reached the shoreline, she hurried to the boathouse.

She peered inside the dirty window panel in the door. Several speedboats and airboats bobbed placidly in the water. No one was inside.

She pulled out Sister Rosemarie's keys surreptitiously and jammed in a few wrong keys before finding the correct one. She slipped inside, closed the door behind her, and pulled the radio out from the bottom of the basket.

Setting the basket at her feet, she leaned against the wall for a moment, breathing hard.

There was no time to waste. She flicked on the radio and pressed the mic. For a second, her thoughts were so jumbled and disjointed, she couldn't remember the order of the dots and dashes.

She hissed a breath through her teeth. *Get it together!* Everyone she loved depended on her. The tens of thousands of people that bomb would decimate were depending on her.

She visualized her drawing pad in her mind's eye. It came back to her.

She keyed in her code name—Rose—so Dakota knew it was her.

The radio crackled. "I'm here," her sister said.

She keyed in the letters painstakingly slowly. I S-A-W I-T. She swallowed. O-N-E M-O-R-E B-O-M-B.

"Did you just say that there's another bomb?" Dakota asked, horror and disbelief in her voice.

Y-E-S I-T-S R-E-A-D-Y.

A sharp intake of breath. "Eden, this is very important. Did you see their plans? Do you know where they're going to detonate it?"

She closed her eyes, saw the maps on the corkboard, one of the U.S., one of Florida, and the words scrawled on the sticky note stuck beside the Florida map. She wasn't sure exactly what it meant, but Dakota would probably know. And if not Dakota, then Hawthorne.

With shaking hands, she coded the first letter.

"Hey!" a voice yelled. "Is someone in there?"

Her heart lurched into her throat. She took two swift steps and looked through the glass panel in the door. Not five feet away, a Shepherd strode toward the boathouse, his brow already wrinkling in anger.

Eden didn't have time to react.

Before she could move, the Shepherd burst into the boathouse.

Get rid of the radio! Eden didn't think—she just acted. She turned and hurled the radio as hard as she could. The radio hit the water with a loud splash. It sank below the surface, down, down, down.

As soon as it disappeared, she knew it was a mistake. Maybe she could've slipped it under her skirt in time, or switched it off and hidden it behind her back...

"What are you doing in here?" the Shepherd demanded.

She couldn't think about what she should've done. There wasn't time.

Eden turned to face him, her back to the water. She shook her head and tried to look appropriately demure and sickly at the same time.

"What did you just do?" His eyes narrowed suspiciously. "I thought I heard voices."

She noticed a few pebbles that had fallen off her shoes from the gravel by the restricted buildings. She stooped, scooped them up, and tossed them into the water.

He stared at her for a moment, then shrugged. "You aren't allowed in here."

She smiled sweetly up at him.

He looked her over, his gaze traveling from the twigs stuck in her hair to her shirt half-hanging out of her waistband to the mud streaking the bottom of her skirt and shoes. "Just because you're the Prophet's new bride doesn't mean you get to do whatever you want."

I hate you, she signed. *I hope you never find anyone to love you for as long as you live.*

"Huh?"

You're as stupid as you look, aren't you?

He stared at her blankly.

She just kept smiling. *You probably have rocks for brains.*

It felt good to insult him in sign language. She wished Logan were here to see it.

"Whatever." The man made to grab her arm but hesitated, as if realizing that he couldn't treat her as poorly as he usually treated the women and girls of the compound. He dropped his hand. "You need to come with me."

The fake smile slid from her face. She clutched her stomach and acted like she was about to heave.

He stepped quickly away. "I know, I know. Straight back to the infirmary you go."

She followed him back, still making herself look sick. It wasn't hard. She didn't need to pretend to feel sick. She still felt hot and light-headed. Bitter acid swirled in her stomach.

The radio was gone now. From here on out, she had no way to communicate with the outside world. She'd managed to tell them about the existence of the bomb, but not where it was headed.

Camp Disney.

She'd done her best. She hoped it would be enough.

2 4
DAKOTA

D akota stood on the dock and stared out at the brackish
water. She gripped the radio in one hand, the page with
Eden's Morse code alphabet key in the other, her arms hanging
limply at her side.

An alligator drifted near the pilings beneath her feet. Maybe
nine or ten feet long, it was a giant primordial lizard with ridged,
leathery skin, a diamond-shaped head like a dragon's, and razor-
sharp teeth.

Monsters of the swamp. So deadly, and yet they rarely
attacked people. But if they wanted to, the damage they
could do...

She'd take those claws and teeth in a heartbeat. There was
plenty of damage she wanted to inflict.

Her call with Eden had been cut short. She'd heard the Shepherd shouting something, then only static. She'd yelled Eden's
name a dozen times, but it didn't matter. Eden wasn't there.

Dakota despised the sour-sick feeling of utter helplessness
churning in her gut. Her sister was somewhere across this very
swamp, trapped by human monsters, and there wasn't a thing
she could do from here to help her.

Yes, there damn well was.

But it was risky. The consequences could be more costly than she wanted to pay. But in the end, she didn't have a choice. There were too many lives at stake.

Julio was right. The existence of another bomb meant this was far, far larger than her and Eden. She had to do the right thing, no matter what.

She hooked the radio on her belt, pulled the satphone out of her pants' pocket, and called Hawthorne—he'd given her his personal number during their earlier call.

He answered on the third ring. "Hit me."

"She saw it, Hawthorne. It's real. The Shepherds of Mercy did this."

"Holy hell."

"How soon can you get in there?"

"I can't say for sure. Fifty percent of our local people—ATF, FBI, Miami police, Broward sheriff's department, even the Army and National Guard—they're either dead or MIA. Another ninety percent have already evacuated ahead of Helen. It'll be our top priority, I assure you. But gathering a team right now—"

"The Prophet—their leader—he's leaving at dawn, and he's taking Eden with him."

"I understand—"

"No!" she shouted into the phone. "You don't! There's another nuclear bomb."

Dead silence on the other end.

She imagined his face—the shock and horror he must be feeling, the same as she was. "Eden saw it. It's real. She said it's ready to go."

"Go where?" Hawthorne asked, his voice strained. "Does she know?"

"She was only able to key in the first letter. A 'C.' She started on the second but didn't finish before she was caught. I don't think she'll get another chance."

Hawthorne cursed. "Did Eden say—does she know when?"

"Only that the Prophet is leaving somewhere at dawn—or before. There's a good chance the bomb is going with him."

"We have to raid that compound. Tonight."

"I know."

"Damn it! Another city...hundreds of thousands of American citizens..." Hawthorne sucked in a ragged breath. "The U.S. is already threatening Iran. Iran is pushing back. So are its allies, Russia included. What do you think President Harrington will do if another bomb detonates on American soil?"

"She wouldn't sit on her hands. She'd strike back."

"She'd have to. And if she was wrong? If we attacked Iran without proof, and then it came out that our own people did this to us, that Iran was innocent after all? How would Iran take that? Lebanon and Syria? Let alone China and Russia?"

Dakota swallowed. She didn't want to contemplate the possible repercussions, didn't know much about world politics anyway. Her life so far had been focused purely on survival.

But she knew human nature. And human nature didn't change—whether you were a homeless street rat protecting your corner, a gangster expanding his territory, or the president of a country on its knees.

Someone hits you? You hit back ten times harder. Or you get your bigger, stronger friends to do it for you.

"If another bomb detonates on American soil," Hawthorne said, "there's a good chance we'll bomb Iran to kingdom come the second it happens. No investigation, no evidence."

Her chest tightened. "It could start a war."

"It could start *the* war. World War III. Mutually assured destruction. World annihilation. Armageddon. We thought thirteen WMDs were bad? Wait until twenty-three thousand nukes are in the mix."

"Let's not get ahead of ourselves." She tried to act like Julio would. He'd be calm right now, steady as a rock. She felt anything but calm. "It hasn't happened yet."

"I already talked to my uncle, General Pierce. He said it was a no-go from the Governor's office, but with this new information...this changes everything. Eden is an eyewitness. And you're both former members of the Shepherds, so your testimony holds tremendous clout."

"We weren't *members* of the Shepherds," she said, forcing her voice to remain even. "We were their prisoners."

"Forgive me," Hawthorne said immediately. "You're right. I'm sorry, Dakota."

"Just tell me we can nail them."

"These are domestic terrorists. The Patriot Act means we can get a warrant without too much difficulty." He snorted. "What am I saying? We're under martial law. The concept of private property no longer exists. Honestly, law enforcement agencies are so splintered and disorganized that disarray doesn't begin to describe it. With the Posse Comitatus Act suspended, DHS can request aid from the Army to assist, even though this is a domestic law enforcement case. Best case scenario, we could send in Spec Ops to go in and clean up."

"But?" Dakota asked, hearing the doubt in his voice.

"But that's not going to happen given the emergency time constraints. There's no time. Too many assets are simply gone, deployed, or evacuated. This is gonna be a last-second mission made up of thrown together units under DHS—ATF, FBI. Law enforcement, U.S. Marshals, whoever we can get.

"As soon as we get the go-ahead, I'm going to call you back so you can tell us everything you know about this place. I've already been looking into things on my end. With everything shot to hell right now, it's a mother, let me tell you. But we've got the satellites in business. A ton of trees blocking our view, but there's clearly lots of activity happening right now. We're working on getting a drone overhead, and Kinsey is checking property records."

She was grateful that he'd taken their conversation seriously, that he believed Eden's account wholeheartedly. He was a good man to have on their side in a crisis. And yet, a chill of unease shivered through her.

"We'll get these dirtbags, Dakota. I promise you."

"There are at least seventy-five women and children in that compound. Not the least of which is my sister."

"Look, forget what I told you before. Even with all that, we're still the best in the world. We'll get the job done, no matter what."

"That's what I'm afraid of. You're going in hot with a bunch of amped-up soldiers and more guns. You can't promise her safety. Or anyone else's."

"We'll do everything we can to protect Eden and the other innocents inside that compound." His voice went hard. "But you must understand, Dakota. There are potentially hundreds of thousands of innocent people in the path of that WMD."

Fear stuck in her throat like a hook. The stakes were enormous—she knew that. Countless more lives would be lost if the last bomb detonated.

And if Hawthorne was right about the saber-rattling occurring on the world stage, the risk of further carnage was an absolute certainty.

Dakota cared. She cared tremendously. She wanted to save everyone just like Hawthorne did. But in the center of those overwhelming numbers and statistics pulsed the heartbeat of one person.

Eden.

"We have to stop that bomb," Hawthorne said.

Dakota swallowed. "I know."

She closed the phone and slipped it into her pocket. She held Eden's drawing pad in both hands, clutching it to her chest until her knuckles whitened.

The smell of smoke filled her nostrils. So much had happened already since this morning, and Ezra's pyre still burned.

For a long moment, she stood there, taking in the miles and

miles of sawgrass, the cypress tree islands and mangroves, the sky dark as slate above them, promising destruction and violence.

She heard footsteps behind her.

"Julio has lunch ready," Logan said. "Was that Hawthorne?"

Resolve burned through her veins. She would do whatever it took. "We called in the cavalry. I know why we had to do it. But Eden could die in the crossfire. I won't let that happen."

"I won't, either."

She turned to face him, the wind whipping her hair, warmth flushing her cheeks, her heart brimming with too many emotions to name. "We need to call the Collier brothers. And Haasi."

25
LOGAN

"And that's everything we know so far," Logan said, stretching out his hands.

The table had been quiet and still for the last several minutes as Logan, Dakota, and Julio explained the events of the last several hours.

Three of the Collier brothers sat at one side of the table, Logan, Julio, and Dakota on the other side. Worn lines creased the brothers' hard, bearded faces. They all wore leather vests, jeans, and worn baseball caps.

Haasi leaned against the counter, her crossbow against the cabinets at her feet.

Boyd was recovering from his bullet wound. Maki was back at Haasi's property watching the kids and guarding the property. And Zander was patrolling US 41 on his motorcycle, watching Mangrove Road for desperate refugees with looting and mayhem on their minds.

Besides, after he'd betrayed them to the Shepherds, no one particularly wanted to see him, and he had no desire to show his face here.

Everyone was on edge. They would be for a while.

"I'll be damned," Archer rumbled, a scowl deepening the

lines around his mouth. He leaned back in his chair, arms crossed over his burly chest. He was an affable giant of a man in his forties, with broad shoulders and arms bulging with muscles the size of footballs.

"I knew evil lurked in that place." Haasi's long gray hair was woven into a braid that hung down her right shoulder. Fine wrinkles netted the dusky bronze skin over the Miccosukee Native American's high cheekbones, her coal-black eyes hard with anger. "I never guessed it could be this..."

"No one did," Dakota said dully. "I lived there, and I didn't know. The Shepherds are cunning. And they only revealed their true intentions to a select 'chosen' few. The rest of them are just misguided sheep who think abuse equals devotion."

Logan watched Dakota carefully. She kept glancing at the bullet holes in the walls, the sandbags still stacked beneath the windows, the faint bloodstains streaking the wooden floor.

The whole cabin smelled of bleach and antiseptic. Julio had spent hours cleaning Ezra's cabin to within an inch of its life.

But the scars of last night's battle couldn't just be scrubbed away. Neither could the memories.

Her expression was tense, sleepless hollows beneath her eyes. Her auburn hair was pulled back into its usual ponytail, and she was dressed in clean clothes—a faded army-green undershirt of Ezra's, lightweight gray pants, and hiking boots.

On the outside, she looked fine. Tired and stressed, but as tough as ever.

It was the inside he was worried about.

"I can't believe it," Jake said, his eyes furious. He was shorter than Archer and slimmer than the twins, his long brown hair pulled into a ponytail at the base of his neck.

He was the hot-tempered brother, the one who'd tried to punch Logan after being taken hostage. It hadn't turned out well for Jake. He seemed to have gotten over it, at least. "All this time, these freaks were operating in *our* swamp. Not fifty miles away! Makes me want to—"

"Knock some heads together?" Archer asked.

"Hell yeah!" Zane balled his meaty hands into fists. "Preferably with bullets."

"They don't get to come in here and try to destroy our country." Jake's features contorted in a mix of rage and disbelief. "I don't care if they were born here. They're terrorists. They deserve death by firing squad."

"Enough talking." Haasi's lips thinned to a grim line. "We can rant and rave all we want. The question is, what are we going to do about it?"

Logan scratched at the scruff growing in along his jaw. "Our friend Trey Hawthorne is bringing whoever DHS could cobble together at the last minute: law enforcement, ATF and FBI under DHS, military police, U.S. Marshals. They're going to raid the compound. They'll stop the Shepherds and find the bomb."

"About time the government showed up!" Archer said.

Haasi slanted her sharp gaze at Dakota. Her head was bent, like she was studying the seams of the table for a solution to the insurmountable problem before them. "Seems risky for those women and kids in there. For Eden."

Dakota lifted her head. "It is."

Julio touched his gold cross. "They'll come in hot. They'll use tear gas, flash bombs, machine guns. Maybe even rockets. It'll be chaotic and dangerous."

"I have to save her," Dakota said in a low hoarse voice. She spread her hands on the table, palms down. Her eyes were shiny. "I promised I'd never leave her. Never, ever."

"I'm sorry, Dakota," Zane said, "but it sounds like a suicide mission."

"Maybe." The dullness was gone from her eyes, replaced with the steely determination Logan knew so well. She lifted her chin, daring anyone to contradict her. "I'm not stupid. I know it's dangerous. But I have a plan."

26

DAKOTA

"We can't go in there to fight," Julio said quietly. "None of us have the training and tactical experience. That's why we called Hawthorne."

"Not to fight." Dakota's jaw flexed. "That doesn't mean I'm putting Eden's fate in their hands."

She spread out one of Ezra's old paper maps of Florida on the table as everyone leaned in close. She drew an imaginary line from the compound's location off Alligator Alley straight down through the mass of green to Mangrove Road.

"The River Grass compound is over fifty miles from here by road. Or, you can take the water. It's not actually a straight line but a labyrinth of winding, snaking channels through the swamp. It shaves off maybe thirty miles. We have three airboats between us, plus Ezra's fishing boat."

"Sounds good so far," Archer said. "Except for the hurricane."

"Hurricane Helen is going to make landfall near Sunny Isles around eight a.m. We're much further inland than the coast."

"It'll still be a brutal storm by the time it hits us," Haasi said.

"We can use the hurricane," Logan said. "The Shepherds will be distracted shoring up their buildings and taking shelter."

"Mother Mary and Joseph," Julio breathed, his face going pale.

"We'll get in and out *before* the hurricane, not during."

Jake shook his head. "I'm still listening, for some insane reason. Keep going."

Dakota took Eden's drawing pad from the corner of the table, flipped past the Morse code and ASL alphabet, and the gorgeous drawings of egrets, turtles, gators, and panthers until she finally reached a fresh page.

She stood there for a moment, her throat tightening, trying and failing to push back the emotions threatening to boil up.

Falling apart wasn't going to save anyone. She had to keep it together.

Logan touched her shoulder. He didn't say anything. He didn't do anything else. He simply sat close to her, the solid strength of him radiating into her own body.

It was all she needed.

She placed the drawing pad in front of her and tugged out the pencil tucked into the spiral. "The compound is shaped like a rough oval. The front gate is to the north; the boathouse, dock, and swamp to the south. This is the huge clearing in the middle.

"The single men's quarters and the family cabins are on the west side. The henhouse, goat and pig pens, and the gardens are all to the northwest behind the cafeteria.

"The chapel is on the southern end, centered between the restricted area and the woods on the west and the infirmary to the east. It's central to everything. The Prophet's house is the biggest and nicest. It's secluded on the east side along with the school.

"The fenced perimeter is patrolled by armed Shepherds at all times. There's razor wire at the top. They say it's to keep the wicked out, but it's really to keep people from trying to escape. At the front gate, there's a platform to the east and another to the west, always manned by sentries with machine guns."

Dakota moved her pencil down near the water. "This is the

restricted area. They keep most of the weapons there. They have a few armored vehicles that would come in and out of the main gate. A helicopter would land in the clearing sometimes to load and unload big crates or transport the Prophet to wherever."

She drew an X over the restricted area. "That's where they must be keeping the bomb."

Archer leaned forward and placed his huge hands on the table. "How would we get in?"

She motioned at the gear, guns, and uniforms they'd confiscated from the dead Shepherds piled in the center of the living room. "We take whatever we can use from them. Their fatigues, their bullet-proof vests, NV goggles, their weapons and ammo. With a bit of luck, we can pass for Shepherds at a distance, especially at night."

Jake nodded, his lips pursed. "Not a bad idea. Until Hawthorne comes. The soldiers will think we're with them."

Hawthorne had sent her a one-word message earlier: *Midnight.* If they were in by ten or ten-thirty p.m., that should give them the time they needed. "We'll be gone before they arrive."

"I can make up some Molotov cocktails for you," Zane offered. "My one-ninety proof special brew burns like a mother. On second thought, I've got better fuel options—gasoline, motor oil, butane, plus tar and petroleum jelly for thickening agents. I can load a bunch of rags and glass bottles in a backpack with padding."

"Thanks, Zane." Dakota turned back to her map. "There's a peninsula on the southwest side. It's narrow—maybe one hundred and fifty yards long, twenty yards wide, and heavily wooded. The Prophet never bothered to fence it. The fence stops at the mainland, at the water's edge.

"A narrow canal runs through the peninsula maybe forty feet past the fence line. Maddox and I used to use it to sneak out. We just had to time it when a patrol wasn't around, and we could get the boat out and through the channel in a few minutes flat.

"We can come in at an angle just east of the peninsula and the fence line. Cut the engines and paddle when we're close so we don't make noise. We can hide the boats in the tall sawgrass."

"They could have eyes on it now," Julio said. "Things change, and Maddox knows about it."

She nodded soberly. "We need to check first. Get close and watch them for a while."

"Surveillance," Logan said.

"They have dense woods all the way up to the fence line. Stupid of them, but it can work for us. We can hike in perpendicular to the fence and set up surveillance posts in the trees using the binoculars and the NV goggles."

Logan studied the map. "We lay low, recon their positions, track their shift changes, observe their defensive strength, and pass that information on to Hawthorne with the satphone. Then when it gets dark, we mount a well-informed snatch and run."

Dakota swallowed the sudden lump in her throat. She was incredibly grateful that he had her back. They were on the same page, working together in sync just like they always had.

It meant more to her than she could ever say.

She cleared her throat. "After we're gone, Hawthorne comes roaring in, destroys the Shepherds' lair, and captures the bomb."

"It won't be that easy," Julio said gravely. "What is that saying? No battle plan survives contact with the enemy."

"There are so many holes in this plan, it looks like Swiss cheese," Zane said.

"I know." Anxiety and frustration twisted in her gut. "It's the best we have."

"I'm in." Haasi lifted her chin. Her eyes were red-rimmed and bloodshot. It hadn't been easy to tell Ezra's old friend that he was dead. She and Haasi had wept together. "Maki will be, too."

"No way I'm staying home for this," Archer said adamantly.

"Count me in," Jake said.

"You promise I won't get shot?" Zane asked.

"No," Dakota and Logan said at the same time.

Archer leaned forward. "Zane. This is for all of us. Think about what you can tell your children and your grandchildren."

"If I'm alive to tell them," Zane grumbled.

"Then I'll tell them how your sorry ass died," Jake said, his eyes blazing. "A hero."

"You didn't sit back on your hands," Archer said. "You were a part of the greatest takedown in American history. Think about when Seal Team Six finally offed Osama Bin Laden. This is even bigger."

"Fine," Zane sighed dramatically. "I'm in. But I'm bringing my Molotov cocktails, just in case."

27
DAKOTA

Dakota sank down onto Ezra's bed. It was covered with a thin, neatly folded quilt dotted with tiny forget-me-nots. Probably bought by Izzy a decade ago.

Her heart contracted painfully as she took in the small spare room. A closet, the door closed. A ceiling fan turning lazily overhead, blown by the wind coming through the broken window. An end table, empty but for a small lamp and a wrinkled paperback book—a Louis L'Amour western. It figured.

The dresser stood across from the bed, so pristine the waxed top glistened in the dim gray daylight. A jewelry box and a photo of Ezra and Izzy were the only knickknacks. In the photo, they were in their thirties, young and full of light and laughter.

Just like everywhere else in the house, the walls were papered with Izzy's black-and-white photographs. Here they were more intimate, somehow. One was a close-up of Ezra looking over his shoulder, grinning at the camera, his eyes bright, the same white grizzled beard but with far less wrinkles lining his weathered face.

Several of the frames were splintered, the glass cracked. Julio had been in here, Dakota realized with a start. He'd swept up the debris, replaced the pictures on the walls, tried to leave it the same way Ezra would have wanted.

She placed her pistol on the nightstand, pulled the quilt into her lap, and twisted the fabric in her fists. A wave of grief throbbed through her. The sorrow ebbed and flowed, barely held back by the dam of her stubborn will.

Not yet. She couldn't let it out, not until this was over.

Her eyes burned. She blinked, the weight of her weariness pulling at her, tempting her with the oblivion of dreamless sleep. As if she'd be so lucky.

She was supposed to be taking a nap. Haasi had insisted. "Did you sleep at all last night? I didn't think so. You're exhausted from one battle and you want to leap headfirst into another? Fatigue will get you killed as easily as a bullet. You need to keep your head screwed on straight."

Haasi had glanced at Dakota's watch. "It's barely one p.m. I'll get water and something to eat ready. Sleep for three hours, then you go."

So here she was, in Ezra's room, using his bed and trying not to fall apart.

She'd stripped off her shirt and pants and wore only a tank top and an old pair of Ezra's basketball shorts. They barely stayed on her hips, but that didn't matter. The cooler she was, the better she'd sleep.

Someone knocked on the door.

Instinctively, she stiffened.

"It's me," Logan said.

Her stomach fluttered despite her exhaustion. "Come in."

He smiled grimly at her as he strode in, shut the door behind him, and sat down next to her. The mattress sagged beneath his weight. She slipped closer to him until their legs were touching.

Heat flushed through her. She cleared her throat and pulled at a loose thread of the quilt, still wadded in her lap. "Can't sleep?"

"How could you tell?" He sighed and rubbed his eyes with

his scarred knuckles. "I need to, though. We both do. Haasi's right. Any reduction in alertness or reaction time could be deadly."

"I feel—I'm worried about the nightmares, you know? And what might happen tonight."

"I can't tell you it's going to be okay," he said heavily. "I wish I could. All I can say is I'm right here. Today, tonight. Whenever you need me."

"I know."

His smile reached his eyes, something shifting in his expression, a flicker of light over dark water. Her belly surged with heat.

He leaned toward her, placed his hand on her shoulder. He rubbed her shoulder blade, his fingers slipping beneath the strap of her tank top.

Every inch of the skin on her back prickled, the scars suddenly itching and painful. Instinctively, she curled away, hunching her shoulders and going rigid.

He lifted his hand. A flash of uncertainty crossed his face. "Do you want me to leave?"

"Yes. I mean, no," she said, suddenly flustered.

She didn't want him to leave. This was her knee-jerk reaction kicking in, that old failsafe from years as an unwanted foster kid, from her time in the harsh and lonely wasteland of the compound.

She swallowed. "I want you to stay."

His gaze roamed over her face, searching, still unsure. He watched her warily, like she was a wild creature who might bolt at any second.

Maybe she was.

She stared straight ahead at the photograph on the wall of Ezra smiling until her eyes blurred. Why the hell was she suddenly so scared? What was wrong with her?

Everything she'd faced head-on—psychopathic religious terrorists, drunken foster parents who used their fists instead of words, a burning, radioactive city—and now she was terrified.

It was stupid. She knew it was, and yet she still felt it, oozing through her like an insidious poison. That deep, primal fear of rejection, of being unwanted, unloved, alone.

She willed herself to meet his eyes. "I have scars."

He didn't hesitate or look alarmed. "We all do."

"Mine are different..."

"They can't be worse than mine." His gaze was steady on hers, unflinching. "You can show me, if you want."

He needed to see her for who she was, all of her, just like she'd seen him out on the water that day on the boat. She needed to trust him fully the same way he'd trusted her.

It was the only way forward.

Screw fear. She hadn't come all this way to back down now.

She forced herself to lean over, twist her torso, and pull back the fabric of her tank top to reveal the dozens of burns that marred her back from the base of her spine to her shoulder blades—the scar tissue seared, misshapen, white and shiny and alien-looking.

"They're ugly," she whispered.

"Nothing about you is ugly," he said, just as soft.

Gently, he touched her shoulder blade. She felt the heat of his fingers grazing her mutilated skin. The scars pulsed.

Memories flooded in—the howling scream torn from her throat, the singed stench of her own burnt flesh, the electric surge of pain so intense it felt like her lungs were collapsing, like she was drowning on dry land.

Everything went blurry. She blinked rapidly. Her brain screamed at her to pull away, to flee, to escape. But she didn't.

The pain was a phantom. It wasn't real.

This room was real. Logan was real.

The only pain was in the memories. In the power she gave to them.

The memories were under her control. She could choose to let them in—or not. She chose not.

The knot in her stomach loosened. The room snapped back into focus.

She turned to Logan. He stroked her cheek, tucked a stray strand of her hair behind her ears. His dark eyes were tender, but there was a ferocity there, too.

He cupped her chin and tilted it toward him. "I told you I was in this, didn't I? I meant it. To the end."

Hands tangling in her hair, he drew her roughly closer. He kissed her. Hard and fierce and full of all the things they hadn't yet said but felt in every fiber of their beings.

She kissed him back, kissed him until her blood was buzzing, until everything that hurt inside her seemed to melt into something warm and right and real.

They lay next to each other, too tired for anything else but desperate for physical contact, for closeness.

Dakota curled into a comma on her side. Logan curved around her, his arm nestled across her ribs, holding her hand.

As she drifted off, she laced her fingers with his, the space inside this little room expanding to fit everything inside them both: all their jagged pieces and hollow parts, and all the ugly and beautiful threads that held them together.

28
SHAY

S hay adjusted the shoulder strap of her backpack and took another shuffling step forward. She'd been standing in a long line of hundreds of people for well over an hour. At least she was almost inside the FEMA in-take trailer for the refugee center nicknamed Camp Disney.

Straight ahead beyond the trailer, she glimpsed endless rows and rows of orderly white tents within the huge fenced perimeter. Behind her, the line straggled almost the length of a football field to the entrance, the gates manned by several National Guardsmen with armored vehicles.

Concrete barriers were set at angles along the road, forcing vehicles to weave slowly and approach the gate single file. Everyone had been frisked—and relieved of their weapons if they had any—before entering the camp.

Shay's stomach rumbled. She took off her glasses and wiped her tired eyes. Even more than food, she wanted to sleep for a week.

The journey from the Miami airport to the town of Kissimmee outside of Orlando was under two hundred and fifty miles. It should've taken three hours. Instead, it took almost eight.

Even with an armed escort and the military clearing the road ahead of them, the convoy of buses was forced to take side roads and alternative routes multiple times. Some areas were still too radioactive to cross, others too dangerous.

Now they stood in this eternal line waiting to be assigned their new living quarters for the foreseeable future. Everything seemed rushed, chaotic, disorganized.

Everyone was dazed, stunned, and vacant-eyed. Some people had only the clothes on their backs. If they'd come from the Emergency Operation Center like Shay, even their clothes weren't their own. Others hiked backpacks over their shoulders or pulled wheeled suitcases at their heels—their entire lives in what they could carry.

The air was hot and cloying, even after seven p.m. Insects buzzed all around her. Somewhere, a guard was shouting orders. A couple of places ahead of her, a mom shushed a crying baby.

"Next!" a voice ordered from inside the trailer.

She moved forward again, stepping into the trailer. A generator whirred quietly. Even with the overworked A/C, the air was still hot and stale and smelled faintly of pine air freshener.

The small building was crammed with dozens of bodies. Something pushed into her from behind. Someone else elbowed her.

"Oops, sorry," Shay said as she accidentally bumped the couple ahead of her.

A Hispanic woman turned and smiled tiredly at her. In her late thirties, she had long black hair, delicate features, and kind but haunted eyes. "No worries, honey. We're all a little clumsy right now, among other things."

"Next!"

The Hispanic woman and her husband stepped up to a rectangular table. Two people sat behind it with "FEMA Recovery Team" pins affixed to their shirts. Several electronic tablets, yellow folders and binders, and various stacks of paper were scattered haphazardly across the table.

At the next table, more volunteers were unpacking large cardboard boxes and handing out emergency bags of toiletries. Boxes and crates stacked in jumbled piles leaned precariously behind both tables.

In the only clear space sat a television placed on a narrow stand and set to one of the local news stations. The news was only about one thing anymore.

"Name, address, and number in your party, please," the female volunteer said in a harsh, nasally voice. "I'll need to see your driver's licenses or state I.D."

Shay tuned out their voices, trying and failing to wait patiently. She tried not to think about how much she missed Hawthorne or how long she'd have to stay in this place. She focused on the television instead.

The newscaster stared at the camera, his face strained. "The U.S. Air Force has dispatched thirty more F-22 stealth fighters to Qatar, again beefing up its forces in the Middle East amid escalating tensions with Iran...Iran shot down two drones yesterday with surface-to-air missiles, claiming the U.S. is invading their air space to search for potential bombing targets. Iran has categorically denied responsibility for the terrorist attacks that have devastated thirteen cities and much of America's infrastructure. This is just the latest in a series of provocations between the US and Iran..."

Despite the heat, Shay shivered. She nibbled nervously on her thumbnail as she watched in growing dread. Several people near her stirred, muttering under their breaths.

"Just bomb them to hell already," one man said.

"And take out Russia while we're at it," another woman said, her voice full of bitterness and rage.

Shay's mouth went drier than it already was. How close were they to war? Before her conversation with Dakota this morning, she would've believed Iran and those Hezbollah terrorists were guilty just like the rest of the country did.

Now she didn't know what to believe.

A ticker below the newscasters' desk reported on more saber-rattling threats from Russia and China, then an update on Helen. The category 3 hurricane was still aiming straight for the heart of Miami, set to make landfall sometime in the morning.

Yet another disaster to make things even worse.

Shay closed her eyes and sucked in a deep breath. She felt worthless here. Her friends were still in the Everglades trying to stop those domestic terrorists. All she could think about was how worried she was for all of them—Hawthorne included.

The FEMA worker's raised voice caught Shay's attention. "Those are the rules. No exceptions."

"We're trying to find our daughter," the Hispanic woman repeated. "We were separated in the attack. Surely, you have a master list of survivors. We just want to see—"

"As I just told you, we will reunite families as soon as possible, but that time is not now."

The woman's shoulders slumped. Her husband put his arm around her. "When do you think—"

"We'll let you know," the woman said curtly. Her face was stony, her eyes devoid of sympathy—or any emotion.

Shay tried to understand how they must feel. The work was overwhelming and never-ending. The crippling desperation, grief, and loss was simply too much for the human psyche to process.

You went numb after a while—and hard. It wasn't an excuse, but some people believed it was the only way to cope.

"Here are your cards. Please head right to make your way to housing. You report for work duty at nine a.m."

The woman hesitated. "Also, we have a place to go. My mother is in Idaho. She'll gladly take us. We were just waiting on our daughter, but we don't want to be extra mouths to feed."

"Ma'am, I am not authorized to allow anyone to leave the premises at this time. It's for your own safety."

"But—"

The FEMA worker frowned, getting irritated now. "I don't

make the rules. We're under martial law. If you don't wish to be arrested, I suggest you move along right now."

The woman's husband squeezed her shoulder. "There's nothing this lady can do about it, honey. Let's go."

They shuffled dejectedly to the second table.

"Next!"

Shay stepped up. She gave them all her info and watched them write notes in various binders and tablets. A printer sitting on the corner of the table whirred to life. "I can help in medical. I'm a nursing assistant."

The FEMA worker barely grunted in response. She pulled out several small slips of paper and rattled off instructions so rapidly Shay had a hard time keeping up. "You're assigned to tent F326. Here are your meal tickets. The times for breakfast, lunch, and dinner are stamped on the back. Your shower days are Tuesdays and Fridays. Report to the hospital at nine a.m."

"Well, um..."

The FEMA worker had already turned to the next group. "Next!"

Shay collected her toiletries allotment—a plastic toothbrush, tube of toothpaste, deodorant, and shampoo/bodywash—and exited the trailer. A soldier directed her into the camp itself. She entered the endless sea of tents crisscrossed by grassy aisles quickly turning to dirt.

The hum of subdued voices filled the air. Several babies were crying. Some adults, too. Everywhere she looked, their faces were the same—hopeless, despairing, defeated.

She kept one hand on the strap of her backpack and held the toiletries bag to her chest with the other. She took a deep breath, steeling herself. She would make the best of things, like she always did, no matter how dire the circumstances.

At least she was safe.

29

DAKOTA

Dakota shifted her hips with a wince. She'd been sitting in the fork of a live oak tree for over two hours. Spanish moss tickled her cheek as she pressed against the bark, angling herself awkwardly to get a better view as she peered through the binoculars.

The branch underneath her swayed, the leaves thrashing. She tightened her grip on the tree limb and scanned the bits and snatches she could see through the foliage.

The semi-tropical forest felt ancient and primordial. Everywhere she looked were spiky saw palmettos and lush ferns, dense thickets of bald cypress, and Spanish moss hanging like beards from ancient, twisting oak branches.

The forest was eerily empty of living creatures. No chattering squirrels. No singing birds, buzzing insects, or croaking frogs. No turtles or raccoons or flighty deer. The wind had even taken care of the mosquitos. The woods were utterly silent but for the rustling and creaking of the trees.

Animals could sense when a hurricane was coming. Those that could, left. Birds flew north, everything on four legs scattering.

Her chest tightened. The animals were a warning she

couldn't heed. They could hunker down in Ezra's shed and outlast any storm, but not without Eden.

She felt the time ticking away, each grain of sand slipping through the hourglass like the ground shifting beneath her feet.

The binoculars in one hand, she fumbled for the earpiece with her free hand, the wire plugged into the radio at her hip, and whispered into the mic. "Alpha, do you have a sitrep?" She asked Logan, using the nickname for situation report Haasi had suggested. "Over."

"The same, over," Logan said.

They'd split up into teams: Logan and Dakota were Team One; Jake and Archer were Team Two; Haasi, Maki, and Zane were Team Three; and Julio was the spotter.

They were spread out over a couple of miles, tucked into trees in the woods outside the compound perimeter. They were closer than Dakota felt comfortable with, but it was the only way to see anything through the heavy leaf canopy. Luckily, the wind swishing through the leaves shielded their movements and masked their noise.

They each wore the radios and earpieces they'd confiscated from the dead Shepherds, along with their clothes and weapons, tactical vests with armored plates, and binoculars and NV goggles. They had water bottles and pouches of venison jerky, compliments of Haasi.

So far, everything they'd reconned was as expected. Guards were patrolling the perimeter, carbines slung over their shoulders. Archer, who had eyes on the front gate, reported that there were four sentries, two at each platform.

The rest of the Shepherds were shoring up the equipment, planting sandbags around the bases of the buildings, and boarding up the remaining windows. M4s were leaning against walls and stacked casually on picnic tables, still within easy reach.

The women and children were busy lugging crates filled with food and jars of water from the kitchens down to the chapel.

Others hauled armfuls of blankets and pillows from the family cabins.

"The chapel is definitely where they're planning to wait out the hurricane," Dakota said. "Looks like they have supplies for everyone for several days. It makes sense. The chapel is big enough for everyone, and it's constructed with thick cinderblock instead of wood."

A white helicopter sat in the center of the clearing. Two armored vehicles were parked a few dozen yards away. The chopper had landed almost two hours earlier. The pilot had greeted some of the Shepherds and headed to the cafeteria. He hadn't ventured out since.

The sun was setting, though she could barely tell through the thick scrim of iron-gray clouds. The natural daylight was so dim that she had to squint to see clearly. Night would fall soon.

Almost time for the NV goggles. They could creep in even closer, then. The Shepherds on patrol didn't appear to carry NV, only high-beam flashlights attached to their belts.

When they'd boated in from the swamp a few hours ago, she had realized right away her original infiltration plan wouldn't work. Two Shepherds guarded the end of the fence line along the peninsula. They didn't patrol every thirty minutes, but remained stationary in a small wooden sentry tower, watching the water.

Luckily, Dakota had the group switch off their motors long before they reached the compound. They'd paddled inland a quarter mile down the shoreline using a wall of sawgrass as cover.

They would need some kind of distraction to draw away those guards. Once the guards were taken care of, Haasi and Maki would have the boats waiting in the cattails on the far side of the peninsula while Dakota and Logan snuck in and grabbed Eden.

Several small tree islands along that side would offer cover while they paddled a safe distance, then motored to safety before the good guys descended with all the fire and fury of hell.

Something stung her shin. Another sting. And another. A

fiery sensation crept up her leg. She glanced down. Her boots were crawling with tiny red fire ants. It figured. Not even a hurricane could faze the tiny indestructible monsters.

She hissed a curse and wiggled her leg, trying to shake them off. It was a stupid move. She knew better. It only made the ants angrier. The stinging worsened.

Forcing herself to move slowly and carefully, she bent down and swiped off as many as she could see. A few remained inside her boot, pricking and biting and stinging.

Maybe she should just take the damn thing off and—

"Something's happening," Julio said in her ear.

The ants forgotten, she brought up the binoculars and scanned the area, her heart pounding. A sudden movement in the clearing snagged her attention. She focused the binoculars.

She could make out several forms standing in a loose circle maybe fifty yards from the helicopter, which she couldn't see clearly, just a glimpse of the rotors. The Prophet's long blond hair was a dead giveaway. That was Solomon Cage beside him, along with Maddox and Reuben.

The Prophet was gesturing wildly. The men were turning and pointing. One of the Shepherds hurried across the clearing, radio to his mouth, probably heading for the restricted area.

Julio was right. "I see lots of movement."

"Are you sure?" Haasi asked. "I can't see anything from here. Over."

"Alpha, what do you see?"

"Looks like fifteen or twenty Shepherds are moving some sandbags around. They're removing them from the cafeteria and the family cabins and repositioning them several yards in front of the chapel. Looks like a wall, maybe. Or a U-shape. Definitely looks like they're creating defensive shooter positions."

An icy chill raced up her spine. "Why would they suddenly change tactics? This doesn't make sense."

"I see more Shepherds emerging from the restricted area," Haasi said. "They're armed to the teeth."

The faint rumble of engines echoed across the compound. "What is that?"

"I can hear the helicopter engine," Logan said. "The rotors are starting to spin. The pilot's back in the cockpit. I think they're going somewhere. Not in several hours, but right now."

"Wait," Haasi said. "I see two armored vehicles departing the restricted area."

"They're heading for the chopper, over," Julio said.

"I've got eyes on it," Logan said. "Holy—"

"Mother Mary and Joseph," Julio broke in, his voice strained. "They're unloading a big long metal trunk from the back of the Humvee. Eight guys are moving it into the chopper. I think that's the bomb."

They were all silent for several sobering seconds.

Dakota's lungs constricted. She couldn't get enough oxygen. "I think they're moving up the schedule."

"They're leaving," Logan said. "Not tomorrow morning. Tonight."

30

MADDOX

The Prophet's satphone rang. He pulled it from the pouch at his waist and put it to his ear. Maddox couldn't hear what was being said, but the Prophet's placid face slowly darkened to a thundercloud. His eyes bulged, his lips thinning into a scowl. "When?"

The voice on the other end said something.

"Your intel better be sound. Or so help me." He paused, his scowl deepening. "Stay in the loop. Notify me if anything changes. We'll be ready."

The Prophet terminated the call and shoved the phone back in the pouch at his belt.

"What's going on?" Solomon asked.

Maddox, Reuben, Aaron Hill, and Maddox's father stood in a loose circle, waiting for orders. The sky was still a dreary gunmetal gray, though dusk was falling fast. The trees swayed in the wind. A bank of black clouds towered in the distance.

They'd all spent most of the day shoring up the compound for the hurricane. The Prophet's helicopter had arrived earlier in the afternoon. In the morning, he'd take it to Montana or wherever he was headed next.

The Bell 429 helicopter was white with blue lettering, *Miami Sand and Sea Air Tours* scrawled on each side. It was the same chopper that had picked up Maddox at the elementary school in Miami after he'd managed to escape the fiery pit of hell itself.

His stomach clenched, a wave of watery sickness twisting his guts. It took every ounce of his will power not to collapse from the stabs of pain searing his intestines. This morning, he'd pulled more than a handful of short blond hairs from his scalp.

The effects of the radiation poisoning had returned with a vengeance.

But he couldn't show weakness. Not here, not now. Sour sweat popped out on his forehead. He gritted his teeth and endured the wave of pain until it subsided.

"What happened?" Solomon asked again. His father wore gray fatigues, not black like the other Shepherds, a large red cross with two swords below it embroidered on his back—a gift from Maddox's stepmother for the Prophet's right-hand man.

"Change of plans," the Prophet said sharply. "We're leaving early. Aaron, gather several men, get the asset and load it on the chopper. It was already supposed to be done by now. Reuben, get your things, find the pilot, and make sure he's ready for take-off."

"Sir?" Aaron asked. "Aren't you leaving tomorrow—"

"You heard the man!" Maddox's father shouted. "Move!"

The Shepherd ducked his head and scurried away, already on his radio.

The Prophet turned to Solomon. "Listen very carefully. This is it. The time is upon us. Armageddon is coming. The final battle."

Maddox's father went rigid.

Reuben's mouth dropped open. "The government is attacking us? *Now?*"

The Prophet paced, his hands behind his back, his face

purpling with rage, a vein pulsing at his forehead. "We knew it was coming, and soon. I'd hoped to escape it by leaving at dawn. But it appears the devil is hard at work. Our source claims our enemy is already on their way."

Maddox went still. The infamous government was finally coming. He'd wondered if they'd ever figure out who was to blame for the attacks. He kept his expression calm, but inside, his heart was jackhammering against his ribs. "That quickly?"

"Their ETA is less than four hours. Clearly, our source is lacking in certain areas. That will be dealt with. Aggressively. But right now, I need the Chosen to prepare for an imminent attack. Forget boarding the windows. Have them move the sandbags into defensive positions, take their shooting positions on the rooftops and in the sniper nests. Bring out the Humvees, the stinger missiles, unload everything we have. They'll be coming with choppers. You need to take them down."

The sky was morose, gray and opaque as dirty dishwater tinged with a sickly, greenish sheen. It was so close he could almost reach up and touch it.

Four hours. Maddox let the words sink in.

His father regained his composure, his expression hardened, his cold eyes steely and determined. "It will be done. And the women and children?"

"Have Aaron gather them all in the chapel. Tell them they're just heading in early before the storm hits. You know what to do."

His father nodded curtly.

"What about Eden?" Maddox asked.

The Prophet's face went blank for a moment, as if he'd completely forgotten about his new bride. "Grab her, too."

"She's in the infirmary, still sick," Maddox said. "Four guards are watching her after they found her wandering around, feverish and delirious."

"I'm sure you'll figure it out," the Prophet spat. "Reuben, be ready. We're leaving in sixty minutes."

Reuben nodded, turned, and jogged toward the men's barracks.

"You're leaving now?" Maddox asked. "Before the battle?"

The Prophet whirled on him. He took two swift steps until he was less than a foot from Maddox and jabbed his finger into his chest. "Are you questioning God now, son? Think long and hard before you answer."

Maddox swallowed. He glanced past the Prophet at his father. Solomon Cage stared back at him, his expression stony, his eyes venomous. "No, of course not."

"God has called the Chosen to defend His kingdom. They will do so with honor and glory, right here, right now. YOU will do so with glory and honor. The angels themselves will come down and fight alongside you."

Maddox said nothing.

"This is the final sacrifice from prophecy. I preached that very message this morning. Were you not listening?" His voice went low and cold. "Did I make a mistake choosing you?"

A deep ugly shame blossomed in his chest. Humiliation burned his face. "I was listening. And no, God did not make a mistake. I am more than ready to fight."

"Then do it. God has told me I have another mission. The fiery flames of God's judgment must reign down once more. I'm taking the final weapon with me while you defend us from the devil himself. Do you think you can handle that?"

"Yes, sir," Maddox choked out.

"Good." The Prophet whirled and strode across the clearing toward his house. His father turned to follow him, but not before shooting a disdainful glare at Maddox.

Maddox stood for a moment, curling and uncurling his hands into fists at his sides, impotent anger slashing through him.

Being Chosen was supposed to change everything. Yet here he was, still the whipping boy, still the object of his father's scorn and derision.

His shoulders trembled, his rage gnawing at his insides like a ravenous cancer. He longed to strangle someone with his bare hands. To kick and punch and hurt until the fury boiling inside him was sated.

If that were even possible.

31
DAKOTA

Dakota's stomach plummeted. Her heart hammered so hard it felt like it might explode.

"We can't let them leave," she whispered, her voice choked. "We have to do something. If they take Eden now, she's in the wind. She'll be gone. I'll never see her again. And that bomb. He's going to blow up another city. He's going to—"

"Bravo, you need to calm down," Julio broke in, his voice tense but steady. "Take a breath. Focus. We need to think clearly right now. We have to. There's too much at stake."

She nodded even though Julio couldn't see her. She forced herself to take a deep breath, to calm her racing heart. Panic wouldn't save Eden. It would only get more people killed. "Copy, Delta."

Her phone vibrated against her thigh. She contorted herself to reach one of the pockets in her new battle belt and tugged out the satphone. She texted Hawthorne an urgent message.

They're leaving now, Dakota texted Hawthorne. *The Prophet and Eden. Bomb on board.*

She'd been texting him intel updates for the last few hours. He hadn't been happy when she told them they were close enough to offer surveillance, but he didn't have much of a choice.

We'll leave now, Hawthorne texted back a second later. *Sixty minutes out.*

Too late.

Chopper's about to fly. Instructions????

A long pause.

Don't engage.

Like hell, she typed back furiously.

Another long pause.

Too Dangerous. Do. Not. Engage.

Screw Hawthorne. They had to move now. After everything the Shepherds had taken from her, after everything they'd done, there was no way in hell she was standing by while the Prophet escaped with her sister.

She shoved the phone back in her pocket. They'd figure this out on their own.

"Guys," Archer said, "if they fly away in that bird before the cavalry arrives, the next time anyone hears about that bomb will be when it obliterates another half million people."

"That isn't happening," Dakota said into the radio. "Not on my watch."

A crackling hiss of silence.

"What's the plan?" Logan asked.

"We better think fast," Jake said.

"Are we all in this?" Haasi asked.

"Damn straight," Zane said.

"Bravo," Julio said. "You know this place better than anyone here. We'll follow your lead. I know you can do this. We're depending on you."

She squared her shoulders, or at least, as best she could halfway up a tree. She'd come this far. She wasn't going to fail now, no matter how insurmountable the odds.

"Our original objective was to snatch Eden later tonight

when it was quiet and most people were sleeping. We have to move earlier than we wanted, but I think that part of the plan can remain basically intact. The place is crawling with Shepherds, but it's getting dark. We're dressed like them. We can still use that to our advantage. Just try not to get too close to anyone. If your cover is blown, start shooting, get to the airboats, and meet at the rally point."

On their way in, she'd pointed out a derelict old fishing cabin about a mile east of the compound, which they could reach by boat or by land. Just in case they were stranded, they'd brought Ezra's fishing boat and stashed it under some branches for cover.

"The critical objective is the chopper," Logan said. "We have to disable it somehow. Maybe he can still drive away with the bomb in the back of that truck, but it'll take longer to get to his destination, giving Hawthorne more time to find him."

"Without the chopper, The Prophet is grounded, and so is Eden," Archer said. "Taking it out gives us the time to go in and extract Eden before the cavalry arrives."

"Why not do both at the same time?" Julio asked. "Seems like it's more dangerous to go in twice. Once the chopper is disabled, they'll be even more wary than they are now. It'll be that much harder to sneak in."

"Agreed," Haasi said. "Something's happening down there. If I didn't know any better, I'd say they've been tipped off about the raid."

"That seems unlikely," Archer said.

"This whole debacle seems unlikely," Zane cut in, "and yet, here we are. Over."

"If they know Hawthorne's coming, that changes everything," Dakota said quietly. "The Prophet will be forced into a corner. He may escape with Eden anyway, via airboat or the road. I think Delta is right. We need to do this at the same time. Disable the chopper and snatch Eden simultaneously. We must get those four guards away from the infirmary. They also have a clear view of that helicopter. Delta, are you still a go to be a spotter?"

She needed Julio to remain in the woods with his eyes on the activity in the compound. She wished they had more people, but they'd work with what they had.

"Absolutely," Julio said. "I'll be your eyes and ears as much as possible."

The sun had finally set. The heavy cloud cover obscured the stars and moon. She could barely make out anything beyond the trees other than dark forms rushing around and flashlights sweeping back and forth.

Dakota reached into a pouch on her tactical vest and pulled out a pair of night vision binoculars she'd recovered from one of the dead Shepherds. She put the normal ones back in the pouch and held the new pair to her eyes. The world transformed into shades of faintly glowing green.

She scanned the area of the clearing that she could see. Her heart sank. "There are four guards stationed outside the infirmary,"

"Damn it!" Zane whispered. "Still? Even with all the frantic rushing around?"

"They're not moving, over."

"Do you still have eyes on the approach point, Zulu?" Dakota asked Haasi.

There was a slight pause. "The patrols have remained in position. So have the guards. They look antsy, but they're still out on the peninsula, over."

Dakota bit her lower lip. "We can't extract Eden or get the boats in close unless those guards are neutralized. That's still our best point of exit. But we're not ready to make our presence known yet. Can we get rid of them without guns? Over."

"I can take them out with my crossbow," Haasi said, barely restrained anticipation in her voice. "I can get up close, nice and quiet. They won't see it coming. That'll clear the way for the extraction."

"We still need a way to get to the chopper," Jake said. "I'm ballsy but walking right up to it might be a bit much, even for me."

"I'm game," Archer said. "I could shoot the engine. It's not going to explode, but the fuel will leak out. Or I could hit the tail rotor with a sniper shot. Either way, the gunshot will draw attention."

"We can't afford to draw any attention our way," Dakota said, "not until Eden is out."

"I have an idea," Julio said. "You can disable the engine by cutting just a few lines. It won't make any noise, and they won't be able to fix it easily. I can talk you through it once you get there."

"How long will it take?"

"A few minutes. Not long."

Jake cursed. "That's a long time to stand around with our arses hanging out."

"We need a distraction," Dakota said. "One big enough to pull away the guards. Or at least most of them."

"Whiskey here," Zane said enthusiastically. He was thrilled about his call sign. "I still have those Molotov cocktails. I'll have to get close enough to throw them, over."

The beginning of a plan formulated in her mind. "There's a thousand-gallon propane fuel tank behind the kitchen. They have a fuel depot near the front gate on the east side to keep the generators and the vehicles running. I'm not sure how big it is, but it's big enough. We don't necessarily need an explosion, but a large enough fire might do it."

"I can work with that," Zane said.

"Team Two, you've got the chopper," Julio said. "Team One is in charge of rescuing Eden. Team three splits up—Zulu stays at the peninsula; Whiskey makes something go boom."

"Got it," Archer said.

"I'll handle the two guards," Haasi said. "Then I'll bring the airboat over."

"This might actually be fun," Zane said with relish.

"It's go time," Logan said. "See you on the other side."

32
DAKOTA

akota took the weird, alien-looking NV goggles out of a
pouch in her tactical vest. She wasn't used to the heavy,
uncomfortable weight of the ballistic plates. She did appreciate
all the cool pouches and gadgets—and the fact that it could save
her life.

She tightened the NV goggles' strap around her head,
flipped down the optics, and turned on the switch. She looked at
Logan's greenish, glowing form. He'd hurried over to her position a few minutes ago.

He gave her a thumbs up. *Ready to go.*

Together, they headed for the peninsula. They crept
cautiously through the woods, keeping parallel to the fence line a
good twenty yards deep until they reached the edge of the
swamp.

They could have tried cutting the fence, but the patrols
passed by every thirty minutes. They would've noticed. Besides,
no one had thought to bring bolt cutters. They could've zip-tied
the cuts in the fence after they'd slipped through. Another
mistake.

They waited for the patrol to turn and head back the other
way. During their short surveillance, she'd noticed a few things.

Since the peninsula already had sentries, the patrol didn't walk all the way to the waterline. Instead, they only patrolled to within a hundred feet or so, then switched directions.

The patrol headed the opposite direction. Dakota checked her watch. 9:29 p.m. They had thirty minutes before the patrol would head back this way.

Haasi was waiting for them. Maki was somewhere nearby, but out of sight. Dakota wanted to help Haasi, to do it herself even, but Haasi had the skillset to get this done. Dakota needed to trust her team.

Haasi held her finger to her lips and pointed fifteen yards ahead. One of the guards stood along the east bank of the peninsula, using NV binoculars to scan the water. Dakota couldn't see the second guard, but the sentry tower was located at the far end of the peninsula.

Dakota and Logan crouched down behind a cluster of saw palmettos, the large, spiky palm leaves shielded them from view. Logan faced north, his spine pressed against hers. He radiated warmth and strength, steadying her in more ways than one.

She wasn't alone. Logan had her back. They all did.

Haasi gripped her crossbow, a bolt loaded, several more ready to go. Moving fast and silent, she turned and disappeared into the trees, circling around to get behind the first guard. Even with the NV goggles, Dakota lost track of her within a few seconds.

She didn't hear the *thwack* of the bolt hitting its mark. She did see the first guard stagger forward, slump to his knees, and topple into the water—a bolt protruding from his throat.

His body sank below the surface and disappeared.

They waited. Dakota shivered as the wind bit at her exposed face and hands. Now that it was night, the strengthening wind had turned chilly.

The wind helped mask their own sounds, but it masked everything else, too. They wouldn't hear the rustle of a bush or the snap of a twig if a Shepherd snuck up behind them.

Even with Logan watching her back, she still felt vulnerable and exposed, like a target was painted over her spine.

A few minutes later, Haasi emerged from the shadows, crossbow still in hand. She knelt beside Dakota and Logan. "The second guard was just checking in. I let him finish his report to give us more time. He never felt a thing."

"Where's his body?" Logan asked.

"With the gators." A smugly satisfied expression flitted across her face. "I confiscated his radio first, so we'll know what they know."

Dakota nodded. "Good work."

Haasi moved east through the woods to get Maki and bring the airboats. Dakota checked her watch. 9:32 p.m. Time to go.

She tapped Logan's shoulder and they both stood.

She eased forward, stepping as carefully and quietly as she could, aiming for the spongy sections rather than twigs and crunchy dried leaves. She strained her ears for unusual sounds even as she tried to keep her own to an absolute minimum.

She crept stealthily closer, Logan right behind her. He was louder than she was, but it helped that the ground they were crossing consisted mostly of grass and weeds.

They stayed in the shadows between the buildings and the perimeter fence. When they reached the infirmary, she halted, heart pounding, and listened.

Voices came from the front of the building—the guards talking amongst themselves in tensed, animated tones.

"I can see you, Team One," Julio said into her earpiece. "Four Shepherds ahead of you. No patrol nearby. You're good for now."

They knelt in a low crouch for ten minutes as they waited for the others to get in position. Her thighs burned. Her pulse thudded against her neck, her palms damp. Every sense was on high alert.

Boom! A massive explosion lit up the entire night.

"What the hell was that?" one of the Shepherds shouted.

"Go find out!" another cried. "Go! Go!"

Footsteps pounded as several men ran across the clearing. More people dashed toward the massive fireball from opposite directions. Shouts and yells echoed, raising the alarm.

"Bravo, you've got one guard remaining," Julio said. "I can't see where he's standing from this angle, but three Shepherds left, so I assume he's there."

Logan drew his combat knife. He pointed at the knife, then himself. He wanted to take the kill.

Dakota nodded. Just by being male, he could get closer to their target before eliciting suspicion. If Dakota got within fifteen or twenty feet of a Shepherd, they'd be onto her in a heartbeat.

Logan rose to his feet and motioned for her to take the right side—he'd take the left.

She unsheathed her own knife and circled the back of the infirmary. The wind moaned around the corners of the buildings. The long grass rustled around her feet.

The squat, square shape of the mercy room loomed in front of her like a green-tinged ghost from her nightmares.

Dakota froze.

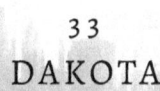

33
DAKOTA

Time slowed. The hairs on the back of Dakota's neck stood on end. Her scars prickled like spiders were scrabbling over her skin.

Three years. Three years since the night Jacob Cage dragged her into that building by her hair. Sickening memories reared up unbidden—the white-hot pain throbbing through every inch of her body, the searing burns pulsing like tiny hearts, the screams for help that never came.

And the blood, spilling across the cement floor in red-black ribbons. Maddox's face, the betrayal and fury in his eyes. *You made me do this. You deserve this. It's all your fault.*

She closed her eyes.

She forced the terrible images back into some deep, dank corner of her mind and shut the door. Forced herself to remember what Sister Rosemarie had taught her.

One, two, three. Breathe.

Those memories held no power over her anymore. She refused to let them.

She opened her eyes. The world around her snapped back into focus.

Dakota turned her back on the mercy room and kept

moving, heading toward Logan. She pressed her back against the wall of the infirmary and peeked around the corner.

Logan rounded the opposite corner and approached the Shepherd standing guard at the door. His shoulders were loose, his body language confident but unthreatening. He still wore his NV goggles so much of his face was hidden. In his black ACUs and tactical gear, he blended right in.

"Hey man, what's with the explosion? I was busy unloading more of those sandbags and missed all the action."

If the Shepherd had any inkling of suspicion, he didn't show it. His carbine was slung across his chest, his pistol holstered. He turned toward Logan. "How should I know? I've been stuck on babysitting duty all day."

Logan laughed heartily. "That sucks, man."

"Tell me about it."

Logan strode right up to the Shepherd and lifted his arm like he was about to slap the guy on the shoulder, man-to-man. Instead, Logan gripped his shoulder with his left hand and drew the Shepherd in close, simultaneously raising the knife in his right hand and sliding it into the side of the man's neck.

Logan yanked the blade out and stepped back.

Blood sprayed in a sweeping arc. The Shepherd clutched at his neck, gurgling, eyes bulging. He sank to his knees. Wet, gasping sounds escaped his shredded throat.

He didn't scream. He no longer could.

After several agonizing moments, he collapsed sideways and fell onto his back.

Dakota stepped out into the open.

Logan blew out a breath as he leaned down and wiped his blade on the dead man's pants. He straightened, sheathed the blade, and looked at her. She couldn't see his eyes behind the NV goggles.

"Ready?" he said in a low voice. "We need to move him around back."

Dakota moved to the body. She wanted to look away, but she

forced herself to look. She recognized the man's medium-brown skin tone, slight build, and narrow features. Aaron Hill.

She swallowed. Aaron had never shown any of the cruelty of the other Shepherds. He'd always been kind to the women, especially his little sister Ruth. "I knew him."

"Now he's dead. Let's go."

Logan was right. None of the Shepherds were good guys. Maybe some of them were just as brainwashed as the women and children, but there wasn't anything she could do about that. She couldn't afford pity. Not now.

"Dakota—"

"I'm good."

She shook off the guilt and stooped, grabbed Aaron beneath his armpits, and helped Logan lug him behind the building next to some bushes. Once that distasteful task was finished, they turned off their NV goggles and flipped up the optics. The lights inside the infirmary would only blank them out.

Logan and Dakota both drew their pistols. They weren't certain what awaited them inside. They weren't even a hundred percent sure Eden was even there.

Time to find out.

Her gun in the low ready position, Dakota held her breath, opened the door, and slipped inside. "Eden—"

Sister Rosemarie stood in the center of the room. "I've been waiting for you."

34

DAKOTA

Dakota took in the familiar room in an instant. She'd certainly spent enough of her childhood here. Everything was the same. The scent of bleach and antiseptic chemicals filled her nostrils. The hospital bed in the corner.

Eden was curled on the mattress.

Dakota released the breath she'd been holding.

Logan aimed his pistol at Sister Rosemarie's head.

"No!" Dakota cried. "Don't hurt her."

Dakota holstered her own gun, crossed the narrow space in several long strides, and wrapped Sister Rosemarie in a giant hug. The woman hugged her back. A lump rose in her throat. Warmth and longing filled her—a longing she'd buried long ago.

Sister Rosemarie gripped her shoulders and pulled her back. She looked into Dakota's eyes and smiled grimly. "Look at you, child. You look like you're ready to take on the world singlehandedly."

"Not singlehandedly. Logan, this is Sister Rosemarie. She's the one who helped Eden and me escape. Please don't shoot her in the head."

Logan lowered his Glock. "You could have said something earlier."

"You've been helping Eden." Dakota's heart swelled. In that moment, she remembered how much she loved this woman. She and Eden owed her everything. "You kept her here in the infirmary away from that monster."

Sister Rosemarie nodded. "And I will continue to help in any way that I can, but Dakota—"

Dakota was already rushing to Eden's bed. "Eden! Let's go!"

Eden was curled in a fetal position. She sat up and smiled weakly. Her long skirt and blouse were rumpled. Her skin was sallow, shadows rimming her glassy eyes.

Dakota inhaled sharply. The room stank of vomit and sweat beneath the bleach and antiseptic. Her gaze drifted from Eden's taut face to the bed behind her. Thick strands of golden blonde hair were scattered across the pillow. Too many of them.

She pressed her palm to her sister's forehead. Her skin was feverish, heat radiating from her body in waves. Dakota ran her fingers through Eden's sweat-dampened curls. Several more strands came out in her hands.

"It's the radiation sickness," Sister Rosemarie said from behind her. "The second stage."

Dakota's heart plummeted. She'd known this was coming. It still hit her like a savage punch to the gut.

There was no time to grieve, no time to worry. All that would have to wait.

"We have to get her to the airboats." She took Eden's clammy hand. "Can you walk?"

Eden nodded. Dakota helped her to her feet.

"Are you sure we can trust her?" Logan glared at the woman suspiciously. "Why are you helping us? You're one of them."

Sister Rosemarie stared back at him. Her gaze never wavered. "I freely admit that I am the worst of sinners. And I will surely answer for every single one of them when the Lord comes for me. But that day is not today. Today, I'm going to do something good. It'll never outweigh the bad, but I choose to do it anyway. Is that something you can understand?"

Logan gave a slow nod, a shadow passing across his features. "I can."

"We don't have much time," Sister Rosemarie said. "Reuben came for her when she was throwing up, fortunately. He said he'd come back right before they took off in the helicopter. I don't know where they're going, but it's not good."

"He's trying to flee before the military comes in with guns blazing," Logan said. "They're not going anywhere tonight, trust me."

"Is it true about the government, then? They're really coming? The Prophet is keeping it from the women and children, but I overheard the guards talking."

"Yeah, and we have to get the hell out of here before then."

Sister Rosemarie went very still. "The children. They're in the chapel already."

"The soldiers know there are innocent women and children," Logan said. "They won't hurt them."

"You don't understand. The Prophet sent them all in. He said the hurricane was going to hit early."

Dakota shook her head. "Not until the morning."

Sister Rosemarie's face went pale. "That chapel is fortified like a bunker. There are sniper positions on the rooftops, and he's dug in sandbag half-walls and sniper positions all around it. The Shepherds are planning to fall back to the chapel."

The realization struck Dakota like a slap in the face. "He's going to use the women and children as human shields."

"Oh, hell," Logan said.

The soldiers would be forced to choose between stopping a bomb that would kill hundreds of thousands and saving a handful of innocent lives.

It wasn't even a choice. Not for them.

But Dakota had a choice.

She knew the smart play. Get her sister and get the hell out before the real soldiers came roaring in and let the chips fall where they may.

Eden tugged on her arm. She signed something, making a motion of crossing her wrists, her hands open, then spreading her arms apart and closing her hands into fists.

Dakota shook her head, not understanding.

Eden mouthed the words.

She understood then. *Save them.*

Dakota turned to Logan. "There's a small rear door in the chapel, through the elders' room. We can get them out. There's room. We have three airboats, plus Ezra's fishing boat. We can take them by land if we have to."

Logan cursed. He tried to rake his hands through his hair, but the band of the NV goggles prevented him. He swore even more vehemently. "Dakota—"

She felt it deep in her bones—the certainty of it. This was what Julio meant. This was her purpose.

She would give them the same choice that she'd be given. She could save them, if they were willing to be saved.

But she had to try, no matter the risk.

"I need to do this."

"I know." Logan stared at her for a long moment. His face was hard as granite, his eyes flashing with the same fire and resolve as her own. "I'm with you."

35
DAKOTA

Static crackled in Dakota's ear.

"Team One, where are you?" Julio asked. "We have a problem."

Dakota keyed the mic. "What do you mean?"

"Whiskey here," Zane said, panting loudly. "I'm still up by the kitchens. I'm behind some storage sheds. No one's noticed me. They're too busy trying to put out the fire...which is, um, spreading. The wind is whipping it into the grass and the trees, jumping from building to building. The wooden structures are flaring up like kindling...over."

"Copy that, Whiskey," Julio said. "Sitrep, Team Two."

"The chopper's toast," Jake said in a strained voice. "There's so much going on, we walked right up without being noticed. We got the job done but were almost discovered by some Shepherds and had to hide behind some cabins, over."

A bit of static interfered, then Zan's voice returned. "... Heading toward Team Two. Don't shoot me, idiots. Over."

"Team One, have you left the infirmary yet?" Julio asked. "I didn't see you."

She clicked the mic. "We're going to the chapel to save as many children as we can."

Silence on the radio. Finally, Julio spoke. His voice was tender but strained. "Dakota, are you certain?"

"I—I can't leave them. Not without giving them a chance. Maybe this is my purpose, Julio. Maybe I'm supposed to do this. This is why I'm here."

"Then go get them," Julio said. "I'll help as much as I can. I'll be praying for you to kick some serious butt."

Dakota managed a grim smile. "Thank you."

She clicked off the mic and turned to Eden. "You're sick. I don't know if you should—"

I'm going, Eden signed defiantly.

"I gave her some medicine that should keep her on her feet for a while," Sister Rosemarie said. "And I'm coming, too. They won't believe you—or trust you. I need to speak to them myself."

"They might warn the rest of the Shepherds," Logan said.

"We'll just have to take that risk." Dakota glanced at Eden and swallowed. "We'll run to the chapel as soon as Julio tells us it's clear. Stay between me and Logan. We'll get whoever will come and then we're heading straight to the boats hidden at the peninsula. Haasi and Maki are waiting. You understand?"

Eden nodded.

Sister Rosemarie took Eden's hand and moved toward the door. "I've got her. You be ready to shoot anything that moves."

Dakota gave her a grateful look. "Thank you."

"It's fairly clear," Julio said into her earpiece. "I count thirty or so Shepherds near the front of the chapel. Another ten or so clustered around the chopper sixty yards north of the chapel. The Prophet's there—looks like he's throwing a temper tantrum. Another ten to fifteen are engaging Team Two to the northeast behind the cafeteria, with more coming. I can't see the fire clearly from my position, but it doesn't look good."

Dakota visualized everything in her head. "Got it, over."

Logan drew her into a quick, fierce hug. He hesitated for a moment, then kissed the top of her head. "I think I love you."

Before she could respond, Logan opened the door, raised his M4 to his shoulder, and darted out into the night.

A fierce tenderness burned in her heart. There was no time to think or react. Or to tell him that she felt the same way.

Dakota motioned for Sister Rosemarie and Eden to go next. Dakota would guard their rear. She lowered her NV optics over her eyes, both to see better and to shield her face. She gripped her carbine, adjusted her sling, and checked her magazine pouch. All good.

She followed them out, shut the door behind her, and paused for a second to get her bearings. The stink of smoke and burning plastic singed her nostrils. The wind whipped at her clothes and hair.

Everything looked eerie and strange with the night vision. The wooded restricted area was directly across from her, maybe half a mile. Three hundred yards to her left was the swamp. The peninsula was on her side, the boathouse and dock halfway between her and the restricted gate.

The chapel stood midway across the open expanse of grass and dirt pathways crisscrossing the compound, the main entrance facing north, the rear door maybe four hundred yards away. Four football fields.

Logan was already moving out, weapon up and scanning for threats. Sister Rosemarie hurried after him, tugging Eden along behind her.

This was it. No turning back. They were all in now.

She tightened her grip on her gun. She was ready to fight, to kill. Woe to anyone who got in their way.

You can end this. Ezra's last words echoed in her mind. *You know how.*

They ran for the chapel.

36
MADDOX

Harrison jogged up to the Prophet, who stood with Solomon, Reuben, and Maddox. "Sir, we have a problem."

"Tell us something we don't know," Maddox muttered.

He'd been overseeing the sniper nests and sandbag defensive positions, as the Prophet had ordered, then heard people shouting about a fire.

The wind had whipped the fire into a blazing frenzy until it had spread into the woods and leaped from the kitchen to the cafeteria and the storage sheds. The gardens were in dire danger as well as the animals—the goat and hog pens, the chickens and rabbits.

Thirty Shepherds had been dispensed to fight the fire on the northwest side of the property, using a hose hooked up to the cisterns and buckets of water. Their fire extinguishers were useless against a fire that size.

The Prophet hadn't seemed to care about the lost buildings or rapidly spreading fire—not after he discovered the sabotaged helicopter.

The Prophet's placid, paternal demeanor had vanished.

"How soon can it be fixed? I need it within the next hour! I need it now!"

"Sir, the repairs are impossible to source tonight." Harrison shifted nervously. "A day or two—"

"More excuses!" the Prophet roared. A vein pulsed in his forehead, the tendons standing out on his neck. "Failure is unacceptable!"

"Everyone's checked in on patrol and sentry duty," his father said, fighting to remain calm, but his left eye kept twitching from the tension and stress. "Except for Sheridan and Roush. I've sent four men to check it out. Another team is searching the compound. No one else reported anything unusual. Our men were right here the whole time."

The Prophet turned on him and jabbed him in the chest with a thick finger. "Well, something happened, didn't it? And on your watch!"

"I—"

"This failure is on your shoulders," the Prophet hissed. "Don't think I don't know what to do with men who refuse to serve the Lord to their fullest potential."

Solomon Cage stiffened.

"Either the government has already infiltrated us, or there's a traitor in our midst. Find out and take care of it! This is not the time for incompetence and inadequacy!"

"Sir?" a bald, middle-aged Shepherd named Corfield asked, raising his voice above the wind and the shouting of those fighting the fire.

"Pull the Humvees in closer to the chapel. Make sure the gunners are ready."

Corfield swallowed. "Closer to the chapel, sir? But our wives and kids are in there..."

"And?" the Prophet snarled.

"Shouldn't we steer the battle elsewhere?"

"The chapel is God's dwelling place. We must be prepared to

make any sacrifice necessary to win this holy battle. It seems your faith—and your courage—has failed you."

Corfield went pale. He stood ramrod straight and wiped nervous sweat from his forehead. "No, of course not. I'll do it now."

"Reuben, get a team to remove the asset from the chopper and move it to the boathouse. Prepare two of the airboats, make sure they're topped off and bring extra fuel."

"Consider it done."

"Bring one of the RPGs."

"They're in the chapel."

"Then get it! Meet me at the boathouse in twenty minutes with eight men."

Reuben nodded and jogged off.

"And the fire?" Solomon asked.

"It's too late. Let it burn."

"It's headed for the chapel," Solomon said. "We could evacuate the children—"

"They stay!" The Prophet scowled, his eyes bulging. "If it's God's will, let it all burn!"

Solomon said nothing, his expression stricken.

The Prophet motioned at Maddox. "Go with Reuben! Get out of my sight!"

Maddox hurried after Reuben without a word. Men were running everywhere like chickens with their heads cut off. Maddox ignored them.

"Maybe we should surrender," Maddox muttered. "Save our own skins."

Reuben shot him a disdainful look. "And burn forever instead in eternal damnation?"

"What if the Prophet is wrong—"

Reuben grabbed his collar and leaned in close, his eyes flashing. "The Prophet is God's voice. He can *never* be wrong."

Anger seared through Maddox. He slapped Reuben's hand away.

Reuben smirked. "Always the doubting Thomas, aren't you?"

Maddox shoved him. "Touch me again, and I'll kill you."

Reuben stumbled. He righted himself, a flicker of loathing passing across his face, as swift and insubstantial as a shadow. Then it was gone. He grinned wide and raised his hands in mock surrender. "Take a joke, man."

Nothing was real to him. Everything was either a joke or a game, a competition of one-up-man-ship.

But it was real now.

Maddox almost wished Reuben had challenged him. Strangling his cousin's thick neck with his bare hands would've been immensely satisfying. Instead, he gritted his teeth, turned on his heel, and strode away.

"Where the hell are you going?" Reuben shouted.

Maddox didn't bother to answer. Let him be the Prophet's errand boy even as death itself loomed over them all. As for Maddox, he didn't intend to become one of the Prophet's sacrificial lambs.

He was sick of Reuben's games. Sick of the Prophet's increasingly insane orders.

But maybe the Prophet was right about something. Maybe this whole damn place really should burn to the ground.

R unning with NV goggles was awkward and dangerous. Dakota's vision kept jostling and she couldn't see her feet. But she kept going.

Some of the Shepherds also wore NV goggles, others swept bright flashlights across the grounds. It was night, everyone looked the same, and they were distracted with other things—the fire, the broken chopper, and preparing for the imminent attack.

The stench of smoke carried on the wind. Dakota could barely see the cafeteria from this distance, but she could just make out the glow of flames in the distance. Soon it would be too bright to use the NV goggles.

She glimpsed movement above her. Snipers were hunkered down on several rooftops behind sandbags piled at the corners. They were focused on the perimeter, the front gate, and scanning the dark skies.

They weren't looking for a woman and a child escorted by two of their own.

No one took notice of them. They made it across the clearing without incident. Logan kept watch outside the back door while Dakota, Sister Rosemarie, and Eden slipped inside.

Dakota flipped up her goggles so she could see. The short hallway opened to the elders' room. The door on the opposite side of the room led to another short hallway, a few storage rooms, and the back door.

Through the hallway, she could make out the raised dais, the big wooden cross, the pulpit, and the main sanctuary with several dozen rows of pews split by a main aisle.

Two wide, propped-open doors at the rear of the sanctuary led to a large foyer. A dozen Shepherds milled in the foyer at the front entrance, their expressions tense as they spoke in low voices she couldn't make out, probably discussing battle tactics and defensive positions.

Dozens of high-caliber weapons were stacked on a table normally used for communion. More guns—AK-47s, M4s, and M16s, a couple of shoulder-fired RPGs—leaned against the wall.

Outside, the wind moaned and howled, but inside, it was warm and cozy. The windows were all boarded up. Candles and solar lanterns provided lighting. The room smelled of beeswax, freshly baked bread, and the lemon-scented lye soap they used to wash the linens.

The pews were filled with women and children. Mothers cradled babies and toddlers in their laps. Small children dressed in long frilly nightgowns and pajamas played between the pews, giggling and chasing each other. Blankets, pillows, and sleeping bags were spread out in the aisles.

Several children had sectioned off an area for themselves, spreading blankets over the backs of the pews. They were huddling beneath their makeshift tents with flashlights and a plate of cookies.

Indignation burned in her chest. These poor kids saw this as a fun event, a sleepover, a reprieve from the unrelenting labor, rules, church and more church they were used to. They had no idea of the insidious threat looming over them.

Dakota remained in the shadows of the hallway while Sister Rosemarie hurried among them, whispering and motioning for them to head for the elders' room. She repeated her speech again and again.

"The government is coming tonight to attack us. They're already on their way. It's going to be a bloodbath. This is not Armageddon, but it's going to feel like it. People are going to die. Not spiritually or metaphorically. For real. But God doesn't want you to die here, like this. We want to help you. Come with us. We'll get you and your children out of the line of fire to safety."

One by one, the women shook their heads—a few apologetic, many of them angry, rebuking Sister Rosemarie in sharp whispers.

A woman stood, a toddler on her hip, and made her way down the aisle to the elders' room. Her expression was fearful but resolute.

Dakota nodded at her. Eden gave them both a giant hug. That was two.

A minute later, two more women; one alone, the other with two whimpering brunette children, maybe five and seven. Three more women and their children followed a few minutes later.

The seconds and minutes ticked by in Dakota's head. She shifted uneasily. Too much time was passing.

Finally, Sister Rosemarie returned to the hallway, her face drawn. "The rest won't come. I can't force them."

"I know."

Sister Rosemarie's mouth contorted, like she was fighting back sobs. "They don't know what they're choosing."

The same anguish twisted Dakota's heart. These people were brainwashed. They couldn't see the truth from the lies—even when it was staring them in the face.

They had tried their best. It was all they could do. "We have to go."

"Wait." A slim, attractive black woman in her forties rose from one of the middle pews. "I'll go. We're coming, too."

The woman eased out of the pew and hurried across the

platform. Her daughter shuffled nervously beside her. With a jolt, Dakota recognized Ruth, the quiet, inquisitive girl in braids who used to follow Sister Rosemarie around everywhere. She looked older now, though she still seemed small and quiet.

The woman pressed one hand to her throat, her fearful gaze darting between Sister Rosemarie and Dakota. "I—I've wanted to leave this place for several years, but I...I didn't know how. If you say we're in danger, I believe you. You've treated Ruth with nothing but grace and kindness. I trust you. We want to leave."

Sister Rosemarie embraced her, tears in her eyes. "I know it's scary, but it's the right thing to do."

"What about my son, Aaron?" Ruth's mother asked. "He's a good boy. He would come with us, I know it."

Dakota tasted ashes on her tongue. Hot shame flooded her.

She'd just watched Logan put a knife through the throat of this woman's son. She'd dragged his dead body across the grass and tossed him in the bushes like so much trash.

She had blood on her hands. They all did.

"We don't have time to worry about him," she said in a choked voice. "We can save you and your daughter right now. It's your choice."

Her eyes wide and fearful, the woman nodded. She gripped Ruth's hand and moved into the elders' room.

"We've got to go now," Dakota said. "We've wasted too much time already."

Rustling and murmurs in the pews drew their attention. Dozens of confused, bewildered, and hostile faces stared back at them.

Several of the women clustered in the middle of the center aisle, conversing in low, tense voices. One of them pointed straight at Dakota. "That's her."

"Stop right there!" Sister Hannah stormed down the aisle, trailed by another woman with a stern, dour face. Her graying auburn hair was yanked back in a severe bun.

An icy chill zipped up Dakota's spine. The second woman

was her aunt. Her real aunt, her own flesh and blood, the woman who'd brought her here after her parents had died all those years ago, when she was just a scared, grieving kid. "Aunt Ada."

"You!" Aunt Ada spat. "Do you know how much pain and suffering you've caused me? How you've shamed your own family with your despicable actions? How dare you show your face here!"

The words stung—but nothing like they would have once upon a time. This bitter, miserable woman had loved nothing more than to use her words to bruise and wound.

She couldn't hurt her anymore. None of them could.

Dakota gritted her teeth. "Don't worry. We were just leaving."

"Oh, I think not." Sister Hannah's eyes blazed with a vicious, almost gleeful zeal. "You're not going anywhere."

38

DAKOTA

"Your husband and the Prophet are going to get everyone here killed," Sister Rosemarie said to Sister Hannah, her voice pleading. "You can't want that."

Scowling, Sister Hannah crossed her scrawny arms over her chest. Her face was gaunt, her watery eyes too close together, her thin mouth like a knife blade. "What is a small sacrifice compared to burning forever in eternal damnation!"

"You would doom your own daughter to that fate?" Dakota asked quietly.

Sister Hannah's gaze flicked to Eden, standing in the middle of the group next to Ruth. For the slightest moment, she faltered, a shadow of doubt passing behind her eyes.

"They want to leave," Dakota said. "Eden wants to leave. You can't keep her here against her will."

Aunt Ada sniffed. "It's God's will she defies, no one else's."

"God's will? Or the Prophet's?" Dakota asked.

Sister Hannah stiffened. Her expression went hard and distant. Whatever flicker of empathy had existed a moment before extinguished itself completely.

"They are the same!" she hissed with renewed conviction. "It is not our place to doubt or question the will of God!"

"Give them their freedom," Sister Rosemarie said. "Give them a choice."

Sister Hannah glowered at them. "*Freedom* is a lie designed by Lucifer and spread by the depraved, wicked heathens to entice us. Just like you're doing right now."

They didn't have time for theological discussions. Dakota turned to her aunt. "You know what happens here. Women and children humiliated, oppressed, and abused. You're one of them!"

Aunt Ada's lips thinned into a sneer. "Obedience and discipline. That's what I tried to teach you. I took you in. I gave you everything you had. And this is how you repay me. I'm your only family!"

Dakota stared straight back at her, uncowed.

She saw them both for what they were—small-minded, spiteful, petty women twisted by their own selfishness and cruelty disguised as piety.

They weren't pious. They were willfully blind.

They held no power over her anymore. What she felt wasn't shame or longing or even bitter resentment—it was a mix of pity and disgust. More disgust. "You're not my family."

Aunt Ada gaped at her.

They would never change their minds. They were already lost.

"You stupid little harlot. If you think—"

"Enough!" Dakota was already turning away. "We have to go."

"Brother Reuben!" Sister Hannah yelled, not taking her eyes off Sister Rosemarie. "We've uncovered a heretic in our midst. An agent for the devil himself!"

"Don't do this!" Sister Rosemarie begged. "Do nothing—that's all I ask. You can stay. Just let us go."

"I'm afraid I can't do that." Sister Hannah smiled like a dog baring its teeth. "Reuben!"

Reuben strode down the center aisle toward them, followed

by two more hulking Shepherds armed with submachine guns. He nearly kicked several children in his haste. They scurried out of his way.

"What's wrong?" He approached the dais. "We don't have time for histrionics, woman!"

"These heretics have turned their backs on God!" Livid, Sister Hannah jabbed a bony finger at Sister Rosemarie and Dakota. "They were stealing my daughter!"

Reuben stiffened when he caught sight of Dakota in the hallway. His expression darkened. "Maddox said you were dead."

"Maddox is a liar." She raised the carbine to her shoulder. She didn't have a clear shot. A dozen women and children huddled between them. "Let these innocent people go, and maybe I won't kill you."

Reuben gave a harsh laugh. "You already know the answer to that."

Sister Rosemarie stepped in front of the group, blocking Reuben's way.

He glared at her. "I always knew you were a despicable heretic. I'll deal with you later. Now move!"

"You will not harm them," Sister Rosemarie said.

He unholstered his pistol and aimed it at Sister Rosemarie's head. "Don't make me shoot you in front of these little kids." His lip curled in derision. "Or maybe it's God's will to put you down like the dog that you are."

Sister Rosemarie drew to her full five-foot-nothing height. "Don't you dare speak for God. You know nothing of Him."

With the butt of his gun, Reuben punched her in the face. The dull thud echoed in the sudden silence.

Sister Rosemarie rocked back, one hand flying to her cheek. She turned her face to the side for a moment. Dakota saw a puffy knot already forming around her right eye and blood dripping from her nose.

But the woman didn't cry out. She didn't cower. Her expression was resolute and fearless. She turned back to face Reuben, still blocking his path.

"Get the hell out of my way, woman!" he snarled.

She was distracting him so they could escape. Dakota gestured to the girls closest to her and pointed through the doorway into the elders' room. *Go*, she mouthed. *Go, hurry.*

Quickly and quietly, the women and children moved past Dakota.

"You always were a boorish brute," Sister Rosemarie said. "Frankly, I expected more from the Prophet's son. But then, you never could live up to expectations."

Reuben took one swift step forward and pressed the muzzle of his gun to her forehead. Several women gasped behind him. The other Shepherds said nothing, their faces expressionless.

Sister Rosemarie didn't flinch.

"The penalty for heresy is death," he said in a low, cold voice. "But you already know that."

"Let her go!" Dakota cried.

"Save them," Sister Rosemarie said to her. "I'm sorry that I couldn't."

Without turning around, she fumbled for the handle of the opened elders' room door directly behind her. She shut the door, blocking herself off from the rest of the group.

Rage slashed through Dakota's veins. She wanted to smash the door down and fling herself at Reuben. She'd rip out his vile, rotten heart with her bare hands. But she couldn't.

Sister Rosemarie had drawn Reuben's wrath to distract him. They couldn't waste a moment.

"What's happening?" Ruth asked tremulously. "I'm scared."

"What do we do now?" one of the women asked.

"Should we go back?" another whispered.

"Go!" Dakota cried. "Go with Logan! I'll be right there!"

A toddler whimpered, clinging to her mother's leg. One of the babies began to cry.

"Go!"

Eden tugged on Ruth's arm, motioning to the women to follow her. The group ran out of the elders' room, down the short hallway to the exit.

Dakota locked the door on her side, looked around wildly, seized one of the wooden chairs and wedged it beneath the door handle. The door was made of reinforced steel, not some flimsy hollow-core construction.

The Shepherds would get through it soon enough, or just run through the church and come after them from the front entrance. But it might give them a minute. It would have to be enough.

She turned to go.

A gunshot sounded. Something heavy thumped against the door.

Dakota froze.

She stared in growing horror as red liquid seeped beneath the door. Blood pooled on the floor, slowly spreading in a widening stain.

Muffled voices echoed through the door. Someone screamed. Then Reuben's voice—cold and smug and self-satisfied. "She got what she deserved."

Reuben had shot her. He'd killed Sister Rosemarie.

39

DAKOTA

Waves of sorrow surged through Dakota, so strong they nearly knocked her off her feet. Her throat tightened, tears stinging her eyes. *No, no, no!*

Another person dead because of her. Another person she'd loved gone forever from her life. It wasn't fair. It wasn't right.

Sister Rosemarie was the best person in this damn hellhole.

Whatever her sins and failures, she hadn't deserved to die.

Dakota gave a sharp shake of her head, snapping herself out of her shock. She couldn't let herself dwell on the horror of what had just happened.

Not if she wanted Sister Rosemarie's sacrifice to mean something.

She buried her grief somewhere down deep and took a breath to steel herself. She had to keep her head clear for the job ahead, no matter what. She still had work to do.

An awful sense of foreboding settled over her. This night of hell was just beginning.

She tightened her grip on her gun and sprinted outside, slamming and locking the exterior door behind her.

Logan was waiting for her at the southeast corner, the women and children huddled behind him. "What happened?"

"Reuben knows," Dakota said breathlessly. "He'll sound the alarm."

Logan adjusted his grip on his carbine. "We have to lay down cover fire or they'll never make it."

Their covert operation wasn't so covert anymore. Now it was time to stay alive. That, and take down as many Shepherds as they possibly could.

The sky was pitch-black. The wind yanked at her hair and clothes. Smoke singed her nostrils. Yelling and shouting echoed from all directions. She flipped down her NV goggles, but they no longer worked. The fire was too bright.

The entire northwest side of the compound was blazing. At least two dozen trees were lit up like torches. The Shepherds had abandoned the fight to put out the fire. The agonizing bleats and cries of the animals trapped in their pens made her wince.

There wasn't a thing she could do to ease their suffering.

"Watch your six!" Julio yelled into her earpiece.

About a hundred yards away, two Shepherds were running toward them from the direction of the boathouse. A third Shepherd was patrolling the fence directly east of them, just north of the mercy room. Maybe four hundred yards.

That familiar tight, panicky feeling plucked at her chest. That terrible sense of everything careening out of control. Every instinct screamed at her to keep her sister right at her side.

But she couldn't. The best way to keep her safe was to let her go.

Dakota grabbed Eden's arm. "I need you to lead the group to Haasi and the boats. Can you do that?"

Eden nodded solemnly, her eyes bright and fierce.

She could do this. Dakota knew she could.

Eden gestured at the group and then took off running. The others followed her. She swayed a little, almost stumbling—she was still sick, damn it—but Ruth jogged alongside her and slid her arm around Eden's waist.

They ran together.

"Hostiles exiting the front of the chapel," Julio warned in her earpiece. "At least ten. No, twelve."

"Over there!" Dakota pointed ten yards left to a four-foot-tall by six-foot-long U-shaped sandbag wall—one of the defensive shooter positions the Shepherds had built. It was unmanned.

It would provide cover from the attackers coming at them from the front of the chapel, but not the ones headed straight at them from the south.

The Shepherds were shouting, waving their rifles but not shooting yet. Everything was confusing in the dark. They didn't want to shoot their own men on accident.

The *rat-a-tat* of a rifle sounded. A round thudded into the dirt a few yards from Dakota's feet.

Instinct took over. She ran for the sandbags and dove for cover.

Logan hurled himself down behind the sandbags beside her. He sank onto one knee, facing south toward the two oncoming Shepherds. He switched the selector to auto and unleashed a hail of gunfire.

The two Shepherds who'd been running toward them from the boathouse jittered like puppets on a string and collapsed.

Dakota spun to the east as she drew the stock firmly against her shoulder, searching through her sights for the Shepherd patrolling along the fence. She found him—he was already laid out flat on his back, a bolt sticking out of his throat.

Haasi had taken him out. She must be covering the women and children from the peninsula.

Eden and the group were halfway across the clearing now, running for their lives.

Please God, protect them.

"Zulu to Team One, I've got the prize in sight," Haasi said in her earpiece. "We had some trouble, but we've already taken care of it."

Dakota didn't have time to respond.

A cacophony of gunfire exploded all around them.

4 0
DAKOTA

Dakota dropped to her knees behind the sandbag wall and flicked the selector from semi to auto. She turned north toward the rush of oncoming Shepherds and rested the barrel on top of a sandbag to steady her aim.

The terrorists were expecting to chase down a group of scared women and children, not meet a barrage of bullets. They certainly weren't expecting to be fired on by what they thought were their own men.

Three of the twelve dropped immediately.

Dakota squeezed the trigger, fired a short burst. The fourth guy's head snapped sideways, blood spraying from whatever pulp of his face remained.

She unleashed burst after burst. Spent cartridges dropped to the ground. The muzzle blasts were almost deafening. Her ears rang from the concussive force.

She drilled the fifth one in the chest with several shots. He spasmed and staggered backward. She lowered her aim and sprayed another across his legs. He went down.

She wasn't as skilled with the M4 as she was with her XD-S, or even the AR-15. But it was getting the job done.

Logan took out two more before the rest got smart and dove

for cover. Two went left and scrambled for the front of the chapel. The other two went right and hid behind the huge armored vehicle.

"Zulu to Team One," Haasi said in her earpiece. "We've got eyes on the prize. They're almost here. We're taking them to Ezra's shed—that bunker. It won't move in a hurricane, come hell or high water. We'll meet after."

"Julio, you should go with them!" She took the brief reprieve to switch out her magazine for a new one in her pouch. She wasn't sure how many of the sixty rounds were left, but it couldn't be many. "Take the boat while you can."

Julio's voice was laced with urgency but remained steady and unflappable. "As long as I can be your eyes and help you, I'm staying."

She swallowed. "Be safe."

"Godspeed," Julio said.

Dakota switched the selector back to SEMI and returned to her post. Eight hostiles from this group were down. Four still alive.

Their backup could arrive at any moment, from any direction.

And they were still outnumbered fifteen to one.

They needed to take these psychos down and they could get the hell out of here.

A Shepherd peeked his head out around the corner of the chapel's concrete wall. It was a mistake. Dakota had him in her sights. She fired twice and his head jerked with a spray of blood.

Nine down.

"We need to make a break for it," Logan said, breathing hard. He ejected his almost spent magazine and slammed in a new one. "We're about to be pinned—if we aren't already."

A Shepherd crouched behind the Humvee fired. The round whizzed by her head. She squeezed off three shots and he disappeared. "There's not much between here and the extraction point. We could make a run for the peninsula and figure it out from there. I'll cover you."

Before Logan could respond, a flurry of rounds ripped through the air above their heads.

"Team One!" Julio shouted through the earpiece. "You've got company behind you. At your five o'clock!"

Logan spun to meet the new threat. "They're coming around the rear of the chapel. I count seven more."

He released a volley of gunshots. They returned fire. Bullets tore into the ground all around them, striking with a rhythmic *thud, thud, thud.*

Dakota remained in place facing their enemies to the north. Adrenaline crashed through her system as she searched for a target. *Come on, come on.*

The engine of the armored vehicle rumbled to life. She watched in horror as the massive machine-gun mounted to the turret began to rotate toward them.

Her heartbeat stuttered. Her insides turned to ice. That beast would tear right through the sandbags and rip them to shreds. They'd be dead in ten seconds.

"Logan!" She shouted over the boom and crack of gunfire. "Move! Go—!"

Another sound rumbled in the background—a dull roar she couldn't place.

"I see the Blackhawks!" Julio's voice blasted into her ears. "They're here. Get the hell out!"

41
EDEN

E den half-ran, half-stumbled across the grassy lawn, the others right behind her. Eden took the lead, Ruth on one side, her mother on the other, the others in a few ragged lines close on their heels.

Four hundred yards. It felt like a marathon, like they were running in molasses. Every cell in their bodies pumped with adrenaline, their hearts hammering, pulses thumping as they fled for their lives.

Gunshots blasted behind her. She didn't pause. She didn't falter. She fixed her eyes on the end of the fence where the peninsula met the water.

Haasi was waiting for them. All Eden had to do was reach her, and they'd be safe.

Her stomach was a sour-sick tangle of nerves. Her skin radiated heat, waves of dizziness pulsing through her head. Her body screamed at her to stop, to rest, to give up for just a little while.

But she couldn't. She wouldn't.

She pushed herself further, forcing one foot in front of the other. *One, two, three. Breathe.* Her fear didn't matter. Nothing mattered but what she needed to do next.

She had people depending on her. She would not let them down.

Ruth gripped her waist. Her arm was slung around Ruth's shoulder. Ruth's mother ran along her other side, encouraging them on.

Haasi was there ahead of her, standing stiff in the shadows, her crossbow tucked into her shoulder, protecting them as they fled toward her.

She fired the weapon. Behind them, a Shepherd howled in agony.

Eden ran faster, her skirt whipping her legs like a flag.

And then they were there, huddling beneath the live oaks, the thick underbrush snagging their clothes. She whirled around, fighting the sour wave of nausea, and checked the group, frantically counting heads. Seventeen souls. Everyone accounted for.

Still, it wasn't enough. So many had refused to come. But she couldn't think about that.

They weren't safe yet.

A dull, thumping roar came from the north. The distant throbbing grew louder. Shouts, screams, and gunfire filled the air.

Helicopters.

"God have mercy," Ruth's mother breathed in horror.

"The soldiers are already here," Maki said. "We must go now! Hurry, hurry!"

She ushered the women and children into the two airboats hidden behind the reeds.

Eden stood there, watching them clamber into the boats, her hands limp at her sides, her feet rooted to the ground.

The River Grass Compound was about to be destroyed. She would never see it again. Everything in her longed to look at it, one last time.

If she dared to turn around, she might turn into a pillar of salt, like Lot's wife. But God hadn't told her not to look back.

And it wasn't Sodom and Gomorrah behind her, as much as it seemed like it.

This had been her home. She was born here, raised here. Every single childhood memory happened in this place. Her father was out there in the middle of all that turmoil. Her mother. Her brother.

They would probably die tonight.

They had chosen to hurt others. They weren't good people. She knew that. She never wanted to see them again, but that didn't mean she wanted them dead, either.

It didn't mean her heart didn't ache with a tsunami of grief and loss.

The good memories filled her mind. Laughing and running with her friends, playing with the goats and chickens, feeding the rabbits every morning. Singing her heart out in the chapel, the hymns so haunting and beautiful it raised goose pimples on her arms. The moments she hid away in the woods to draw and think and dream. The times her brothers loved her and everyone was happy.

She was afraid to turn around, to look.

She did it anyway.

4 2

LOGAN

The fleet headed in fast and low over the trees, streaking across the darkened sky. It was impossible to count how many in the darkness, but if Logan had to guess, it was three or four. One long oversized one with two rotors—probably a Chinook, for troop transport—was flanked by several smaller, faster Blackhawks.

His heart surged in his chest. An aerial armada. It was both the most beautiful and the most terrifying thing he had ever seen.

With a shout, the gunner swung the massive turret around and aimed it toward the air assault bearing down on them. More screams and shouted orders filled the air. Logan and Dakota were forgotten. For now.

A series of muzzle flashes flared from the opened doors of the helicopters. The door gunners on the choppers were aiming for the sniper positions at the rooftop corners of various buildings to keep them from blasting the choppers out of the sky with shoulder-fired rocket-propelled grenades, or RPGs.

A deafening howl erupted as the belt-fed machine guns roared to life and began pounding the compound with machinegun fire.

KYLA STONE

Logan and Dakota hit the ground at the same time, hands over their heads, pressing themselves against the U-shaped sandbags. Maybe it wasn't the right move, but it was all fear and instinct now.

The sandbags were their only protection, and it wasn't much. Their backs and heads were completely exposed to an aerial attack. Logan cringed, flinching away from the shattering gunfire above them. Bullets could drill into their exposed bodies at any moment.

Dakota shouted something. Logan answered, but he couldn't even hear himself.

Their voices were lost in the ear-splitting roar of gunfire, the deafening whine of the turbines, the thunderous throb of the rotors.

Time slowed. Each frenzied second felt like eternal minutes as everything played in awful slow motion.

Logan lifted his head at the same time as Dakota, their desperate gazes meeting, silent communication passing between them in an instant. This was no place to sit out a full-blooded, guns-blazing assault. They couldn't stay here.

They needed to get the hell out now or they were liable to get killed by friendly fire. The soldiers would be high on adrenaline and combat, and in the smoke, noise, and confusion, they'd kill first, ask questions later.

No way in hell Logan was going out like that. Not after everything they'd already survived. There was no fear anymore, no doubt. Nothing in his mind at all but keeping himself and Dakota alive.

Dakota mouthed a word. Or maybe she was shouting. He couldn't tell, but he knew what she meant—the fence.

Get to the water, the fence line. Haasi and Maki had fled with the airboats, but Ezra's fishing boat was still hidden a mile out. They could seek shelter in the woods, get Julio, and make a run for it.

He locked eyes with Dakota and nodded.

180

That silent, icy calm descended over him. His heart hammered in his throat, adrenaline spiking.

Logan leapt to his feet and spun, weapon up and ready, scanning for hostiles to provide covering fire for Dakota. He felt her spring up next to him, her back pressed against his.

They took it all in a few terrible heartbeats. They stared, awestruck, as the battle unfolded around them.

At the chapel, several dozen Shepherds turned to face the oncoming onslaught. Several men stared dumbly up at the huge aircraft suspended in the sky above them, buffeted by the heavy winds. Most of the Shepherds were already shaking off the fear and confusion and forming a coordinated defense.

They fanned out behind the sandbag defensive positions, releasing a blistering barrage of machine gun fire, several of them leveling rocket-propelled grenade launchers at the incoming choppers.

Two of the Blackhawks dipped and veered away as heavy groundfire peppered their sides. The nearest Blackhawk leveled out around fifty feet above the ground. It swerved hard left away from the chapel as the armored vehicles aimed and fired their massive guns.

The choppers weren't targeting the chapel outright with their big guns. But they couldn't avoid the casualties of the women and children locked inside. Not unless they established a precision attack from the ground, which the Shepherds were effectively driving back.

For now, the Prophet's human shields ploy was working.

A huge flare stabbed the darkness, spitting fire skyward. An anti-aircraft gun. It was stationed somewhere near the restricted area—the actual buildings were blocked by the trees.

More Shepherds had dug in defensive positions near the woods between the restricted area and the men's barracks. Pencil-thin lines of flame spit out as the Shepherds' gunners fired continuous heavy-duty rounds.

The choppers kept low and fast over the trees. The tree cover kept them hidden until the last possible moment, and even then, they were flying so low and fast that it was difficult for the Shepherds to acquire a firm target and fire.

As tracers looped toward it, one of the Blackhawks banked hard with a shriek of its turbines. Leveling out, it fired several rockets at the sentries' platforms on either side of the front gate. A sheet of flame flared above the trees.

A second Blackhawk hovered near the Chinook as it roared in toward the western side of the compound near the burning cafeteria and outbuildings. The Chinook descended, machine-gun fire slamming into its sides. The Chinook swerved but kept flying, coming in low for a landing.

Logan doubted off-loading troops from the Chinook in a hostile fire zone was their first or second choice. But they couldn't land further away and hotfoot it to their target, not with the compound the only clearing in the dense, swampy jungle large enough for landing within fifteen miles.

With a throaty growl, the Blackhawk raked the ground around the cafeteria, the gunners unleashing a fury of covering fire as the Chinook touched down. Dozens of soldiers spilled from the rear ramp, armed with heavy-duty weapons, ammo belts, plates of body armor, and military gear.

The Chinook lifted off again, the whine of the turbines revving to a fever pitch, like the roar of some great, ferocious beast. It tore skyward at full throttle before heading north and speeding out over the Glades toward Orlando.

Two more choppers hovered over several buildings along the eastern and western perimeters, probably searching for their specific landing zones and fast rope insertions. The nearest one held steady near the infirmary and mercy room as black-clad soldiers roped rapidly to the ground, agile and lethal as spiders.

Dakota seized Logan's arm, her fingers digging hard into his bicep, shaking him from his horrified stupor.

Time to run.

43
EDEN

Eden took a deep, steadying breath. *One, two, three. Breathe.*

She was brave enough to face this, to watch the destruction of her past. A part of her needed to see it.

As the rest of the women and children took their seats in the airboats, Eden turned around. In the distance, the army helicopters were dark hovering shapes roaring in low over the trees and blazing buildings, their bellies flaring red. Bursts of flame spewed from the metal beasts like fire from a dragon's throat.

Tiny figures fled from the onslaught. Small and large muzzle flashes erupted from the darkened ground like pops of fireworks.

And everywhere the fire blazed, eating up the buildings and spitting out smoke, soot, and death. People were shouting and screaming but she couldn't hear them anymore over the feverish shrieking of the helicopters and the thunderous *boom, boom, boom* of their weapons.

It wasn't just the bad burning up. It was the good things, too.

Even though she knew in her head that there was no other way to stop the evil in this place, everything about it felt wrong

183

and sick and twisted her insides with conflicting emotions—love, grief, remorse, justice, relief, fear.

Tears gathered in the corners of her eyes and leaked down her cheeks. She wasn't grieving for the Shepherds or even for her parents. She was grieving for the ones still back there, the children no different than she was. And for herself.

Haasi came up beside her and wrapped her in a fierce hug. "You did it, girl. You did it."

Eden nodded dully. She didn't feel proud right now. She felt sick.

A hot spike of watery pain lurched in her guts. Darkness wavered at the corners of her vision, and she swayed on her feet.

"The hard part is over now, honey. It's over." Haasi took her hand and guided her into the boat while Maki kept the rifle up and ready to fire. "We have to go now."

Eden slumped into the bottom of the boat, her back pressed against the legs of the children crammed onto the bench behind her. Haasi was wrong. The hard part wasn't over.

The truly hard stuff—the grief, the mourning, picking through the pieces of the past to choose the things you wanted to keep and the things better left behind—that would take a long, long time.

Ruth squeezed in beside her. Her small face was terrified but brave. "It'll be okay. God is still with us."

Eden hoped that was true. Her heart ached with worry for Dakota, Logan, and Julio. They were still out there somewhere. They were the ones who mattered most.

She whispered a prayer for them.

Even as she felt herself fading, something niggled at the back of her mind. She was forgetting something crucially important. Something she was supposed to tell Dakota.

The radiation sickness had muddled her thoughts, and in the chaos and tension of the rescue at the chapel, it had slipped right out of her head.

Unconsciousness was pulling at her, blurring her vision,

tugging at each tendril of thought and unraveling it. She blinked hard, forced herself to focus. She couldn't let herself go yet.

Too many people were depending on her. She hadn't let them down. She wasn't going to start now.

And then she remembered. She dug inside her pocket and pulled out a wrinkled, sweat-dampened piece of yellowed paper. She'd written two words on it earlier in the infirmary—the message for Hawthorne she hadn't been able to relay on the radio.

She would pass it on. The rest was up to Dakota and Logan.

The airboats roared to life, their fiberglass hulls vibrating. As the flames consumed the compound, Maki and Haasi directed the boats out into the swamp, fleeing toward safety.

Eden had faith. In God. In her friends, in Dakota. And in herself.

Today, she'd fought back.

She hadn't let the fear destroy her. She hadn't let the Shepherds steal everything that mattered. They'd done their worst, and they would still lose tonight. She knew it with every fiber of her being.

Eden reached up and untied the blue ribbon hiding her neck. She had no need of it. She let the ribbon slip from her fingers, closing her eyes as the wind whipped it away, lost forever to the night.

44
MADDOX

Maddox was almost to the men's barracks when he heard it. He froze, straining his ears to catch any strange noises over the wind, the roaring fire, the shouting men.

A faint, dull roar reached him. He strained his ears over the wind as gradually the sound strengthened into the *whump, whump, whump* of approaching rotors.

He craned his neck and gazed up at the black expanse of the sky. To the north, a dark shape moved fast and low over the swaying trees. Then another. And another.

The night filled with a hail of gunfire and the wails of the dead and dying. Everything was chaotic, haphazard, disorienting.

Maddox ran for the cover of the closest barracks. A long, sparse cabin with bare pine plank walls and boarded windows, it wouldn't provide much cover against the heavy firepower pounding the compound, but it was all his panicking mind could think of in the moment.

He stood in the doorway, stunned and shell-shocked. He watched the carnage playing out like some horrible, jerky, slow-motion movie that wouldn't stop playing, that he couldn't seem to turn away from no matter the revulsion roiling in his stomach.

Judgment Day was here, he realized with a terrible jolt, just like the Prophet had foretold. But it wasn't their enemies' judgment day. It was the Shepherds'.

Fear paralyzed him, trapping him in a blank void of indecision. Would he rush out there, a brave and courageous warrior of God, to fight against trained soldiers, to die valiantly if that was his calling?

Or would he fall the second he hit the battlefield, strafed and riddled with bullets, his body torn to shreds? Would he die alone in the dirt and muck, his lifeblood soaking into the swampy ground, no one to mourn him or even notice he was gone?

Dread surged up from the pit of his stomach, a dizzying, raw terror clamping down on him. A vision of shrapnel shredding flesh and red-hot lead splintering bone—all of it his own—flashed before his eyes.

No. He refused to die like that. He'd fought too hard to stay alive. Sacrificed too much.

He was no idiot. There was only one way this ended. The enemy was too strong, too powerful. The Shepherds would ultimately lose to the government's coordinated assault. That the Prophet no longer seemed to care about the compound itself was evidence enough for Maddox.

To the south, near the gate to the restricted area, he saw his father, instantly recognizing the gray battle fatigues and the large red cross on his back. Several Shepherds were with him, shouldering RPGs and aiming for the helicopters wheeling and diving overhead like great predatory birds.

Maddox should go join him. Fight by his side for glory and divine honor and to defend the home that was now blazing up all around him. If he were a good son—if he were Jacob—that's exactly what he would've done.

But he didn't.

Maddox didn't move.

45
LOGAN

E verything that had come before was leading up to this moment—this one moment that would test Logan to the fullest, would push him to the brink and past it, forcing him to confront death itself.

He was scared—any sane human being would be—but he was also determined, focused, undaunted.

Death would not have him. Nor Dakota or Eden or anyone he cared about. Not today.

He pushed Dakota out ahead of him. She sprinted across the open ground. In two strides, he was at her side. She took the right, he the left, searching for threats as they ran.

His pulse thudded against his skull. Every breath ripped from his chest.

His carbine set to automatic fire, he unleashed a barrage of firepower as he advanced. One Shepherd clutched at his gut with both hands, dropping his rifle. Logan hit another one with a shot between the eyes. A third and fourth, he drilled new holes into their skulls. The fifth went down as Logan strafed his kneecaps with bullets.

He fired again and again and again, with skill and precision. He killed every Shepherd that came within range of his weapon.

The world was distilled down to its purest form—kill or be killed. The red mist of combat descended, the air heavy with the scents of gunpowder, coppery blood, and the stench of death.

Gone was the numbing darkness. Gone was the searing *need* and sour-sick lurch of despair. Gone was the monster.

It was only him.

He was liberated, made new, reborn in battle. There was nothing but the white fire of righteous rage blazing through him, nothing but the relentless desire to win, to defeat his enemies, to waste this place to ashes, to fight the good fight and prevail.

He was in total control.

He whirled, sighting two more Shepherds bearing down on a soldier crouching behind the shattered remains of the mercy room. He unleashed a long burst of automatic fire. They crumpled and didn't get back up.

The thump and boom of grenades clashed with the juddering clatter of machine-gunfire and the shouts and cries of friends and enemies alike. One of the windows broke in the chapel; the high terrified screams of women and children lacerated the din of battle.

Dakota fired several short bursts, aiming to the west and taking out a few Shepherds hiding near the families' cabins. Several more huddled behind a defensive sandbag wall returned fire.

Bullets zinged and whistled all around them. Dirt and clods of grass kicked up as rounds struck the ground only feet away. They desperately needed cover before they were cut down in the crossfire.

A massive live oak with a trunk thicker than a tire stood less than ten yards to the southwest. He dove for the ground and army-crawled, Dakota right behind him. Bark exploded from the trunk above their heads as they made it to the tree and circled around to the relative safety of the other side.

Smoke from the fires and from white phosphorus grenades

poured across the compound, making it difficult to see anything. Flashes of small explosions and muzzle fire mingled with the dull orange glow of multiple fires lighting up the night.

It was too bright for the NV goggles. He had only his own eyesight to rely on now. Logan ejected his nearly spent magazine, slapped in a fresh one from his battle belt, and adjusted his grip on his gun. He peered around the trunk.

The *whomp, whomp, whomp* of spinning rotors blared as aircraft wheeled and swooped overhead, dodging the enemy fire blasting the sky, the tracers like laser beams from a sci-fi movie. The *crack-crack-crack* of gunfire splintered the air.

Soldiers raced between the buildings. A team kicked in the front door of the infirmary and let off a series of flashes and loud explosions—flashbangs and smoke grenades. Smoke billowed from the broken door and the windows.

They cleared the building and repeated the process with the mercy room. On the northwestern side of the clearing, a second fire team was doing the same. Soldiers darted from building to building as the other members of their teams provided covering fire. They pushed south and east toward the chapel and the restricted area beyond it.

From the roof of the chapel, a hidden gunner unleashed a massive .50 caliber M2 machine gun, deafening as a buzz saw as it ripped the ground to shreds. Chunks of dirt and glass blew high in the air.

The huge bullets tore into the walls of the infirmary, massive chunks of wood exploding like splinters. Two soldiers jerked and fell, their bodies pulverized.

The Shepherds repulsed the attack, pushing the soldiers back with heavy, sustained gunfire. The whoosh-crash of an incoming RPG filled the air. Several soldiers went down in the explosion.

Another burst of gunfire. This time from behind them. Logan whipped around. Four Shepherds were closing in on their position—fifty yards to the southwest and moving fast.

He and Dakota were about to be pinned down.

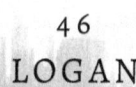

46
LOGAN

L ogan motioned to Dakota to get her attention and
pointed toward the fence. She signaled that she
understood.

Trying to keep as much of his body behind the tree as possible, he squatted, braced himself, and took careful aim. He refused to shoot a soldier. They were the good guys. But the soldiers would still slaughter them without a second thought, believing they were the enemy.

His heartbeat slowed; his breathing steadied. Aim. Exhale. Squeeze. As Dakota raced across the exposed ground, he opened fire.

Three Shepherds dropped immediately. The fourth returned fire. Bullets slammed into the trunk above his head. He didn't wince or duck. He remained steady, kept shooting.

Two rounds struck the fourth one in the center of his tactical vest. He jerked and fell to his knees. Logan ended him with a headshot.

He swept the grounds, searching for Dakota.

She'd disappeared. One second a dark retreating blur in a landscape of fire and destruction, the next second she was gone. She was safe in the woods or the water. He had to believe that.

He was about to run after her when an explosion shattered the air seemingly right above his head. The blast was deafening.

One of the RPGs had hit a Blackhawk. It careened across the sky, a tail of fire spiraling after it, lethal blades churning furiously.

Instinctively, Logan dropped and flattened himself against the ground. The tree trunk shuddered as the floundering helicopter whooshed past, its metal belly scraping the canopy. The downdraft battered him with a storm of wind, leaves, dirt, and debris.

With a screeching, sputtering howl, the aircraft plunged to earth.

The ground shuddered beneath Logan. A wave of heat struck his body. He kept his head down for several endless moments, his heart pounding, forgetting to breathe.

Finally, he pulled himself to his feet, leaning hard against the tree, his ears ringing. Fire and smoke exploded from the wreckage like terrible fireworks. One of the soldiers trapped inside shrieked in agony.

Logan forced himself to look away and scan the grounds, searching for movement, for the glint of a weapon in the woods, between the buildings, on top of a roof. Whoever had brought the chopper down—Logan wanted his head on a spike.

There. Near the restricted area. Just inside the scrim of trees less than four hundred yards to the west—three Shepherds with RPGs on their shoulders, aiming at the next Blackhawk.

None of the soldiers on the ground had made it this far south yet. Logan was the closest.

To get the shot, he'd have to move out from behind the shelter of the oak and completely expose himself. If he didn't take it, the Shepherd would obliterate another chopper, kill even more of the good guys, the soldiers risking their lives to end this madness.

He could keep running. Or he could do something.

Only one option was acceptable.

He crept out from behind the tree. He dropped to one knee and took aim with his carbine, focused the man's head in his sights.

Recognition jolted through him. During their earlier surveillance, Dakota had pointed out the bizarre red cross emblazoned on this man's fatigues. *Solomon Cage.* Maddox and Eden's father. One of the men responsible for the brands scarring her back.

Fresh fury burned through him. He longed to torture this asshole, slowly and painfully like he deserved. But there was no time. He had a job to do.

"We've been burned!" Jake yelled in Logan's earpiece. "We're still trapped behind the barns and we're taking heavy fire!"

Julio responded, but Logan didn't hear him.

He pushed back every distraction, blocking out the stink of sweat and gunpowder, the screaming and gunfire. He fixed his gaze on his target. Exhale. Aim. Squeeze.

Logan fired.

47

MADDOX

Maddox watched from the barracks as the Shepherd with the first RPG jittered and fell from enemy fire. His father stepped forward, grabbed the massive thing, and shouldered it himself. A second Shepherd stood next to him, another rocket at the ready.

Solomon Cage aimed and locked on one of the Blackhawks strafing the grounds near the restricted area, where several Shepherds were taking cover in the strip of woods. The RPG fired at the chopper in a trailing arc of fire.

The rocket struck its mark. The tail exploded, and the bird began spinning wildly, rotors whomping. The chopper crashed to the ground in a fiery burst of flames and smoke and twisted metal.

A soldier limped from the crash, shrieking, his back, arms, and head on fire. Maddox watched in mesmerized fascination as the man staggered and sank to his knees, flames licking his face, his fingers, his thighs. He collapsed face-first to the ground, still burning.

The Shepherd handed Maddox's father another one. He aimed at the next Blackhawk, this one bearing down on the Prophet's house.

Movement across the clearing drew Maddox's attention. Maybe a hundred and fifty yards away, a Shepherd was acting strangely. He was kneeling out in the open, weapon braced against his shoulder, preparing to fire. He wasn't facing the enemy onslaught; he was facing the restricted area—and aiming at Solomon Cage.

Maddox peered through his scope. In the fiery light, he glimpsed a strong, scruffy jaw, bronze skin, and tattoos inking the man's forearms where the sleeve of the black fatigues had been pushed back.

Maddox's heart bucked against his ribs. That was no Shepherd. That was one of Dakota's men—Logan.

How the hell...then he remembered. Reuben had sent out a warning over their comms, but Maddox hadn't heard it clearly. He'd been distracted. Moments later, they'd been attacked.

A bizarre mix of outrage and grudging admiration roiled in his gut. The wily vermin had managed to sneak into the compound after all, right in the middle of the firefight of the century. They truly were relentless.

If Logan was here, then Dakota was here somewhere, too. If she was, then that meant—but there was no time to consider the ramifications.

Logan was about to kill his father. He had to do something.

Maddox stepped out of the barrack's doorway to get a clear shot. He raised the M4 and sighted the Hispanic guy's head.

You could do nothing.

Maddox hesitated. Waves of electric, feverish heat rolled through his body. Explosions and gunfire roared all around him. Smoke and cordite stung his nostrils.

Hatred twisted and churned within him, writhing like a snake eating away at him. He would never be anything to his father. Would never escape his scorn and derision.

Unless...

You could let it happen.

KYLA STONE

A strange numbness stole over him. Everything faded away. He could barely hear a thing but for his thudding pulse.

His finger stilled on the trigger. He looked up, waiting.

He didn't have to wait long.

Logan fired. *Boom!*

His father's skull exploded.

Maddox blinked, but the sight was seared into his retinas. Blood was everywhere. His father's body crumpling, collapsing, his arms and legs suddenly limp with no brain to signal the muscles, tendons, and nerves.

The RPG thudded to the ground and rolled harmlessly in the grass.

The Shepherd beside his father spun around, firing indiscriminately. A moment later, he fell, too.

For an endless moment, Maddox didn't move, just stared in dull horror at his father's body.

Nearby gunfire jolted him out of his fugue. The numbness dissipated beneath an onslaught of pain and rage, warring emotions bubbling to the surface— resentment, admiration, jealousy, love, loathing.

His father. The man he'd both hated and adored. Who'd held so much power over him his entire life.

Solomon Cage was dead. A corpse. Gone in the blink of an eye. Another dead body leaking blood in a blood-soaked ground.

The heavens didn't open to receive him. There was no glory, no fanfare. Nothing.

A vile, wriggling shame filled him. *Your father is dead. You watched him die. You're either a coward or a monster. Which one is it?*

Maddox held all the power. He controlled who lived or died. He was better than both his brother and his father, now.

Maddox chose monster.

He swung the muzzle back around and aimed at Logan. Time to take him out. His hands were damp and shaking, the sights wavering.

He squeezed the trigger.

Logan stumbled.

A hit, but not a kill shot. Maddox shifted, raised the carbine slightly, forced himself to focus, to steady his treacherous hands.

Logan hobbled for the cover of the tree line. Maddox smiled as he sighted the man's skull. He'd never make it—

Four Shepherds darted out of the Prophet's house and aimed RPGs at the Blackhawk screaming by overhead. A thunderous blast and the house behind them disappeared in a gout of smoke and blazing flames. The roof collapsed under the force of the explosion.

A third Shepherd staggered out of the smoking ruins. Another grenade blast, and he was thrown into the air and came down in pieces.

On the western side—Maddox's side—more than a dozen soldiers were attempting to work their way down to the other side of the chapel to trap the Shepherds in a pincher. They were already near the family cabins. They'd reach Maddox sooner rather than later.

No time to aim and fire again. Maddox whirled and ran for his life.

48

LOGAN

Logan limped behind the corner of a long narrow building outside the perimeter of the woods just as a massive explosion somewhere behind him trembled the ground.

He scanned wildly for any threats but saw nothing. The soldiers on the ground hadn't made it this far yet, and the remaining Shepherds were clustered in and around the chapel.

He longed to go after the scumbag who'd shot him, but the coward had slipped away through the trees into deeper woods. And Logan was in no shape to go after him.

He clenched his teeth against the eye-watering pain. It felt like a burning poker jabbing deep into the bone, like someone had taken a blowtorch to the muscles, tendons, and flesh of his left calf.

He let his weapon hang from its strap and bent down, jerked up his pantleg, and probed at the wound. A deep gash tore through the meat of his left calf. The raw pink of muscle peeked through the leaking blood and shredded skin.

He flinched at the gory sight, but he wasn't giving up or going down, wasn't going to hunker down somewhere to wait it out. He was part of a team—not just with Dakota but all of them. They depended on him.

He'd do what brave soldiers had done for hundreds of years before him: he'd grit his teeth and carry on fighting. He'd see this thing through to its bloody end.

But first, he had to stop the bleeding, or he wouldn't be doing anything. He fumbled for one of the pouches in his tactical vest and pulled out a vacuum-sealed Israeli compression bandage, Celox clotting granules, and hemostatic gauze.

He poured on the Celox, packed the wound with the gauze. Wrapping his calf, he slipped the elastic bandage through the compression bar, pulling it snug and making sure the absorption pad covered the wound. Finally, he twisted the closure bar like a tourniquet to make it tight.

It still hurt like hell, but it would keep him on his feet for a while. He rolled down his pantleg and gripped his gun.

He needed to get to Dakota, needed to—

A soldier barreled around the corner, gun up and aimed straight at Logan's head.

"Don't shoot!" Logan dropped his weapon and thrust his hands in the air. He sank to his knees, his heart jackhammering wildly against his ribs. "I'm a friend! I know Hawthorne! Don't shoot!"

"Holy hell!" The soldier's brown face was covered in black and green camo paint. He barely looked human. "Logan? Is that you?"

Logan sagged in relief. "Hawthorne."

"You're lucky as hell I saw you take out that RPG. Otherwise, I would've severed your spine from your brain before you'd taken a single step. I don't miss those shots."

"I never doubted it."

Hawthorne cursed. "You look just like them! What were you thinking?"

He took several deep breaths to steady his nerves. "Dakota's idea."

"Why am I not surprised?"

"It worked until you showed up early."

"I was trying to save your sorry butts." He held out his hand.

Logan took it and allowed the man to pull him to his feet. "I'll thank you once we get out of this dumpster fire alive."

"We will. Stay close and give me that M4 for now. The last thing we need is some trigger-happy chap blowing your head off right next to me." Hawthorne smirked. "Brain matter is so hard to get out of my hair."

Logan was still too rattled to appreciate the gallows humor. Giving up the gun made him feel exposed and vulnerable, but Hawthorne wasn't wrong. At least he still had the Glock and his combat knife. "Dakota—she's in the woods along the southeast perimeter."

"I'll send Kinsey to get her."

"Julio is still in the woods, too. He's dressed like I am, like the Shepherds. Jake, Archer, and Zane Collier are friendlies pinned down on the eastern side somewhere near the animal barns and sheds."

Hawthorne scowled but merely shook his head in resignation. He slung Logan's weapon across his chest. "I'll radio it in. You fools are lucky as hell you're still alive."

He hurried after Hawthorne, each step sending jarring pain spiking up his spine.

Hawthorne rounded the corner in a crouch, alert and ready. He stopped so suddenly, Logan nearly bumped into him.

The chapel was burning. Black smoke boiled from the cracks between the boards nailed over the windows. Agonized shrieks and wails echoed from inside the walls.

"Sitrep, Alpha Team!" Hawthorne shouted into his radio. "Did we do that?"

"No, sir!" Even through the static, horror and disgust laced the female soldier's voice. "They set it on fire—they're doing it to themselves."

Hawthorne stared, horrified. "This is turning into a dumpster fire. We go in now! Save who you can. End this and get the hell out!"

They unleashed havoc. The men fired rockets into buildings and hurled grenades through windows. The Blackhawks swooped and dove, unleashing a terrible, monstrous firepower on the remaining Shepherds.

A series of explosions shook the compound to its foundations. Rows of cabins and concrete-block buildings collapsed as gouts of flame and belches of smoke shot skyward, blotting out the already black sky.

The aircraft's turbines whined and screamed like some horrible predator hunting its prey. The huge rotor blades blasted a powerful downdraught, mingling with the strong wind to create a furious cyclone beating at the roofs and windows, the grass, bushes, and trees, and everyone trying to stand upright, friend and foe alike.

Machine guns on both sides roared as huge rounds chewed up the ground, the buildings, the bodies unfortunate enough to be in the line of fire. Everywhere, muzzle flashes and spitting bullets, spent shells spinning into the air in clattering clouds, men screaming and shrieking and killing.

Death rained down with the vengeance of some terrible, mythic god bent on the annihilation of every living thing he'd ever created.

Within minutes, the compound was a smoking, shattered ruin.

49

MADDOX

C rack! Thump!

Maddox spun to his right, carbine up, breathing hard. Cold sweat broke out on his brow. Ten feet into the trees, a branch as big around as his thigh had broken off and smashed to the ground, taking several smaller branches with it.

He sagged against the wall in relief. He was deep in the restricted area, near the comms shack. He had no plan other than to escape the rampaging slaughter by any means necessary.

The wind whipped through the trees and howled around the corners of the buildings. The peppery tang of cordite, the stench of things burning, and the musty smell of mud, peat, and rotting vegetation stung his nostrils.

Faint snippets of voices reached him—jumbled, clipped, and anxious. Maddox edged against the wall and peered around the corner.

Seven shapes moved in the shadows about forty yards away, hustling toward him through the trees. Four lugged a large, heavy object between them, two more striding along on either side, rifles up and scopes scanning the forest for threats.

There was no mistaking the confident gait of the last figure, the long yellow hair fluttering behind him. The Prophet.

For an instant, Maddox hesitated, startled. The Prophet was running away. That was clear. Leaving the rest of his men behind to die glorious deaths for him.

A surge of loathing filled him. His home was being razed to the ground. His stepmother was trapped in the chapel, maybe being burned alive. Everyone he knew was dead or in the process of dying. His father was dead.

You let him die.

The Prophet was getting the hell out. And he wanted in. Nothing else mattered.

He squashed the rage and hatred welling in his chest, his knack for self-preservation kicking in. He'd survived worse than this. He always survived.

"Don't shoot!" he called just loud enough for them to hear. He stepped out from behind the comms building, hands in the air, M4 lifted above his head. "I'm a friendly. Don't shoot."

Something pressed against the back of his skull. The hard muzzle of a gun.

Maddox nearly pissed his pants. He hadn't even seen the Shepherd scouting ahead, keeping hidden in the cover of the trees. The guy had gotten the drop on him way too easily.

He was distracted, off his game. It had almost cost him.

"Don't shoot," he said again.

"You sure about that?"

Maddox exhaled a sharp breath. "Reuben."

"In the flesh," Reuben said, a sneer in his voice.

The two Shepherds straight ahead leveled their carbines at him.

"It's Maddox." Reuben removed the muzzle from Maddox's skull. "Maddox Cage."

The Shepherds lowered their weapons but remained on high alert. Maddox recognized them now: the two trigger-happy guards were Huffman and Kirby, Reuben's buddies.

He only knew two of the four carrying the load: Dave Clarke

and a skinny guy in his thirties named Nash—he'd had a family here. Probably now he didn't.

They all looked shaken, their faces drawn. Nash stank—dribbles of vomit stained the front of his chest.

It was easy to believe in war and sacrifice before you actually had to live it.

Only Reuben seemed unfazed.

"We have to go," Kirby said tightly.

"You look like hell, man," Clarke muttered. "You all right?"

Maddox wished he still had the wall to hold him up. Sweat drenched his back beneath his tactical vest, his legs weak and wobbly. His whole body felt like it was burning up from the inside out.

The radiation sickness.

He forced himself to straighten, pushing the pain down deep. If he showed weakness now, they might leave him behind. "I'm fine."

"He's alive, which is more than many of your brethren can say." The Prophet's face was smudged in soot and ash, his features rigid from the incredible stress, but he seemed otherwise unhurt. "Where's Solomon?"

Memories seared his mind—his finger tense on the trigger, his father's head centered in his scope, then Logan Garcia's. The moment of hesitation. The terrible *boom* amidst the cacophony of the battle, his father's body dropping to the ground in an explosion of red.

"My father—" He cleared his throat. "My father is dead."

"Damn it!" the Prophet roared. "How the hell did that happen?"

Several of the men glanced at him, startled.

Maddox opened his mouth, said nothing.

The Prophet's eye twitched, his mouth tightening. "God has called him to his glory. His sacrifice shall be rewarded."

"Copy that," Reuben said into his radio. He motioned at the

group. "The enemy infiltrated the chapel. The compound will be overrun soon. We need to keep moving."

The Prophet's face showed no emotion. "They did what was required of them?"

Reuben gave a curt nod. "They were faithful to the end."

The Prophet fell into step beside Maddox. Maddox felt the man's eyes on him, studying him, his gaze calculating. He raised his voice just loud enough to speak over the wind whipping at their clothes. "It's a miracle you're here, son. I need your help."

"Name it," Maddox said without thinking.

"With our chopper MIA, we need to use the airboats. Your father told me you can navigate like no one else. You know all the secret channels. I've already called it in. A bird will meet us at an extraction point off highway 27 in approximately two hours. We have only a small window to get out before the hurricane hits and we're trapped, which will only give our enemies more time to track us down."

The Prophet was still trying to convey the steady calm of a man of faith, a man God would never allow to die. But Solomon's death had clearly shaken him. The tension in his shoulders and the sharp, agitated tone of his voice gave him away. "Do you understand the urgency?"

"Perfectly." Maddox glanced at the large object his fellow Chosen soldiers carried. It looked like some kind of high-tech metal trunk. "Is that the bomb?"

"The most important part. A few pieces had to be dismantled temporarily. You might call it a suitcase bomb now. But don't worry. Five kilotons are plenty for our purposes."

The Prophet slapped him hard on the back. Maddox forced himself not to flinch. "With your father gone, you're the one I depend on, son. I know you can get us out of here. God Himself shall reward you."

Reuben glanced sharply back at them, his expression inscrutable.

Once, Maddox had longed for such accolades. Once, he would've beamed with haughty triumph. Now the words sounded hollow, just the empty manipulations of a pathetic man desperate to save his own skin.

They reached the fence and the end of the restricted area. Kaufman and Kirby laid down cover fire while Reuben sprinted ahead. He reached the boathouse, took cover, and added his own fire to drive back the enemy.

Maddox kept his weapon up and ready as he edged out from behind the fence. The boathouse stood less than four hundred yards straight ahead, the shoreline ten yards to his left.

To the north, fires raged across the compound. Small dark shadows darted around the buildings. Muzzle flashes burst here and there. The *rat-a-tat* of machine guns battled with the roar of the fire and the wind thrashing the cypress and oak trees, many of them on fire.

Nearly every building was smoke-blackened, some of them burning, others crumbling. The walls still standing were peppered with bullet holes and huge jagged holes from the air assault.

Corpses—both Shepherds and soldiers—were scattered everywhere.

He couldn't see his father's body from here. His stomach lurched. He swallowed back sour acid as a wave of watery cramps wrenched his guts. Competing emotions tore through him— grief, satisfaction, triumph, guilt.

As he turned away, something snagged his attention. Beside the mercy room, the infirmary blazed, great gouts of flame leaping for the sky. "What about Eden?"

"Forget her!" the Prophet snapped. "She's not important anymore."

That didn't make sense. But right now, nothing made sense. God's army was supposed to annihilate the wicked. Instead, they were the ones being slaughtered. The Prophet was supposed to protect them all. Instead, he was saving his own skin.

The son was supposed to protect the father, not stand by and watch his death.

"But—"

The Prophet grasped his arm roughly and shoved him forward, his eyes flashing with impatience—and fear. "Just run!"

50
SHAY

S hay trudged back toward the general direction of her tent —or she was trying to. She'd gotten turned around somehow.

Curfew was at nine-thirty p.m., but it was already well after ten-thirty. Everyone was supposed to be in their designated tents, including her.

After dinner, she hadn't wanted to sit uselessly in her tent, so she'd searched out the Red Cross hospital tents and checked herself in as a volunteer. She'd wanted to help tonight, but the nurse turned her away and told her she needed rest first.

All the tents and rows looked the same, especially in the dark. There were signs, but she must've missed one somewhere...

She hesitated.

Heavy clouds had rolled in over the evening, completely blotting out the stars. Powerful spotlights beamed around the fenced perimeter, but deeper in the interior, shadows lurked everywhere she looked.

Someone was crying. It was close by, maybe just the next tent over.

She still had her pack with her. Hawthorne had told her to take it with her wherever she went, no matter what. She planned to do exactly that. She thought about trying to use the satellite phone's screen to light her way, but she wanted to conserve the battery. There wasn't a charging outlet in her tent.

Her feet ached, and her stomach growled. Earlier, she'd stood in line for fifty minutes for cold pasta, lumpy spaghetti sauce, and a pile of soggy canned green beans. The portions were small. From the grumbles and complaints of those in line with her, the camp had apparently begun cutting rations several days before.

The mess tent she'd been assigned to was only one of many. The FEMA staff were doing the best they could, but they were simply overwhelmed. They had an entire city of refugees to care for. They had too many people, too few supplies.

She didn't blame anyone, but she still felt grumpy and tired all the same. She just wanted to collapse into her cot and fall into an exhausted sleep.

If she could sleep. Thoughts of her friends in the Everglades were constantly on her mind. And Eden, trapped in that terrible place with those violent homegrown extremists.

She hadn't heard an update from Hawthorne in hours. She knew he had a critically important mission regarding the Shepherds of Mercy, but he wasn't at liberty to give her the details.

During dinner, a few National Guard soldiers had set up a battery-operated radio at their table. Shay had caught a few snippets of the news as she waited in line for her paltry meal.

The announcer spoke in a clipped British accent. "Ashkan Houshian, the nuclear scientist who defected from Iran and sought asylum in Sweden in 2016, now claims Iran has a secret nuclear weapons program, though Iran continues to insist that they've been abiding by the JCPOA signed in 2015...Houshian claims that Iran not only has enough enriched uranium to make a bomb, they already have several nuclear warheads and enough material for the thirteen WMDs detonated on American soil...

"Meanwhile, Putin claims America is 'provoking a war' and insists Russia will not stand by and allow the U.S. to invade yet another country without proof...a top Kremlin official stated, 'We are not the aggressors here. America is a bully. And the world will not abide by it any longer. If America uses nuclear weapons against Russia's allies, Russia will have no choice but to retaliate with nuclear force.'

"In her Presidential Address last night, President Harrington had this to say: 'The United States will not be cowed by any nation. We have a right to seek justice for our fallen friends and family, and we will do so as we see fit. We remain the most powerful nation in the world. God bless America...'"

Many of the people milling about were too tired or numb to pay attention to the news anymore. It was one cataclysmic disaster after another. More death, more destruction, more terrible news.

But others stopped, turning to listen. A few covered their mouths with their hands. Several shook their heads angrily.

"What are we waiting for?"

"The longer we wait, the weaker we look!"

"Will we even survive another war?"

"If Russia nukes us..."

"Let them try. The U.S. will bomb them out of this century."

"What if Russia sends their fifty-megaton Tsar missiles? What if they send a hundred nuclear missiles at once? Can we stop them, then?"

"Our anti-ballistic missiles will stop any nuclear attack."

"Just like they already did, right? If you still think the government can protect us, look around you! They can't do jack squat."

Shay had retrieved her food and hurried to an empty seat at the end of an overcrowded plastic table. Her hands had trembled as she inhaled her meal as quickly as she could.

She hoped the news was wrong. She hoped Hawthorne could stop whatever new calamity was marching inexorably toward them.

She just wanted him to be safe. She wanted them all safe.

Something rustled behind her.

Shay tensed. She spun around, searching the shadows, her heart hammering.

It was probably nothing. Likely a squirrel. Or someone rolling over in their cot. It wasn't like the heavy canvas tent walls offered soundproofing or much privacy.

She turned back around, started walking faster.

The soft weeping had stopped.

More footsteps behind her.

Her heart jolted. Before she could move or react, something barreled into her. The force of the blow knocked her off her feet. She struck the ground face first, barely getting her hands beneath her to prevent a mouthful of dirt.

Pain stung her knees and radiated from her hips up through her diaphragm. She sucked in a sharp breath, but no oxygen reached her lungs.

Agony exploded across her rib cage on her right side. Something had struck her—or kicked her. A shadow loomed over her. A person.

Someone was attacking her.

51
LOGAN

The battle was over.

Sound slowly returned to Logan's ringing ears. His tunnel vision faded. He wiped the specks of blood from his face and limped after Hawthorne, wincing as pain spiked up his leg.

Shrapnel, shell casings, and spent munitions scattered across the trampled grass. Confiscated weapons lay in random piles— AK47s, M4s, M16s, RPGs.

Dead bodies lay everywhere. A dozen soldiers searched the dead, a half-dozen others guarded a handful of surrendered Shepherds on their knees, their hands zip-tied.

Two soldiers tended to the small huddle of surviving women and children they'd managed to rescue from the chapel. They were covered in soot and ash, coughing and crying.

A medic moved among the walking wounded, tending to cuts from shrapnel and a few shallow gunshot wounds. One of the Blackhawks had already medevacked the critically injured.

"Archer and Jake are headed your way," Julio said into Logan's ear. "They're starting to comb the woods for survivors. I'm hightailing it to the fishing boat while I still can. See you at Haasi's."

"Thank you." Logan could still barely hear his own voice. "For everything."

Archer and Jake made their way toward him, shuffling between two soldier escorts, their weapons confiscated. They were dirty and blood-spattered but appeared unhurt.

"Where's Zane?" Logan asked.

Archer's soot-smeared face was streaked with tears. The big man didn't try to hold them back. He wept without shame or embarrassment.

Jake's face was dirty but dry. His entire body was thrumming with grief and pain and rage. "He's gone. Zane is dead."

Archer stared blankly at Logan, not really seeing him at all. He was still trapped in the chaos and madness of the battle. "We were careful, hunkering down and not drawing attention to ourselves. We got pinned between a sniper and a cluster of 'em hiding behind the cafeteria. We got drawn into the battle. We had to engage. Zane took out three of them with another one of his cocktails and a few well-placed bullets. Jake got the sniper, and I took out the last two...but not before they got off one last shot."

"A damned ricochet took him out," Jake spat, a bitter fury scraping his voice. "He was worth more than this whole stinking compound! Worth a thousand of these crazy savages!"

Cold anger burned through Logan. Fat, jovial Zane with his jokes and his moonshine, his shaggy beard and his outsized pride in those Molotov cocktails. He should've grown old living large in the swamp he'd always called home, riding hard on his Harley, bouncing a half-dozen wild-haired children on his knee while he told tales of that fated day he'd helped save America.

Instead, he was dead. Killed by a bunch of evil freaks. What an utterly senseless waste.

"I'm sorry," Logan said lamely. There was nothing else to say.

Archer spun in a slow circle, his big hands limp at his sides.

His eyes were glassy. "Tell me we caught the spineless slimeball. Tell me this was worth it."

"It was worth it," Hawthorne said in a low, hard voice. "And we'll nail the Prophet. I can promise you that. He's here somewhere. We'll find him."

Archer gave a small nod of acknowledgment. Jake stared at the burning chapel and said nothing.

Hawthorne gestured to a couple of his soldiers. "Get these two some medical care and get them into a Blackhawk."

"Is it over, then?" Logan asked.

Hawthorne nodded heavily. "The fire teams on the ground are spread out with interlocking arcs of fire. Every avenue of approach is covered. Most of the buildings are secured or destroyed—including the sentries at the front gate and the snipers on the rooftops. We're closing the net on the restricted area, flushing out the last few hostiles. Our boys are going through the chapel, searching for innocent survivors. Not that there are many left."

His mouth tightened in a grim line, his eyes flashing. "Those savages killed their own...When they knew they were surrounded, that it was over, they set the chapel on fire, with the women and children trapped inside with them..." His voice trailed off, unable to continue.

Logan said nothing. There wasn't a thing to say to make such an atrocity palatable. The depraved things humans did to each other...Maybe God, if He existed, was justified in annihilating mankind after all.

If Logan were a god, maybe he would obliterate them all, too. And they would deserve it. But then, so did he.

If Dakota were here, she would tell him most people sucked, but the few good ones made the rest worth it. And she would be right.

But right now, he didn't feel it. Right now, he wanted to break bones, smash faces, strangle every Shepherd he could get his hands on.

Except most of them were already dead.

Logan should've felt buzzed and high on the momentous victory. But the wreckage of the downed Blackhawk, the dead soldiers, and the smoke still burning from the chapel—and the heavy knowledge of whose bodies lay inside it—overshadowed it all.

They'd defeated the Shepherds, but at what cost?

5 2
SHAY

P anic seized Shay. Her lungs were burning. She couldn't breathe. Her diaphragm spasmed, the wind knocked out of her.

She tried to roll onto her unhurt side, to get to her feet and figure out what the heck was happening. White stars danced in front of her eyes.

"Just stay down!" a deep male voice growled.

The shadow leaned over her. Hands grabbed her roughly and jerked at the straps over her shoulders. He was trying to take the backpack. Trying to steal it.

She couldn't let that happen. She flailed, trying to claw at her attacker's arms. It was so dark, she couldn't make out any details, just a looming dark shape.

She still couldn't get any oxygen. Her head was pounding, her ribs aching.

Her attacker yanked the backpack straps over her arms, scraping her skin. He was going to get away with all her earthly belongings. Her satphone. She couldn't lose it.

She grabbed for the backpack, closed her fingers around one of the straps, and jerked it toward her. The attacker whirled and smacked her across the face, knocking her back on her butt, her glasses half-falling off her face.

Her assailant ripped the backpack from her hands.

"Hey!" a voice shouted. "Stop that!"

A woman dashed out of a nearby tent. She held a fist-sized rock in one hand. Without hesitating, she hurled it at the attacker.

He ducked with a grunt. The rock glanced off his right shoulder. He cursed as he turned back toward Shay and aimed another savage kick at her ribs.

Shay managed to dodge it. She rolled out of the way, dirt, twigs, and pebbles digging into her spine. She clambered shakily to her hands and knees. Pain spiked up her ribs and she sank back down again. "Give it back!"

"Shut up!" someone yelled. A baby started crying.

No one else left their tents.

The woman ran at Shay's attacker, slapping at the guy with nothing but her bare hands. "Leave her alone!"

The attacker shoved her to the ground. He backed away, glaring between the woman and Shay. He spat a final curse and took off running in the opposite direction, Shay's backpack bouncing over his shoulder.

After passing about ten tents, he darted between the rows and disappeared into the shadows. Shay wanted to run after him, but the pain was too much. Her lungs were burning, her ribs spiking with pain. It was still hard to breathe.

"Stupid mother—" The woman let out a string of curses in Spanish. She held her side and took several deep breaths, then reached out her hand and helped Shay to her feet. "Sorry, haven't done that in a while. Since high school if I'm being honest. Should we run after him?"

"No—" Shay gasped. "That sounds like—a terrible—idea."

She wasn't Dakota. She had no weapon, no self-defense moves. It was probably stupid to fight the scumbag in the first place. Her ribs would be suffering the consequences for a while.

She fixed her glasses and bent over, forearms on her thighs, sucking in beautiful mouthfuls of oxygen and trying not to cry.

"What good is a prison without the guards?" the woman quipped.

Shay gave a bitter laugh, wincing at the sharp jab between her ribs. She straightened and gingerly explored her torso with her fingers. Her right side was extremely tender, but nothing was broken. With some ibuprofen, she'd be fine in a few days.

"Thank you." She took a better look at the woman. It was dark, but she could see clearly enough this close. She recognized the familiar long black hair and delicate features. "You were in front of me in line when we checked in."

The woman nodded. "Small world."

A soldier jogged between the rows of tents toward them, flashlight beam bobbing ahead of her. She wore fatigues with a handgun holstered on one hip, a taser on the other. "Is there a problem? Someone reported screaming."

Shay explained what had happened.

"Are you okay?" the soldier asked. "Did he hurt you? Your cheek looks bruised."

Shay raised her hand to her face. "I'm fine. I just want my things back."

The soldier shook her head. "I'm sorry. I truly am. We're enormously understaffed. Believe it or not, a black market crime syndicate sprang up within a day of setting up camp. Not many people came in with their own stuff. Everything from cigarettes to conditioner to tampons are in high demand."

The pain in her ribs and her stinging cheek were nothing compared to the theft of the phone. She'd just lost her only way to communicate with Hawthorne and make sure her friends were still alive.

Hawthorne was her connection to something outside the devastation of the bombs, something bright and good amidst the despair and hopelessness overpowering everything else. He was her light in the darkness. Knowing she could talk to him, even for a few minutes a day—it was enough to keep her going.

"Ma'am, I'm really sorry," the soldier said again. "I'll get your information and radio it in, but I can't promise you anything."

"I understand," Shay said, trying to be polite, but her eyes were wet, her throat tightening.

A few minutes later, the soldier was gone, and Shay and the woman were alone again.

"Thank you," Shay said again.

"For what?" the woman said bitterly. "He got away."

"For trying. For helping. Not many people would do that."

The woman smoothed her loose, ill-fitting clothes. Her posture was perfect, and she moved with an easy grace. "It was the right thing to do."

"Too bad that rock missed. It would've been a solid hit."

"I was using it to keep the tent flap closed properly." The woman wiped at her red-rimmed eyes. "I didn't even think about it. I just grabbed it and ran."

Shay hesitated, feeling suddenly awkward. "Were you the one crying a few minutes ago?"

The woman stiffened, embarrassed.

Heat shot up Shay's throat into her cheeks. She shouldn't have said anything. "Sorry, it's none of my business. I am—or was—a nursing student. I guess trying to help is in my nature."

"I understand completely. My husband is a pediatrician..." She sniffed and wiped at her face. This is all just so hard. The terrorist attacks. The fires and radiation. Everyone losing their homes, being separated from family members and not even knowing whether they're alive or dead..."

Shay remembered how the couple had asked about their daughter at the FEMA intake trailer, how quickly their loss had been dismissed.

"I'm so sorry." Her heart ached for this woman, for all the broken, torn-apart families. "I'm Shay, by the way. I don't even know your name."

"Gabriella," the woman said. "Gabriella Ross." She stared down the long, endless row of tents, her eyes dull with grief. In the distance, the fence hemming them in gleamed faintly, illuminated by the lights. "Well, I better get back to my husband. He's still sleeping in our tent. I hope we can meet again, but under better circumstances."

"Me too," Shay murmured.

Gabriella began to walk back toward her tent, her shoulders slumped in the darkness. She looked so lost, in so much pain.

Shay watched her go. She didn't want to intrude where she wasn't wanted. She didn't know Gabriella or whether the woman would welcome or resent her interference.

But still...she felt a tug on her heart. She couldn't bear to just leave her like this, alone in her misery. It didn't matter that they were strangers twenty minutes ago. It wasn't in her nature to leave anyone hurting if she could help it.

Shay said, "Wait."

53
SHAY

Gabriella Ross turned around in the darkness and faced Shay, her eyes white in the shadows of her face.

"Where were you when it happened?" Shay asked gently. "Where are you from?"

Gabriella sucked in a ragged breath. "We're from Miami. My husband was supposed to be downtown when the bomb detonated. I picked him up for a long lunch and a shopping trip to this specialty art store at Miami International Mall. We were looking for a gift for our daughter. She'd just won this art contest, and I wanted to show her...to show her how proud we were..."

Her face crumpled. "Thirty minutes earlier and my husband and I would have been dead. But if I was at home with her, I could have saved her..."

Shay's heart went out to her. Her own eyes teared up. She held out her arms, and the woman collapsed against her. Pain shot through her ribs, but she gritted her teeth and endured it.

"You can't think like that," she said. "It'll just tear you apart."

"I know. I know. I just...everywhere I go, I keep searching for her, keep thinking I'll see her face. It's the not knowing. We may never know what happened to her..."

Millions of grieving family members were experiencing the same horror and heartache. So many bodies were burned beyond recognition, simply incinerated where they stood, or buried beneath mountains of concrete. Their families would never know how they died. Or even if they were dead for certain.

She was used to helping with physical wounds, but the emotional wounds caused by these attacks were even more devastating—and longer-lasting.

The psychological toll couldn't be measured, not like the billions in property damage, the millions of sick, injured, and dead. The despair and grief seldom left physical markers, but the trauma was crippling all the same.

She just held the woman, offering whatever comfort she could. She held the woman and let her cry. Maybe that's all you could do in the end.

After several minutes, Gabriella pulled away. She wiped her reddened eyes. "I'm sorry. I'm such a mess."

"Tell me about your daughter," Shay said. "Talking helps, I promise." It was the not talking, the ignoring and burying the pain down deep that made everything so much worse. "I would love to hear about her."

She gave a sad, broken-hearted smile. "She's so beautiful. Short and chubby, blonde-haired and blue-eyed. The opposite of us, but that doesn't matter. She's smart. An artist in the making. You should see her drawings. They're like extensions of her soul. She's so talented."

The back of Shay's neck prickled. The woman's description sounded so much like...but no, it wasn't possible. It couldn't be possible.

"We searched for her every day at the EOC. There were just so many people...we'll search here, too. My husband, he's giving up hope. He's a man of odds, percentages. The chances are dismal, I know that. He's just so exhausted and heartbroken.

Frankly, so am I. But I can't stop. I can't give up, no matter how unlikely it is, how terrible the odds."

"You're her mother."

"Thank you for saying that. It matters more than you could ever know." Gabriella sniffled. "She's mine in my heart. One hundred percent. I can't imagine loving her more. She's our foster child, but we're going to adopt her the second the state allows us to."

Shay felt lightheaded. It wasn't a symptom of the attack. Something was happening, something she could hardly believe. "Is she...is your daughter mute?"

Gabriella's eyes widened. Her gaze filled with desperate hope. She seized Shay's arm. "What do you know? Have you seen her? Do you know where she is?"

Shay stopped breathing. Her whole body was tingling. It couldn't be...could it? Was this really happening? Here in the midst of turmoil, hardship, and despondency? In this desolate, miserable place, surrounded by darkness, was it possible that they'd stumbled upon a miracle?

Shay placed her hand over the woman's hand and squeezed. "Gabriella, tell me your daughter's name."

"Eden. Her name is Eden."

LOGAN

"Logan!"

Logan whipped around, adrenaline spiking, weapon raised.

"It's me." Dakota emerged from the darkness like an avenging angel. She cradled the M4 across her chest, her knife and pistol sheathed at her waist. She was coated in mud, her cheeks scratched and bloodied, sweaty tendrils of her auburn hair clinging to her forehead.

His heart surged with relief.

He wanted nothing more than to brush the hair back from her face and draw her to him hard, to feel her beating heart against her own chest and make sure she was still here, still alive, still real.

"Are you okay?"

She nodded tightly. "You good?"

She was checking in with him, making sure his head was straight. His body may be battered, but he wasn't broken. Not anymore. They'd dashed into the jaws of hell and stolen from the devil himself, then destroyed his lair to seal the deal.

He was good.

Her gaze dropped to the blood caking his left shin.

He shifted, easing the pressure—and the pain. Now that the adrenaline was fading, the sharp throbbing had returned with a vengeance. "It's just a scratch."

Captain Rachel Kinsey jogged up beside Dakota. In her early forties, Kinsey looked faintly Middle Eastern, with tan skin, dark eyes, and inky black hair cut in a tousled pixie. Logan hadn't seen her since their time at the Emergency Operations Center in the airport, when she and Hawthorne had helped them escape the mandatory FEMA camps.

She grinned at him, the dimples in her ruddy cheeks giving her an impish look. "Glad to see you're still alive, Garcia."

He managed a grim smile back. "Not as glad as I am."

"Where the hell's the Prophet?" Hawthorne said into his radio. "Kill or sighting confirmation? Team Alpha? You have anything? Over."

"That's a negative," a voice crackled. "Forty-six confirmed kills at the chapel. Physical description doesn't match any of them. Over."

"No dice on the barracks or weapons depot," a third soldier said.

Logan touched Dakota's shoulder. "I killed Solomon Cage."

She grimaced. "Good."

Hawthorne's radio crackled again. "Fifteen more confirmed kills. No sign of the target. Or the bomb. Over."

"He must have it with him." Kinsey half-faced away from them as she scanned the tree line to the east, her weapon lowered but still ready.

"All teams, keep looking!" Hawthorne keyed off his mic and cursed. "How the hell did he escape our net? He's gotta be in the woods somewhere."

Logan spun around, searching the darkness, the wavering shadows between the burning buildings, the smoke blowing almost sideways, the wind whipping the blaze into a frenzy as the flames lit trees, underbrush, grass, anything it touched.

"There!" Dakota shouted. "He's there!"

She took off running toward the dock and the boathouse. The building wasn't on fire yet, but a large tree beside it burned bright.

"Wait!" Hawthorne sprinted after her. Three of the soldiers followed him, including Kinsey.

Logan didn't hesitate. He ignored the eye-watering pain and ran haltingly after them. A wind gust hit him, and he almost went sprawling. He managed to stay on his feet and reached the dock just as Dakota pointed out several lights bobbing in the distance.

Hawthorne swore a blue streak. He reached for his radio. "I'll send in a search team to sweep the swamp with more air support."

Logan's earpiece crackled in his ear. Haasi's voice came on the line. "Everything good here. We've got seventeen rescues and we're headed to the second rally point. Just pausing for a minute to let you know before we're out of range. I have a message for you from Eden."

Logan and Dakota exchanged a strained glance. "What is it?"

"She gave me a yellow notepad with the words 'Camp Disney' written on it. She seems to think you'll know what that means, over."

Logan's heart stopped beating.

Beside him, Dakota went rigid. She stared at him, her eyes wide. "That's what Eden was trying to tell us before. The bomb's target. It's Camp Disney."

Hawthorne whirled on Dakota, his face ashen. "That's where FEMA set up the refugee camp. Every refugee in Florida is there. Over two-hundred thousand souls." He took a ragged breath. "Including Shay."

For a terrible moment, no one moved. Logan's mouth went bone-dry. Not Shay. Shay was supposed to be safe. She was supposed to be healing people, making a difference, all the good things that Shay did so well.

She was the best of them, and she belonged far, far away from this hellhole.

"Are you sure?" Kinsey asked. "The refugee camp?"

"In a perverse way, it makes sense, doesn't it?" Logan said darkly. "If they took out another city, it'd be rough. But hit the refugees who've already lost everything but managed to escape with their lives? It's like when enemy combatants attack medics, hospitals, or schools. It's a blow intended to devastate morale. To break our spirits."

Exactly." Hawthorne's voice was tight with barely restrained panic. "We cannot let that happen. But the choppers have limited fuel and still need to make the return trip to get out of the path of this hurricane. Additional air support is incoming, but their ETA is still twenty-five minutes out."

"That's too late." Dakota hooked her thumb at the boathouse. "We can take an airboat."

Hawthorne nodded. "I'm going after him."

Kinsey touched his arm with her free hand. "Count me in."

"I know the Glades," Dakota said. "I can take you."

"You shouldn't even be here! I'm not taking a civilian—"

"There's no time!" Logan said sharply. "Listen to her!"

"I know where the Prophet's going," Dakota said. "At least while he's in the swamp. He's heading southeast. There's a channel that'll take you all the way east almost to Highway 27, where there's an isolated private boat dock and a clearing large enough for a chopper to land. There's an old dirt road leading to 27, too, if he calls someone to come get him with a vehicle. I'd bet you anything he's going there."

The wind roiled the black water, churning like some great monster writhing below the surface. The bobbing lights grew smaller and smaller.

If that psychopath escaped after all of this, after all they'd suffered, endured, sacrificed, and fought through, if he detonated that bomb—

No. It wasn't an acceptable option. They had to stop him, no matter what.

Dakota gave them their best chance. And wherever Dakota went, Logan vowed to be right beside her.

He would die for her, this girl who'd taught him how to truly live. But he didn't want to. He wanted to spend the rest of his life by her side, taking on every threat and fighting for all the things that mattered.

No way in hell were they sitting this one out.

"This is bigger than rules and protocol," Logan said. "We know the risks. We're willing to die to stop that bomb, same as you. Let Dakota do her thing."

"They're right," Kinsey said. "He's already getting away."

Dakota jabbed her finger toward the swamp. "We have to go after him right now!"

Hawthorne ran a hand over his bald head and gave a heavy, defeated sigh. "Fine, but—"

Dakota was already running toward the boathouse.

The others followed her, Logan limping more slowly, holding the weapon Hawthorne had returned to him. Kinsey got on her radio to report the new information regarding the bomb's target and request backup.

Hawthorne had his satphone out and was desperately calling Shay. He shoved it back in its pouch on his belt with a curse. "She's not answering."

"We're going to save her," Dakota said. "We'll stop him. We have to."

LOGAN

The boathouse was on fire. Orange tongues raced along the roof. They only had a few minutes before the whole building went up in flames.

Logan tried the door. It was locked.

"I'll take this," Kinsey said.

Logan moved aside and Kinsey threw a hard front kick to the right of the door handle. Two more powerful kicks and the door splintered and swung open.

Dakota and the others raced inside, covering their mouths and coughing. Logan hobbled after them. A wave of heat struck Logan's back. Smoke swirled along the ceiling. Acrid smoke stung his nostrils.

There was space for six or more boats, but only four floated in a row on either side of a center dock—two airboats, a small fishing boat, and a speedboat. Two large roller doors took up the far wall. They were open.

Dakota grabbed a picture frame from the nearest wall, opened the faux frame, and fumbled through several sets of keys. She seized two.

Hawthorne pointed to the sleek red-and-white speedboat. How about that one?"

"The water's too shallow. We'll destroy the propellers and wreck the motor. We have to take the airboats. They sail on the top of the water." Dakota clambered into the first airboat and pointed to the second one behind her. "Get in."

The airboat was like the ones Haasi and the Colliers owned, but larger and fancier—built of fiberglass, about eighteen feet long, and powered by six-cylinder aircraft engines. A huge fan was encased in a metal cage mounted to the hull. The elevated driver's seat was bolted to a square platform lifted several feet in the air, with the passenger seats anchored below it.

Dakota pulled her earplugs out of her pocket, removed her radio earbud, and stuck them in her ears. "It's going to be loud. But so is theirs."

Logan grabbed his own ear protection from a pouch on his vest and stuck them in.

Hawthorne slid into the boat behind Dakota and sat awkwardly on the passenger seat, M4 in hand and ready to go. "We should take two boats—four in one, three in the other. Anyone else know how to drive these things?"

None of the others said anything.

"I sure as hell don't," Kinsey said.

"How hard can it be?" Hawthorne shrugged. "It's just a boat, right?"

Dakota eyed him. "For starters, an airboat doesn't have brakes and there's no reverse. So no, it's not just a boat."

"Holy hell," Hawthorne muttered.

She glanced at Logan. "He can do it."

She'd shown him how to drive one a few times during their time at Ezra's cabin, but that was it. He balked, about to protest, but she shot him a desperate look.

She trusted him to do this. He needed to do this.

"Yeah," he said. "Okay."

"Kinsey, go with him," Hawthorne said. "Greer and Seong, you too. Briggs, you're with us. Keep the lights off as long as you can. Use your NV goggles. They won't hear our engines with theirs going just as loud. We need that element of surprise."

Logan and Dakota both nodded.

Favoring his left leg, Logan stepped clumsily into the boat, coughing from the smoke, trying to cover his mouth while keeping his balance. He sat on the seat mounted in front of the cage that housed the propeller.

With the weight off his wounded calf, the pain lessened slightly. He'd be fine. He would see this through, no matter what.

"Be judicial with your firepower," Hawthorne said as a final warning. "The Prophet likely has the bomb with him—or at least the nuclear part of it."

"Will the bomb detonate if we shoot it?" Dakota asked.

"Nope. But that doesn't mean he doesn't have a handheld detonator."

Logan flipped the NV goggles over his eyes, adjusted the dial, and the world once again transformed into shades of green. He put the key in the ignition, pumped the choke three times, and turned the key.

The engine belched smoke and roared to life, the propellers spinning. The whole airboat shook and vibrated.

Greer, a Caucasian guy with a trim mustache, and Seong, a young Korean-American soldier with acne still dotting his oily forehead, each took a passenger seat while Kinsey took the one closest to Logan.

Logan couldn't hear the hiss and sizzle of the flames over the growl of the airboat engines, but he could feel it—savage and hungry. The whole boathouse shuddered as a powerful gust of wind tore through the building.

Time to go.

Hawthorne waved his hand, motioning them forward. Dakota fired up her engine, and the airboat surged through the mouth of the boathouse.

Easing the throttle forward, his heart hammering against his ribs, Logan followed Dakota into the swamp.

DAKOTA

Dakota drove the airboat with white-knuckled hands. She glanced at the small GPS screen out of habit, but it wouldn't tell her what she needed to know, not out here. She was going by memory and skill now.

The airboat skimmed the surface of the water, bumping over the small, choppy waves. They sped through one winding, twisting channel and then the next.

She visualized everything in her head, each tributary like arteries, veins, and capillaries, the lifeblood of the Everglades. It was so easy to get hopelessly lost. So easy to wreck your boat and find yourself trapped in the wilderness with no way out.

But she knew this wilderness. Even after all this time. She knew the airboat trails and the locations of open-water troughs unencumbered by sawgrass. She expertly navigated through the jungle of dense vegetation, avoiding masses of tangled water-anchored plants, randomly jutting stumps, and floating logs.

In the green glow of the NV goggles, the tree islands floated out of the darkness like alien life forms. The four lights of the speeding airboats several hundred yards ahead of them gleamed and flickered in and out of view like fireflies.

The engine roared and rumbled beneath her, her ponytail whipping against her neck and shoulders. She couldn't help thinking of the last time she'd fled on an airboat in the middle of the night.

Memories flashed through her mind—the red eyes of the gators like demons in the moonlit night, the panicked desperation churning in her belly, Eden bloody and barely conscious beside her.

This time, she wasn't the one fleeing her pursuers. This time, she was the hunter.

She didn't know for certain whether it was Maddox up ahead, but she had a strong hunch. The lead airboat moved with expert precision. She would've already caught a lesser driver.

The Prophet was smart. He knew the swamp was the one thing Maddox Cage knew better than anyone else.

But that didn't mean Maddox wouldn't make a mistake, or that she couldn't find a way to exploit a weakness. She already saw one.

The fleeing airboats were sticking with open water, steering clear of the waist-and-chest high patches of reeds, sawgrass, and willow bushes to avoid the risk of getting stuck or slowing the airboat.

It meant their path was more meandering. The lead boat also had the added weight of several hundred pounds of whatever the hell that nuclear bomb was made of.

She and Hawthorne didn't. It made them faster.

"Short cut!" she shouted to Hawthorne, who nodded tightly. He gripped the handrail like his life depended on it. So did Greers, the soldier with them.

She hammered the throttle and angled them into the sawgrass at full speed. It was all or nothing. She knew never to stop or slow down in grass or they might not be able to power out of it. They didn't want to get stuck.

The airboat's bow smashed through the grass, the entire boat quivering with the jarring vibrations, bits and pieces of freshly flayed vegetation flying up in a hailstorm of green confetti.

The razor-sharp sawgrass sliced at her hands and face, stinging like paper cuts. At least she was wearing pants, boots, and long sleeves this time.

She kept the control stick rigidly in place and pushed her foot all the way down on the gas. She had to be completely focused. Nudging the stick left or right even a little could throw the hull off balance and send them sprawling.

A couple of teeth-rattling minutes later, they shot out of the sawgrass into open water.

It worked. The next time they caught sight of the lights, they were only a hundred yards away, then seventy-five. The fleeing airboats drifted in and out of sight amongst the sawgrass, cattails, and mangrove hammocks.

Each time they appeared, they were closer, the lights larger and brighter.

Dakota's heart hammered in her ears. She licked her dry, chapped lips. What she wouldn't give to gulp down a gallon of Gatorade right now.

A large tree island with a channel running through it loomed ahead of them. The Shepherds had gone straight through. She almost followed them but held back at the last second.

She remembered this stretch. The mouth was wide, but it quickly narrowed, the tall cypress trees closing in on either side, the canopy cutting off the sky, their branches reaching out to snag your clothes, scratch your arms and legs, bumping and clawing at the boat.

It would slow them down. Maybe enough that Dakota could get the drop on them this time.

She mashed the throttle and roared ahead, aiming to circle the sprawling island instead of jetting straight through it. The boat skidded into the turn. She spun the wheel, angling hard to take the corner tight and gain even more precious seconds.

They came out upon a wider, open section of water. She let up on the throttle so Logan could catch up. In deep water, airboats sank lower. The steering got sluggish, less responsive, and prone to rolling. She needed to be careful.

Logan motored up beside her. She motioned to him with one hand and pointed ahead. He nodded. She cut the engine, letting the airboat drift to a stop about thirty yards away. Logan did the same.

Hawthorne had moved from the bench to the floor of the boat, kneeling stiffly and bracing himself between the aluminum seat at his back and the boat's side on his right, his carbine up and ready to fire at a moment's notice.

She tapped his shoulder to let him know. *Get ready.*

If she was right, the Prophet would come skimming out of the dense foliage and they could take him by surprise, broadsiding him with a barrage of bullets.

Thirty seconds later, they heard the guttural roar of approaching engines. Dakota tensed, made sure the safety was off the M4, and steadied her stance, which was difficult with the boat undulating beneath her.

Bright beams cut a swath across the water. The harsh white light screwed with her night vision, and the device overloaded, blanking out for a moment.

She adjusted her grip on the M4 and flipped up the goggles. Hawthorne had already anticipated the problem and turned his off. The lights from the Shepherds' airboats were enough to see by.

They waited, barely breathed.

The lead airboat eased out of the tunnel at no more than ten miles an hour. Their lights were directed ahead. Dakota and Logan's boats remained in darkness.

The Prophet sat stiffly in front of a huge metallic box. Behind him, Maddox Cage drove the airboat, two Shepherds hunched at the bow.

The second airboat appeared behind the first. With a jolt, she recognized Reuben in the captain's chair. Four Shepherds were crowded in front of him, all armed with carbines.

Hawthorne raised three fingers. *Three, two, one.*

A fraction of a second later, Dakota fired.

57
DAKOTA

Dakota braced herself, aimed at the skull of the closest Shepherd in Maddox's boat, and fired. Her first shot missed. The airboat rocked and she shifted her aim a little lower.

Hawthorne unleashed a short burst, and the man next to her target toppled.

Logan, Kinsey, and the two soldiers with them opened fire on the second boat. One Shepherd grabbed his thigh and went down screaming.

Shouts rose above the guttural roar of the engines. Reuben immediately ducked while simultaneously hitting full throttle. The Shepherd with the wounded leg lost his balance and toppled into the water. The other two Shepherds crouched and returned fire.

Bullets whizzed by her head. Several more plunged harmlessly into the water on either side of the airboat. With their boats already moving, the Shepherds' aim was heavily compromised. So was their own.

She aimed again, mindful of the encased bomb and tracking ahead of the lead airboat as Maddox hammered the throttle, too. This time, she trained her sights on the second Shepherd's center mass—a larger, easier target.

It didn't matter if she hit his ballistic vest. She needed the force of the impact to knock him out of the airboat. Neither Reuben nor Maddox would stop or go back for anyone.

They were twenty miles into the middle of nowhere. It might as well be twenty thousand. No one was swimming back home.

She fired a quick double tap. The Shepherd fell, his gun flailing wildly. He toppled backward and plopped into the water. Reuben's airboat nearly decapitated him as it thundered past.

The two fleeing airboats flew through the black night. In the lead, Maddox sped full tilt on a southeasterly course, followed closely by Reuben. They whipped around the cypress hammock and disappeared from view.

Dakota let the carbine hang from its sling and fired up the engine. It coughed and roared to life. She mashed the throttle and gave chase.

The swamp was a maze, a carnival of mirrors, an endless labyrinth of mangrove tunnels and sawgrass corridors. But it didn't matter. She was just as good as Maddox.

No way were they escaping.

The air was chilly, the wind nipping at her exposed skin, yet rivulets of sweat traced her spine and pooled at the small of her back. Every muscle in her body was tensed and aching. The thunderous roar of the engines blasted her eardrums.

A barrage of bullets struck the water. She barely heard the *crack, crack, crack* of the shots. Dakota flinched and tried to swerve out of harm's way. Too late.

Two rounds punched through the hull of their boat. A third struck Greer in the side of the head.

Dakota stared, stunned, as the soldier spun from the impact. He collapsed, his body flopping bonelessly, his bloody head bashing the gunwale.

Hawthorne started to turn toward him, but both of his hands were occupied by the rifle. Greer's body rolled into the water.

Dakota didn't have to look back to see if he was still alive. She'd glimpsed the gaping hole in his head. He was gone. There was no time for mourning or second-guessing.

Another flurry of rounds peppered the water just ahead of them.

She had to get them out of the line of fire, or she and Hawthorne were just as dead. She pushed the control stick forward to shift the rudders, channeling the air into a sliding right turn at high speed.

Hawthorne held the handrail in an iron grip. They both leaned to counter the centrifugal forces tugging at them so hard the hull lifted right out of the water. They nearly tipped.

She straightened their course and risked a quick look to the west—the direction the gunfire had originated. Reuben's airboat had circled around and rushed them from the rear.

Only two Shepherds were left in the boat—Logan's team had taken out the other three. One machine gun could kill them as easily as four.

The gunner aimed his weapon. They were only forty yards behind them. Too close.

"Go!" Hawthorne shouted. She saw his mouth move, but barely heard him.

More rounds punched the water only a few feet to her left. She flinched. Her heart in her throat, she spun a sharp right. She had to figure out something, and fast, before the next bullet hit its mark.

They were running out of time. Reuben was right on their tail. And Maddox and the Prophet were pulling away.

58
LOGAN

Logan got off a few more shots before the second boat peeled away. He was forced to sling the carbine over his shoulder and focus on keeping them from crashing into a tree island or submerged log at forty miles an hour.

He could barely hear the barrage of the bullets over the roaring engines, but the splashes repetitively pockmarking the water surrounding Dakota's airboat told him what he needed to know.

"Go! Go!" Kinsey shouted. "Let Hawthorne take the Prophet. We need to take these guys out of the picture! Now!"

Reuben's crew were trying to circle around and come at Hawthorne and Dakota from behind while Maddox and the Prophet escaped. They couldn't let that happen.

He pushed the throttle and went after them. The aircraft propeller spun, the fiberglass hull vibrating as they tore through the night.

In front of him, Kinsey braced herself. Out of the four they'd started with, she and Logan were the only ones left. Both sides had taken heavy losses. Reuben's airboat was also down to two men.

He chased them through the maze of sawgrass as tall as his

head, swerving left, then right again, twisting and winding through the serpentine pathways. Tunnels and narrow channels appeared out of nowhere. The airboats zigzagged through the perilous maze of water and grass, Logan in hot pursuit. Finally, painstakingly, yard by yard, he drew closer, until he was within a hundred yards.

They exchanged volleys of gunfire. Gunshots zipped past him. He couldn't hear them, only caught the spray of rounds striking the water all around them, felt the occasional thud of a bullet punching through the hull.

Kinsey returned fire, cursing loud enough for Logan to catch a few shouted insults.

Both sides missed repeatedly. Long, endless minutes passed. Every muscle in his body strained, taut and aching, the tension winding tighter and tighter in his gut.

The airboat was difficult to maneuver. He hated his own incompetence. One wrong move would crash them into a tree island or tip them head-over-heels into the water at forty miles per hour.

Either way, Reuben escaped and went after Dakota. That option wasn't acceptable.

Everything in him tunneled to a singular, absolute focus, one all-consuming purpose. Nothing would stop him.

The Shepherds' airboat sped around a large island covered in trees and thick underbrush. Small glowing eyes peered at them from the bank. The trees shuddered and swayed in the wind.

Logan followed. Not wanting to tip, he let up on the throttle as he rounded the bend as tightly as he dared, only a few yards from the muddy shoreline.

More open water spread out straight ahead of him, the next patch of sawgrass a couple of hundred yards away, the channel through it as wide as a small river. The island was to his left, some cattails and a raft of floating water-plants to his right.

His breath caught in his throat. He slowed the airboat and

peered into the quivering shadows lurking beyond their lights. Where the hell was the second airboat?

In front of him, Kinsey twisted in her seat, scanning the horizon, just as confused as he was. The Shepherds' airboat had disappeared.

Apprehension prickled the hairs on the back of his neck. Logan released the throttle and seized his carbine.

Maybe they'd kept going around the island, circling it like some horrible game of Ring Around the Rosie. Unless it was a—

Out of the corner of his eye, he glimpsed a flash of movement.

Twenty yards ahead, the Shepherds' airboat burst out of the shallows on the far side of the tree island. Their blazing lights nearly blinded him.

The airboat charged, jets of frothy foam spraying as it bore down on them, on a direct course to ram straight into the bow.

Adrenaline surged through Logan's veins. He had no idea what to do. He couldn't brake or reverse this stupid thing. He dropped the gun and hammered the throttle instead, trying to outrun them, but it was too late.

They were dead in the water.

The attacking airboat broadsided them, striking with the force of a speeding train. The hull caved inward. The boat lurched wildly.

They capsized as a wall of water surged over the gunwale.

Kinsey toppled over the side into the water. Logan toppled back against the caged propellers as the boat keeled over.

Pain seared his left calf as his leg struck something. He flailed, losing his grip on the boat and grasping for purchase. His hands found only empty air.

He tumbled into the swamp after Kinsey.

59

LOGAN

L ogan barely managed to suck in a shallow breath before he went under. The cold water shocked his system. The water was deep, dark, and murky. He couldn't see a thing.

Panic gripped him. He floundered, his legs thrashing. Water poured into his boots. His clothes were heavy, and the tactical vest weighed him down like an anchor. He forced himself to stop fighting and let himself sink, tried not to think about gators taking savage bites out of sensitive body parts.

His feet touched the thick muck of the bottom. Electric pain shot through his entire leg. He nearly gulped in a mouthful of brackish swamp sludge. Willing himself to ignore the pain, he pushed off with his good leg, kicking hard, swimming upward with powerful strokes.

He broke the surface, sputtering and coughing, blinking water out of his eyes and trying to get his bearings. He'd come up on the far side of the boat. The airboat had tipped over, the propeller end sagging deep in the water.

He was still alive, that was what mattered.

The water was black and foul. His nostrils filled with the dank scent of wet things, of decay. He didn't want to know what nasty bacteria might be seeping into the opened flesh of his leg, bandaged or not.

He needed to get out of the swamp. But right now, it offered the cover he desperately needed. He blinked again, wiped his face, forced himself to calm the hell down and take stock.

The M4 was gone. He'd had it slung loosely on his shoulder so he was free to drive the boat unhindered. His NV goggles had been knocked off his head, too. But he still had his Glock in the concealed holster at his back and the combat knife sheathed to his belt, along with several spare magazines.

His leg hurt like hell, but that was to be expected. His right shoulder was throbbing. He must've banged it on the propeller cage as he was hurled over the side.

The thunderous growl of the airboat engines had gone quiet. No shouting or gunfire. The only sounds were the low moan of the wind and the creaking branches on the nearby island.

He strained his ears. A splash came from behind him, then to the left.

He jerked his head toward the noise. A falling branch? Maybe a gator. Or one of the Shepherds. He couldn't decide which threat was worse.

Cautiously, careful not to splash, he kicked his good leg and swam slowly around the edge of the waterlogged boat.

About ten feet ahead of him, he spotted a dark shape. His heart jolted. A head protruding from the water. It was small and oval-shaped with short spiky hair standing on end. *Kinsey.* She was still alive.

He scanned left and right. To the east of the island, about thirty yards from him, the other airboat was stuck in a large clump of swaying cattails. The bow was crumpled like a soda can, but the thing was upright, lights still blaring. It seemed empty.

Was someone lurking in the bottom of the boat? He couldn't tell from his low vantage point. Part of him wanted to shoot the damn thing to hell for sinking them. It'd do double duty and take out any potential threats, too.

But if the Shepherds were lying in wait on the island, he'd give away his position.

And they needed a boat to get the hell out of this damn swamp. If their radios were out of range this far out, Dakota might not be able to find them.

First, though, he had to take out the Shepherds.

They needed to be very, very careful.

"Kinsey," he whispered as quietly as he could.

She jerked around, saw him, and paddled over, keeping her hands underwater.

"This is a nightmare," she hissed when she was two feet away. "I think I'm dying."

"You're not dying. I think both the Shepherds are on the island. They could be in the boat, though. I think we should circle around in the water and head inland only when we reach the southern tip of the island. They'll expect us to climb ashore here where the boat capsized. We can sneak up on them from behind."

"Okay, yeah. That's smart." Kinsey's eyes were wide and white in the dark shadows of her face. "I'm terrified of the water. I watched Jaws as a kid. Scared me to death. I live in Florida and I've never even been in the ocean."

Logan started swimming parallel to the island. They were twelve or fifteen yards from shore, maybe. "There are no sharks in the Everglades. Dakota would've told me."

"There are other things with teeth," she murmured.

He was well aware of that fact. He was trying his best not to think about the giant prehistoric predators lurking in the depths, maybe drifting toward them right now, maybe hunting them.

They were already being hunted by predators of the human persuasion.

He took slow, careful strokes, constantly scanning the shoreline. Mud, weeds, logs, swaying trees, wavering shadows. Not for the first time, he wondered how Dakota could love this place.

Everything about it was hostile to humans.

"How big you think this island is?" he asked under his breath.

"Maybe a half a mile? How far do you think we've swum?"

"A hundredth of a mile."

"I hate you," she whispered. "Hawthorne may like you, but he has terrible taste."

"Can we please focus on the task of not getting ourselves killed?"

"Definitely. Getting out of the water would help with that."

"Not yet."

She blew a frustrated breath through her teeth. Jerk."

"You have NV goggles on you?"

"I lost them in the water. But I have a monocle in my vest."

"That will help."

"This wind will help shield our movements, too."

They swam in silence. Things brushed against his legs—a rock, a submerged log, a fish. Maybe something else. He jerked away, recoiling in alarm.

Something splashed behind them. Kinsey gasped and floundered like a drowning cat. She seized his arm and gripped it so hard her nails dug into his skin.

The same primal terror clawed at him. His pulse thudded against his skull. His mouth was bone-dry. Every instinct in his body screamed at him to get out of the damn water as fast as he could.

But they couldn't. Not yet.

After several more minutes, his feet touched bottom, and he slogged through the murky water, his boots sinking deep into the muck. His calf pulsed with pain with every step.

He ignored the pain, pushed down the terrifying images of twenty-foot alligators his frantic brain kept conjuring into existence. He concentrated on watching for movement in the trees.

Everything looked the same. Muddy banks. Heavy under-brush. A blackened, desiccated tree trunk, two massive logs beside it. Trees and shadows constantly swaying.

Kinsey rushed ahead of him, frantic to get to the relative safety of the bank. She clambered through waist-deep water toward the shore, trying not to splash but not doing a very good job.

"Kinsey!" he hissed.

One of the logs moved.

60
LOGAN

Kinsey froze.

She was still in the water. Logan was only a few feet behind her.

Not ten feet away, a huge alligator hinged open its jaws and hissed. Its long heavy tail switched. Its leathery scales shone wet and black.

The thing was a Goliath, fourteen or fifteen feet long and probably half a ton.

A cold, primal terror slithered up his spine.

"Whatever you do, don't move." He had no idea if that was true, but it seemed reasonable that frenzied splashing would draw the ancient predator's attention.

Keeping his own movements slow, he reached beneath the water for the Glock at his back, wishing desperately that he still had the M4. A barrage of 5.56 rounds would rip the monster into ragged chunks before it could move.

He had no idea how many 9mm bullets it would take to bring it down. A lot, probably.

The beast would reach them first. The thing was massive enough to take Logan's head off with one savage snap of its jaws.

Kinsey whimpered. Her breathing came in ragged gasps, her

249

shoulders shuddering like she was about to hyperventilate. He didn't blame her.

The beast slid into the water so fast Logan barely had time to react.

It swam toward them.

Kinsey squeaked.

Logan pulled out the gun, finger on the slick trigger. The muzzle wavered. He wasn't sure where to aim. He tried to get a bead on wherever the creature's brain was located.

"Shoot it!" Kinsey cried.

But something made him hesitate. If he missed the kill shot, the sudden blow could provoke the thing into attacking.

The alligator swam closer. Not five feet away.

Logan stopped breathing. His finger tightened on the trigger, began squeezing.

The alligator turned its massive head. It kept swimming, drifting by so close, little ripples of displaced water lapped at Logan's waist.

Logan watched the Leviathan cruise past in horrified fascination. The spade of its enormous head and narrow snout. The teeth sticking up from its jaws, huge and gleaming and razor-sharp. And the long wide oval of its back, the muscular tail drifting behind it like a log.

It swam another twenty feet before sinking below the surface.

As soon as the monster was gone, Kinsey lunged forward, sloshing through the water and staggering up onto the muddy bank. She whirled, gun out, splattering water everywhere as she aimed at the second log.

It didn't move. It was just a log.

Logan hobbled out of the water after her. His wet clothes stuck to his body. The wind was cutting and viciously cold. His leg ached.

He hoped he wasn't infected with some rare bacteria that

would infect his bloodstream and eat his brain. This swamp could kill a man a million different ways.

Kinsey sank down onto the muddy ground, tucked her knees under her chin, and hugged her legs. She sucked in rapid, shallow breaths. "Worst. Idea. Ever."

"You're still alive, aren't you?"

"Barely. That gator nearly killed me. I about had a heart attack."

He'd felt the same, but he didn't say so. "I don't think that was a gator."

"What do you mean?"

"It had a narrow snout, and its teeth were showing. Dakota told me there's still a few crocodiles out here. She said they're more aggressive than alligators."

Kinsey shuddered. "I don't want to talk about it anymore."

Logan adjusted his clothes and the soaking wet tactical vest and examined the Glock 43. He checked the chamber and the magazine. Fully loaded, a round chambered. Several loaded magazines were tucked into his battle pouch.

Kinsey scrambled to her feet and did the same. She shouldered her rifle and carried her pistol instead. She pulled a long metal tube from a pouch at her waist and threaded it onto the end of her pistol.

A silencer wasn't nearly as silent as Hollywood suggested, but the moaning wind, creaking branches, and thrashing foliage just might give them enough cover.

Kinsey pulled a Gatorade from another pouch. She shared several mouthfuls with him.

The electrolyte-filled drink slid down his parched throat, re-energizing him. He wiped droplets from his chin with the back of his arm. Time to end this and get back to Dakota.

He took a slogging step into the black, sucking muck. It gave him an idea. He bent down, grabbed a double handful of mud, and smeared it across his face and the back of his hands. Kinsey did the same.

He motioned for her to follow him into the woods. "Time to hunt."

Kinsey's expression tightened. She nodded, deadly serious again. "We see them together, you take the left, I'll take the right. If we need to open up on them, I'll go low, you go high."

"Got it."

Together, they moved deeper into the island. They were both shivering from the brutal cold of the water. Logan's boots sank into the spongy peat. Rotting vegetation gave off a rank smell. The shadows were thick and wavering, the darkness dense beneath the heavy tree cover.

Every thirty or forty feet or so, they paused to listen and watch. Kinsey used one hand to hold her monocle to her eye and scan the dark shapes of trees and underbrush ahead of them.

Logan was limping, but the adrenaline shooting through his veins kept the pain manageable. Each step they took was cautious and careful as they eased past whipping palms and ferns and paused to move rattling branches aside.

Every sense was on high alert. Every muscle was tensed, ready to spring into action.

Thirty excruciating minutes passed. Then forty-five minutes.

The black sky opened up and rain sheeted down. It stung his face and bled into his eyes.

More agonizing minutes passed.

The rain slashed sideways. The thin pine trees were bent like penitents. The wind nearly flattened him against tree trunks as he slogged forward. He could barely hold himself upright, the wind howling and shrieking, driving leaves and broken twigs into their faces.

Around the hour mark, Kinsey paused to scan with the monocle and stiffened. She raised her hand and pointed to the northwest. She handed Logan the monocle.

Using his free hand, he peered into it, his eye adjusting to the greenish surroundings. He could barely see through the wind and rain.

Through a break in the swaying trees about twenty yards ahead and to the right, the dark shadow of a figure stood with his back to them.

He was facing the shoreline, carbine in his hands, an attached, mounted light slowly scanning the water. The figure was too slim to be Reuben. Beyond that, Logan couldn't make out any defining features.

He didn't need to. The man was a Shepherd. That was all they needed to know.

Kinsey took the monocle back and gestured to herself, then the suppressed pistol. She wanted the kill. She crept forward, searching for a better angle.

Gun up and ready, Logan moved out to cover her and scanned for the second Shepherd—Reuben. He didn't see him. Didn't hear any twigs cracking underfoot or a hushed voice.

That didn't mean he wasn't there.

Wet leaves slapped at him. The dense foliage began to thin, with patches of open clearing as they edged closer to their target at the shoreline. He could see a little better, too.

The ground beneath him grew wet and spongy. His feet sank to his ankles with every step.

The water was creeping over the banks, gradually spreading and running in streams through the trees. Water swirling everywhere, rising and rising and rising.

They needed to get the hell out of here before the entire island flooded.

About twenty feet from the water, Kinsey stopped, finally close enough to get a clear, unobstructed kill shot. She situated herself beside the trunk of a cypress tree, set her stance, and aimed her pistol with a two-hand hold.

Kinsey fired two shots. The Shepherd's head jerked back. He collapsed into the shallow water with a dull *splat*.

She turned toward Logan, grinned, and gave a thumbs-up sign.

One down. One to go.

Boom! The crack of gunfire exploded. *Boom! Boom!*

61

DAKOTA

Dakota chased Maddox and the Prophet through an ever-narrowing maze of mangrove trees. Hawthorne got off a shot whenever he could, but he had to be careful of the bomb.

At least Logan and Kinsey had lured the second boat away. She hoped they were fine, but she couldn't worry about them now. One hundred percent of her focus was on catching Maddox and putting an end to this, once and for all.

Maddox kept up a steady zigzag pattern, twisting and turning, trying to shake her. She gritted her teeth, gripping the throttle with whitened knuckles.

For three years, she'd run from him, scared and alone. He'd hunted her, flushed her from the refuge of Ezra's, sent her fleeing into the dangerous streets of Miami.

And still he hadn't given up, as tenacious as a bulldog with a bone.

She was the hunter now.

The stakes were higher than they'd ever been. If they got away, that bomb would obliterate thousands of lives, including Shay's.

Dakota wouldn't let that happen.

One, two, three. Breathe.

Her shoulders ached, her muscles trembling, but her focus was absolute.

She kept on him, tailing every figure eight and abrupt course change, every intricate maneuver as Maddox desperately sought an advantage—and didn't find one.

Slowly, slowly they drew inexorably closer, until finally they pulled to within ten yards and were racing through Maddox's churning wake and trail of broken lily pads.

A narrow mangrove channel appeared ahead. Almost too narrow for the airboats. Almost. Maddox angled wide to avoid it.

Dakota made a split-second decision. She was on the outside and could force them in. Going full throttle, she used her airboat's lighter weight and faster speed to her advantage. She slid up on their port side and began crowding them.

She nudged the control stick forward and banged into the other airboat's gunwale. She pushed and shoved. At the last possible second, Maddox gave in and angled sharply into the channel, probably hoping she'd ram into the mangrove trees rushing at them instead.

She didn't.

Dakota rolled the airboat into a tight righthand turn, let up on the throttle, and skimmed into the narrow passage, narrowly missing the jutting roots of a huge tree. She slowed as they dodged and weaved through the mangrove jungle's twisting corridor. On either side of the boats, leaves and branches whipped by in a dark blur, mangrove leaves slapping the hulls.

They were trailing their quarry by only thirty feet when Maddox abruptly cut his engine. The airboat's beams lit up a huge cypress that had fallen across the channel, its shaggy roots jutting twenty feet into the air above them.

The mangroves on either side were too thick to pass through. There was no going around it. There was nowhere to hide, no cover. And nowhere to run.

This was it. The end of the line.

The hairs on Dakota's neck stood on end, her adrenaline surging. She cut her own engine, slewing sideways to keep from drifting too close. Both pairs of searchlights blared, providing enough ambient light for everyone to see clearly.

"They're trapped," she said in a low voice.

"Careful now," Hawthorne murmured. "Trapped animals are the most dangerous. People can be the same."

"Ezra used to say the same thing." She braced herself between the captain's seat and the starboard side, raised the stock of the carbine to her shoulder, and aimed through her sights.

Hawthorne pressed his feet against the metal storage locker, shoving himself back and wedging his torso firmly against the seat. Now he had both hands free to shoot. "If you see a shot, take it."

"Got it."

Hawthorne trained his rifle at the airboat. He raised his voice above the wind. "Surrender now and maybe you can still get out of this alive!"

The Prophet and Maddox stood next to each other near the bow, the big metallic box behind them. Maddox gripped an M4, the muzzle shifting from Dakota to Hawthorne and back again.

The Prophet's gaze locked on Hawthorne. His hands were at his sides. He appeared to be unarmed. He sneered. "I know your tricks. You'll shoot me dead the first chance you get."

The Prophet raised one arm, lifting his hand toward them so they could see that he held a small black object. "This is a detonator. It's rigged to the nuclear bomb behind me. If I press this button, it will explode."

Beside her, Hawthorne swore.

"Maybe you think the Everglades is the best place for this bomb to go off. Less casualties. Right, officer? Maybe you're thinking you'll sacrifice yourselves for the greater good. Maybe you think it'll be worth it if it kills me and keeps the bomb from destroying another highly populated area. It's not. In this wind? The fallout will spread for hundreds of miles. Tens of thousands of people will still die slow, horrendous deaths. If I were you, I would think twice."

The Prophet's gaze shifted from Hawthorne to Dakota. "I see the harlot of Babylon still lives." He shot a murderous glance at Maddox. "I was told otherwise."

"Don't you talk to God?" Dakota snapped. "I would think He'd tell you."

Maddox let out a snort.

The Prophet stiffened. "Kill them, Maddox. They're wasting our time."

"Can you kill both of us before one of us gets off a shot?" Hawthorne asked. "Fifty-fifty chance I drill you right between the eyes and you're dead before you even twitch. Are you willing to take that risk?"

Dakota doubted the odds were fifty percent. Probably much less. But it was possible. They might kill him before he pushed the button. Or they might not. But if they were wrong...the consequences would be catastrophic.

The boat rocked beneath her feet. The wind whipped strands of stray hair into her eyes. She blinked to clear her vision. Tension thrummed through her body, every muscle tensed.

"Then it appears we've reached an impasse," the Prophet said. "Time is ticking. You feel that wind? Smell the ozone in the air? The hurricane is coming. Just a few hours away now. It'll tear these boats apart like match sticks. What will you do then? I'm willing to die for the cause. So is Maddox. We can wait you out."

Their airboats were drifting slowly closer, rocked by the small waves tugged by the wind. Twenty feet away now.

She had to do something to break this stand-off. But how to break it in their favor? The Prophet held the power with that detonator. She'd be damned if she wasn't going to take it all back.

Hawthorne shifted slightly, trying to keep his balance in the swaying, lurching boat. "Put your weapons down. If you voluntarily surrender now, I will personally see that things go easier for you."

The Prophet laughed, his eyes flashing. "You see the lies they spread, son? They're like maggots. Fleas and cockroaches. They infest everything they touch."

"Maddox," Dakota said. "You need to kill him."

Maddox flinched. His eyes darted to hers and then away.

"He's the reason your father is dead. He got your stepmother and all the others killed, and then he ran away like a coward. Does that sound like God's prophet to you? He's a charlatan, a snake-oil salesman. And a liar."

"Make her stop talking!" the Prophet yelled.

She ignored him. "Don't die for this man. He abused you, Maddox."

"Kill her already! Kill them both. I have faith in you. God's hand is with you. Do it!"

"This is the man who ordered you to be whipped, again and again. This is the man who overlooked you, shamed you, made you feel like you were never good enough."

"Shut up!" Maddox screamed. His gun wavered. "Everyone just shut up!"

The trees thrashed. A gust of wind knocked into the boats, rocking them, dragging them closer. Fifteen feet away now.

Dakota's muscles ached from the strain of gripping her weapon, holding it taut against her shoulder. Her arms were leaden, the M4 felt it weighed fifty pounds.

The Prophet still held out that damn detonator, taunting them.

"He sent you into Miami after me. He knew about the bomb. He left you there to die, Maddox. Why the hell are you still protecting him?"

Out of the corner of her eye, she saw Maddox's muzzle track

ever so slightly to the right. He was going to take out Hawthorne.

Dakota's finger tightened on the trigger. She had to do something. At the last second, she shifted the muzzle lower. Exhaled, squeezed the trigger.

The gunshot exploded the night air.

62

LOGAN

"**L**ook out!" Logan shouted.

Kinsey staggered back, her mouth opened wide, shock and pain registering on her face. Another *boom* cracked the air. Bark shattered two feet above her head. Kinsey collapsed.

Logan didn't have time to see if she was okay. He whirled around just as a huge shape barreled out of the darkness not five feet to his right. *Reuben.* The Shepherd lowered his shoulder and rammed into Logan, knocking him back into a cluster of spiky bushes.

Logan's hand struck a branch as he fell. The Glock went tumbling into the dark.

Adrenaline surging, Logan leaped to his feet. Pain speared through his calf and radiated from his shoulder. Mud, twigs, and bits of rotting leaves clung to his clothes and exposed skin.

Several rounds smashed into a tree to his left. He ducked, ears ringing, frantically searching for the source of the gunfire.

Reuben stood several feet away, a couple of cypress trees and a thin scrim of leaves between them, his M16 leveled at Logan's head.

He'd missed the first few shots. But he was close. Too close.

Next time, he wouldn't miss.

261

There was no time to think. Only act. Still half-bent in a crouch, Logan charged him. Reuben swung the muzzle his way, trying to find a good shot between the trees, but Logan was already on him.

He came in low and knocked the muzzle aside. He rose to his full height and seized the man by his throat. Logan slammed him back against the trunk of a thick cypress tree and followed up with a swift, powerful left punch to his groin.

Reuben let out a strained *oof*, curled into himself, and sagged like a rag doll. He fell to the ground. The M16 skittered away into the underbrush.

Logan kicked Reuben savagely in the head. Once, twice. Reuben's eyes rolled into the back of his skull, his mouth open and puckered like a dying fish.

Logan stumbled as eye-watering agony seared his leg. He bent and gingerly felt his calf through his pants. That was a mistake. White-hot pain blazed so intensely that blackness hovered at the edges of his vision. His entire leg felt hard, hot, and swollen. His hand came away bloody. He'd torn the muscle, doing even more damage.

Wind-driven branches flailed at him, the rain stinging like stones. The trees cracked in protest. The storm groaned like a living thing.

Keeping one eye on Reuben, he wiped the blood on his pants, shuffled to the spiky bushes, and kicked at the rotting leaf litter on the ground, searching for the Glock.

He caught the slight metallic gleam at the base of a slash pine a few feet away.

Movement snagged the corner of his eye.

Reuben clambered to his feet, breathing heavily and bleeding from a cut along the side of his head. He was a boulder of a man, solid and muscular, and easily outweighing Logan by forty pounds. He flexed and unflexed his fists. "You're gonna die for that."

Logan dove for the Glock. With an electric shock of pain, his leg gave out on him. He fell to his hands and knees. Sharp prickly plants scraped his palms. The watery muck sucked at his legs.

Reuben seized him from behind, lifted him, and flung him against a tree. His head struck the slender pine. Stars sparked across his vision. His brain went foggy.

He stumbled, righting himself slowly, using the trunk to hold himself up as he turned back around to face Reuben.

"You!" Reuben snarled. "I remember you. You're Dakota's little errand boy."

Logan could just make out the man's face—flat, cold eyes and a slash of white teeth. It was dark now, but Logan remembered exactly what the terrorist scumbag looked like.

He remembered Maddox and Reuben standing in front of Ezra's cabin, both of them arrogant, bristling with aggression and rage, holding a limp Park between them after they'd beaten him to a bloody, senseless pulp.

He remembered the flicker of dark pleasure in Reuben's eyes when he'd pressed the muzzle of his pistol to Park's head.

Logan hated him for that. He would kill him for it, too. "And you're nothing but a psychotic terrorist freak."

Reuben smiled, shadows playing across the broad planes of his face. "I was there, you know. I drove the van to Miami. I was the one who parked it in front of Miami Tower. I watched all those clueless sheep walking right by it. They had no clue, man. No freaking idea their judgment was upon them."

"You're insane."

"Take it up with God if you've got an issue, man." He sneered. "But it won't be heaven you see next. All you heathens belong in Hell."

The evil men Logan had known in his past life were demons, killers and fiends, lovers of chaos and destruction. They wore their true selves on their sleeves—in their combative stances, their lethal stares, the aggressive ink staining their arms, backs, and faces broadcasting their threat, their capacity for violence.

These fanatics pretended they were different, but they weren't any better. They were worse: hiding their true natures, cloaking their depravity in religion, justifying their bloodlust as they destroyed cities, professing their piety while beating little girls.

An image of Dakota flashed through his mind. The puckered, ridged scars mutilating her back. The pain in her eyes. The ugliness she'd endured.

A dark, dangerous rage flared through his veins. And with it came the deadly calm. The cold certainty—he and Dakota would end this, once and for all. Right here. Tonight.

Logan would kill Reuben for Park. He would kill him for Dakota. He'd kill him for the city of Miami, for all the dead and the people who loved them.

The exhaustion faded away. The agony in his leg and the ache in his shoulder faded. The wind and the rain and the muck were nothing.

He was the darkness, and the darkness was in him. This time, it was everything good and right and just.

And then he was moving, springing up and lunging, attacking with the ferocity of a rabid dog.

63

DAKOTA

wo more gunshots followed right on the heels of the first.

Dakota's ears rang from the blasts, like her brain had just been shaken inside her skull. She looked up from her sights. It took her a second to refocus.

Time seemed to slow down. Everything happened in slow motion.

Beside her, Hawthorne expelled a sharp, pained breath. The carbine slipped from his fingers, banged against the side of the airboat, and fell with a splash.

Hawthorne sagged and toppled into the water.

Dakota didn't have time to react, to feel anything other than a flash of horror.

Maddox had dropped his M4. He gripped his lower stomach beneath his vest with both hands. Black blood poured between his fingers. He stared across the water at her, face slack, eyes wide with shock and disbelief, as if he never believed she'd actually shoot him.

The Prophet stood next to him, the same stunned look on his face. He still held the detonator, but his hands hung limply at his sides.

Without a sound, Maddox spun toward the Prophet. In one fluid movement, he seized the Prophet's arm with bloody hands, and knocked the detonator from his fingers. It clattered to the floor of the boat.

"No!" the Prophet shrieked, leaning for the detonator.

It all happened in a few short seconds. Dakota watched, frozen and helpless.

Maddox reached for something at his belt. He withdrew a combat knife.

The Prophet flailed his hands, screaming something unintelligible. He lost his balance, stumbled back against the trunk.

Maddox lunged at him, knife raised.

The Prophet shifted at the last second, sliding sideways on the lip of the trunk. Maddox fell against him. The knife sank into the Prophet's right side and slid between his ribs.

Maddox yanked the knife out, raised it to stab again, but his hands were so slick with blood that it slid from his fingers and clattered against the hull.

The Prophet managed to shove Maddox off him. A gust of wind tore through the channel and the airboat listed. Knocked off-balance, Maddox staggered. The back of his knees struck the portside hull, and he pitched over the side.

A loud splash, then nothing.

With a groan, the Prophet collapsed into the bottom of the boat.

Dakota shook off the shock. She peered down into the water, her weapon up and ready to fire. The boats were too close to each other, less than ten feet away. She moved to the bow, then the stern.

Still nothing.

Something splashed behind her.

She whipped around and moved so quickly to the starboard side that the boat rocked dangerously. "Maddox?"

"No," a familiar voice wheezed. "It's me."

Her heart jolted. She lowered her gun. "You're alive!"

"Hurts too much to be dead." Hawthorne's smooth brown head barely bobbed above the water. "Help me up?"

She braced herself, reached down, and gripped his wet forearm. He was lean, but his height made him big and heavy, especially with all his soaking wet gear. She gritted her teeth, hauling back with all her strength.

With her help, Hawthorne clambered over the starboard side, grunting and groaning as he drew himself to his feet. Water dripped everywhere. Dark, watery blood leaked from a ripped hole in his upper left arm.

He swayed a little as he unholstered his pistol.

"Are you okay?" she asked.

"Never better."

"You got shot."

He winced. "Just nicked me. I hope."

"I think the Prophet's still alive."

He nodded. The airboats were so close, their sides bumped against each other. He stepped gingerly into the other boat and scrambled around the large trunk to the stern.

"Yeah, he's still kicking." He aimed his weapon at the Prophet. "Do not even *think* about moving."

"What about the detonator?" she asked.

He searched the floor of the boat. "It's right here." Keeping the gun trained on the Prophet, he squatted with a wince, picked it up, and slid it carefully into a pouch on his tactical vest. "That could've gone badly."

She didn't want to think about why Maddox stabbed the Prophet. She didn't care why. "Lucky for us, it didn't."

"I'm going to secure him with zip ties, and then we can head back. I don't know how long we've got before this storm gets real. And I probably need a hospital."

She peered into the water, scanning the surface carefully with the carbine. She'd shot Maddox in the stomach. There was a good chance he was dead. There was a better chance he was still alive.

It didn't matter that he'd switched sides and neutralized the Prophet.

As long as Maddox held breath in his lungs, he was dangerous.

64
LOGAN

Reuben juked. He moved with surprising agility for such a large man. Logan's right fist grazed Reuben's chin as he spun left.

Logan adjusted, gritting his teeth against the pain spiking up his leg, and hammered Reuben with a strong left jab. It landed solid, knuckles crunching bone. Reuben stepped back with a curse, his nose spurting blood.

With a guttural shriek, Reuben ran at him.

Logan jumped out of the way, his leg almost buckling, and shot a left jab to the back of his head. A lesser man would've fallen, but Reuben shook it off like a dog shakes off rainwater.

Reuben whirled and battered Logan with a fierce barrage of blows like sledgehammers—a left, right, another left. One hit his shoulder, pain exploding with furious electrified shocks up and down the nerves of his arm. He staggered and sucked in a sharp, pained breath.

Reuben was an experienced fighter. Normally, Logan could hold his own. But his opponent was bigger, stronger, unhindered by injury.

The radiation sickness had taken its toll. The battle for Ezra's cabin only twenty-four hours ago had depleted his body's resources. Now he was hurting, exhausted, and pushing himself beyond his limits.

It didn't matter how determined or courageous he was—his body was going to break.

Trees shuddered, the thinner branches twisting and whipping. A branch thick as his wrist hurtled through the air, narrowly missing his head and striking Reuben's right arm.

Reuben let out a curse and grabbed at his bicep.

Logan spun and lurched in the opposite direction, using branches and tree trunks to hold himself up. He broke from the tree line out onto the open bank.

"You're dead, man. Dead!" Reuben shouted. "Why are you still fighting? Give up and I'll kill you mercifully, I promise."

The relentless rain bore down on him. The roaring wind nearly toppled Logan off his feet. He shifted his balance and turned to face the Shepherd, hobbling on one foot.

Reuben stood just past the trees a few yards away, watching and waiting, a vicious smile plastered across his face.

He knew he was on the edge of victory. It was only a matter of time. "You lost, man. It's over."

Logan managed a weary grimace. "Who says I lost?"

Reuben went very still, suddenly realizing he wasn't the prize.

Logan's goal was to pull Reuben off Dakota and Hawthorne so they could catch the Prophet and stop that bomb. Dakota was the one who'd always wanted to save the world so badly. Now he did, too.

Whether he lived or died here in this swamp, he'd done what he meant to do. He'd already won.

With a roar of outrage, Reuben came at him. He pummeled Logan with a fresh flurry of blows. Every punch struck him like a battering ram, knocking him back. Wearing him down, punch by bloody punch.

His boots slid and splashed in the ankle-deep water. He fell to one knee, panting. He barely heard the storm over the throbbing of his own heart. The pain was grinding away at him. The exhaustion sucking at his legs, constricting his lungs.

Logan couldn't last much longer. He'd asked too much of his body, forced it to carry him past the point of endurance.

He needed to ask it for more.

Just a little more.

Wearily, he managed to push Reuben off him for a moment and stagger to his feet. He could barely stand straight.

Reuben lunged again, aimed a right hook, and nailed him in the jaw with explosive force. Logan took the hit without dodging and went down. His leg shot between Reuben's, his left ankle hooking behind Reuben's right.

As he landed back-first into the water and muck, pain spiking along his spine, the ground slamming his wounded shoulder with hammer force, he jerked Reuben's leg out from under him.

His own leg exploded with fiery jolts of agony. His vision went red. Black swam around the edges.

He wasn't done yet. He had to finish this—stab him, strangle him, break his neck—whatever it took.

Reuben was already rising heavily to his feet, spitting a rotting leaf from his mouth, his hands curved into bludgeoning fists.

Logan flipped onto his stomach, sucking in ragged breaths, and tried to stand. His left ankle buckled and collapsed beneath him. His injured leg couldn't hold him up any longer.

The muck sucking at his hands and knees, the stink of rot and decay strong in his nostrils, he scrambled through the flooded, soupy vegetation for the shoreline.

The water would offer buoyancy, help keep him on his feet until he could finish this. It was his only chance.

"You think you're gonna just swim away?" Reuben

demanded from behind him. "Didn't you listen before? You're already dead, man. You just don't know it yet."

Half-falling, half-sliding down the mud-slick bank, Logan launched himself into the water. Ice-cold water engulfed him to his waist, stealing his breath.

Their airboat had sunk completely, but the second airboat still drifted twenty yards from the shoreline, the dented bow caught in a clump of cattails whipping in the wind. The boat's lights swayed and flickered across the water.

Reuben plunged after him. "You're gonna pay for burning the compound. I'm going to kill you slowly. Painfully. I'm gonna chop off your fingers one at a time and feed them to the fish."

Logan didn't bother to answer. He needed every ounce of energy he could muster. Clammy sweat coated his skin. The chilly wind stole every bit of warmth from his body. He was shivering, trembling, his body wracked with spasms of agony.

He backed up, hobbling on one leg, bending his knees to take the pressure off his throbbing calf. The cold black water reached his chest.

Beneath the surface, he drew his combat knife.

Reuben splashed noisily toward him, his own knife drawn.

The water made their movements sluggish, like the fight was happening in awful slow motion. Reuben swung and Logan ducked and dodged out from beneath the blade cutting through the air. It scraped harmlessly across his tactical vest.

Logan flicked the knife and slashed a bloody line across the Shepherd's face. Reuben roared and threw a vicious punch.

Logan ducked sideways, but he was slowed by the water, the unrelenting pain, and his lame leg. Reuben's blade sliced a shallow wound on his right shoulder.

Logan lost his balance. Gasping, he sank below the surface and inhaled a mouthful of putrid water. He gagged, every instinct screaming to thrash to the surface for precious oxygen.

Instead, he forced himself to remain underwater. He

couldn't see a thing. Cold darkness clawed at him. Black water swirled and boiled all around him.

He felt rather than saw Reuben's presence looming over him, bending down for the killing blow.

He felt himself fading, felt the sweet release of unconsciousness sucking at the corners of his mind.

Logan gathered the last of his strength.

65

DAKOTA

Harsh shadows wavered over the cypress roots from the fallen tree jutting above their heads. The tangled roots of the mangroves on either side of the channel provided dark pockets to hide.

"Leave him," Hawthorne said.

She shook her head. How could she explain that she couldn't just leave him? How could she describe how her stomach was tied in knots with a tangle of competing emotions she didn't even know how to describe? A mixture of hate, shame, love, resentment, and loss.

"Maddox. You're going to die out here." Her pulse thudded in her ears. Her palms were clammy. "You don't want it to end this way."

The scars on her back prickled and ached with old phantom pains. She needed to see him dead. She'd believed him dead too many times to not see it with her own eyes.

But it was more than that.

"I know you," she said, raising her voice over the strengthening wind. "I know you don't want to die alone."

"I'm turning this boat around," Hawthorne said. "We have to go before this storm kills us. Kinsey radioed for an extraction before we got out of range. Several Blackhawks will be there to greet us and get us the hell out of here."

The wind whipped the trees. Leaves and small branches tore past them. Dakota had to brace herself to keep from tipping out of the boat. The temperature had dipped another ten degrees in the last hour.

Hawthorne was right. The hurricane was coming. She needed to remember her priorities. Some things mattered more than vengeance. "If Logan and Kinsey haven't made it back, we'll have to search for them. I'm not leaving the Glades without Logan."

Hawthorne's mouth tightened. "Don't worry. Neither am I."

Dakota turned toward the captain's seat and raised her voice over the wind. "Last chance, Maddox."

Something splashed in the water several yards to her left.

She spun and aimed at the threat, finger on the trigger.

A dark head appeared in the shadows beneath one of the mangrove trees. Her heart stopped. Maddox was alive.

He swam awkwardly to her airboat, splashing wildly.

"Don't do that. You'll attract the gators."

Even as she spoke, she caught sight of a pair of eyes just above the waterline. They glowed in the searchlights. Maybe ten yards behind him, drifting closer.

She reached out her hand. "Get in!"

Maddox hesitated.

The beast cut a V-wake in the water as it glided slowly closer, its great leathery back up, tail sweeping back and forth, its knobby head protruding, marble-sized eyes shining orangish in the light.

"You want to be eaten alive?" Dakota asked. "You get to choose how you die."

Maddox took her hand. He cried out in pain as she pulled him up. Hawthorne came over to help. The second they hauled

Maddox into the boat, Dakota put her knee on his chest and forced him down.

She frisked him quickly. Hawthorne handed her a pair of zip ties from his battle pouch, and she cinched Maddox's hands together at the wrists.

Hawthorne moved back to the other boat to keep an eye on the Prophet.

"I can't—breathe," Maddox huffed.

She moved her weight off him and sank back onto the nearest passenger seat.

"How the tables have changed, haven't they?" He coughed, spitting water. "I have to say, even I'm impressed. It hurts like a mother, though."

"I'm not doing this with you."

"What do you mean? I kept the bomb from blowing us all to kingdom come. I stabbed the Prophet for you, didn't I? You should be thanking me."

"You kidnapped my sister and gave her to a monster. You murdered Nancy Harlow. You murdered Yu-Jin Park. And you murdered Ezra Burrows."

"I had to. It wasn't personal." He shifted, grimacing as he tried to stop the blood dribbling from the hole in his belly. "And you shot me. Everything's fair in love and war."

Anger slashed through her. She tensed, fighting back the urge to shoot him again. Soon. But not yet. She had a vow to keep. Several, in fact.

She rose to her feet.

His eyes widened. "Where are you going?"

"I'm doing exactly what I promised. I'm going to kill the Prophet." She adjusted the sling across her chest and gripped the M4. "And then I'm coming back to finish killing you."

Dakota left Maddox where he lay and leapt into the second airboat. It slewed and rocked beneath her weight. She stumbled, striking her shin against the corner of the metal trunk, and righted herself. She raised her weapon.

The Prophet was propped awkwardly in the stern of the boat, his back and shoulders squished against the captain's chair. His hands were zip-tied tightly in front of him. Hawthorne had bound the bullet wound in his side with Quick Clot and a compression bandage.

He would live if they got him medical aid soon, if one of the Blackhawks medevacked him to the nearest functioning hospital.

That wasn't good enough.

She pushed past Hawthorne and stood over the Prophet, her muzzle aimed at the spot between his eyes. A fire was eating her up inside, burning through her rib cage, boiling her blood, searing every inch of her skin.

"Dakota, don't," Hawthorne warned. "He needs to stand trial. This isn't the way to do this."

She didn't move. "I'm cutting the head off the snake."

"I may be the snake, but I'm not the head!" the Prophet blubbered, hands raised defensively, eyes bulging. "Please! Don't shoot me! I'll tell—I'll tell the government everything!"

She shook her head in disgust. He'd claimed he was the voice of God. Acted like a god himself in human form. In the end, he was nothing but a sniveling coward.

She placed her finger on the trigger.

"We aren't the only ones behind this!"

"More lies won't help you."

"Dakota!" Hawthorne said again.

She applied pressure with the pad of her finger. The trigger started to move.

The Prophet's eyes widened in terror. "Wait! Wait! Don't kill me. You'll never find out the truth if you do! You think a bunch of fanatic nuts could pull this off? You think we snuck fourteen nuclear bombs into this country without help? You don't even know who really did this to you!"

Dakota hesitated.

"You keep me alive, I'll tell you everything. You won't get the ones truly responsible without me! You need me!"

"You can't kill him," Hawthorne said.

"I'm making no promises." A chill raced up her spine. She kept the muzzle aimed between his eyes. "Now talk."

He gazed up at her, hatred mingling with the fear in his eyes. "We had help. We were sponsored."

"By who?"

"Russia."

66

MADDOX

Maddox felt dazed, shaken. He was lightheaded from the loss of blood. Pain throbbed through every cell of his body.

He stared across the airboat at the Prophet in shock. Russia? No. It couldn't be. It made no sense...couldn't make sense... Maddox shook his head in disbelief.

And yet, he couldn't dismiss the Prophet's words, for they had the terrible ring of truth.

"You still don't get it. Even after all of this," the Prophet spat. "America is a prideful Jezebel. The wicked believe they're invincible. They think the world worships the ground they walk on. That they are powerful, prosperous, and beyond reproof. But they are nothing like that. America is a nation of lost, lonely, angry, desperate people, bristling with dissension and hatred.

"It was so easy to manipulate them. They followed me like pigs led to the slaughter. Hatred is malleable, so malleable. And Americans are full of hatred." His voice still had that powerful, hypnotic cadence. He didn't sound scared anymore. He sounded proud and boastful, just like he did every time he took to the pulpit.

"I don't understand," Dakota said. "Russia helped you do this?"

The Prophet pointed at Dakota with a bloody finger. "You will never understand because you are willfully ignorant. America was the leader of the world, the superpower of super-powers. But not anymore. This country is blinded, arrogant, corrupted. It allowed others to rise above it—China, Russia."

"Why?" Dakota asked.

"Putin knew America was trying to destroy Russia, that Washington would depose him in a heartbeat if they could. He knew about the government's spies and assassins, how Washington would love nothing more than to place one of their own puppets in Moscow and control Russia themselves. Only Russia is powerful enough to do anything about it. Only Russia can match America on the military stage—jet for jet, missile for missile, warship for warship, nuke for nuke.

"But war isn't fought like that these days, is it? Wars are fought in the shadows. The weapons are subversion and misdirection. Propaganda and misinformation. Hacking social media accounts. Infiltrating national power grids. Interfering with elections to plant doubt and suspicion. To turn the people on each other and watch them destroy themselves from within. This was the natural next step. And America never saw it coming."

The Prophet coughed and winced. His face contorted in pain. "America fights its wars in other people's countries. Proxy wars in Syria, Iraq, Libya, and Yemen. Ukraine and Afghanistan. The government brought this on themselves. Washington was too cocky to ever believe the ultimate proxy war might be fought on their own soil. They were too blind to see it coming. Even now, they're still blind. But now they're crippled, too."

"You planted the evidence to make it appear Iran was guilty," Hawthorne said, his voice raw with barely restrained outrage. "You wanted America to rush into an invasion, just like they did with Afghanistan. You wanted Washington to nuke them in retaliation. And then..."

"The compound was supposed to be discovered—and the evidence," Maddox said weakly. "To lay the blame on us."

"When Russia struck back on behalf of their beleaguered allies, it would be justified," Hawthorne said. "Russia would have the support of the U.N., China, the Middle East."

The Prophet smiled, that same menacingly benign smile Maddox had despised for so many years. Maddox wished he could smash it right off his face.

"Did you know that I once played poker? A vice I have willingly sacrificed. But there are lessons to be learned if you pay attention. You cannot play each hand as its own. You cannot even play each game. You don't play the cards—you play your opponents. You give them fake tells, play bad hands purposefully, bluff. You train them to expect certain things from you at a certain time. You wait and watch and learn. And then, when you're ready, you spring the trap."

"America is already on her knees from the terrorist attacks you orchestrated. Another strike would decimate us, set us back decades at least."

The Prophet shrugged. "That was Russia's plan, not ours. Take your grievances up with them."

"You're an American," Hawthorne said, disgust in his voice. "Why would you collaborate with a country that hates us and plot to destroy your own nation?"

The Prophet sneered. "This is your America, not *my* America. It's not God's America. We wanted the old government destroyed, and so did Russia. We shared a mutual enemy. It was cunning, using a country's own people against them. It fit our own plans, so why wouldn't we? They offered the resources we needed to bring about the New America as God commanded. They gave us money, weapons, and the nukes. It was like God Himself had provided us a lamb for the burnt offering."

"What about after?" Hawthorne asked. "Is Russia planning to invade? Do they want to bomb the whole country into the middle ages? What's their end game?"

The Prophet shrugged, wincing. "They want the old America destroyed so they can be the most powerful country in the world. Russia always seeks power. They've always wanted to be the best. What do we care about any of that?"

Maddox stared at him, too stunned to think clearly, just trying to comprehend how rapidly everything he thought he knew had been turned on its head.

His entire life was a lie. Everything he'd ever been taught to believe in was nothing but a manipulation, a con game.

It was all beginning to make sense. The pieces fell into place with an awful clarity. The letter he'd witnessed the Prophet writing in a foreign language. The Russian nuclear physicist. All the money so easily wired in whenever they needed it.

That's why the Prophet said to leave the evidence in the restricted area. That's why he no longer cared about Eden's fate, or anyone's for that matter. The Shepherds had served their limited purpose.

The Shepherds existed to do the dirty work for a terrorist.

Maddox shuddered. He couldn't stop shivering. The wind was cold, so cold.

"Did my father know you were in bed with a foreign nation?" he asked.

The Prophet curled his lip in a pained sneer. "Your father was a simple man. Loyal when given orders, but too myopic to do what was necessary for victory, to understand the complexities of the war we are fighting. To save America required grave sacrifices. Only I was capable of doing what was required."

"You didn't even need Eden. She was just a ploy, a pawn."

"She was necessary," the Prophet hissed through bloody teeth. "God told me to marry her to seal—"

"Lies! All you do is lie!" Indignation burned in his chest. He may have hated his father, hated his stepmother and Reuben and everyone else, but he loathed the Prophet even more.

If he had the strength, he would stab him again and do it

right this time, until he was good and dead. Better than dead. Let *him* be the sacrifice, the sanctimonious ass.

But he didn't have the strength. The pain spread like a red stain behind his eyes. His arms and legs were going numb. Everything was starting to fade.

Sounds were coming from far away. His thoughts were slow and foggy.

With every beat of his heart, more blood leaked out of him. It drenched his shirt beneath his vest, dripped in rivulets down his stomach and hips, puddling on the floor beneath his back—hot, wet, and sticky.

He wished he'd killed the Prophet himself. He wished he'd done that, at least. One good thing. Something to be proud of.

"We still won." The Prophet sucked in a wet, ragged breath. "We were the ones who destroyed your cities—"

"Enough!" Dakota snapped. "Save the rest of your grandstanding for Guantanamo Bay."

Maddox watched dully as Dakota flipped the carbine and smashed it against the side of the Prophet's skull. The man's eyes rolled into the back of his head.

Maddox slumped, unconsciousness darkening his vision.

Fear ate at him like acid corroding his insides. He didn't want to die. He was afraid to die. Death was still coming.

It would have come for him anyway. The radiation sickness was a poison destroying him slowly, insidiously. He hadn't escaped after all.

At least it was Dakota, he thought dimly. At least it was her.

67

LOGAN

His knife gripped low at his side, Logan crouched in the muck, anchored both feet beneath him, and propelled himself upward with a ferocious leap. Excruciating pain bit into his calf. But it did the job.

He surged toward Reuben, angling the blade up as he stabbed with all his might. The blade slid just below the lip of Reuben's vest into his soft unprotected side, puncturing his kidney.

A hot rush of blood gushed into the water, pouring over his hand as he withdrew the knife and stabbed a second and third time, sharp and savage and furious.

Logan yanked the blade out, pushed away, and broke the surface of the water, coughing and sputtering and blinking water from his eyes.

Reuben staggered back, clutching at his side, the whites of his eyes wide and wild. "You stabbed me!"

"That was for Dakota. And for Park."

Something moved in the water behind Reuben. Something long and dark and deadly.

It happened in an instant.

The water exploded. An enormous creature erupted from

beneath the surface, jaws hinged wide as it launched itself at the Shepherd. It seized Reuben's right arm in its jaws and shook its head, tail thrashing, the water frothing.

Logan watched in horror, too stunned to move.

Reuben shrieked, a high howling cry of pain and terror. He fought, beating at the beast's leathery head with his good hand.

It didn't do any good.

The gator dragged him beneath the surface. The water churned and boiled as the creature spun with its prey. Its tail thrashed violently. A furious froth of foam and spray shot up.

The creature pitched and rolled and spun. The water boiled. Reuben flailed. An arm breached the water, fingers splayed wide.

And then, just as quickly, the water quieted.

Less than thirty seconds later, only bubbles and a faint rippling gave the monster's presence away.

Logan shuddered and shook himself from his stupor. He had to get the hell out of the water. There might be another one. Or maybe this one was still hungry.

He didn't know if that beast was an alligator or a crocodile. Frankly, he didn't care.

He was just grateful he was still breathing.

He sheathed the knife with a shaking hand and sloshed toward the flooded bank, limping heavily, his left leg dragging, nearly crawling as pain battered every inch of his body.

Water poured off his skin. He was coated in gritty sand, mud, and bits of decaying leaves and twigs. His wet boots sank into the water and muck, making sucking squelch sounds with each painful, hobbling step.

He retrieved his Glock. He almost didn't find it, but it had snagged in the brush just above the rising waterline.

He made his way through the trees, pausing at each one to rest his throbbing leg, the wind whipping at his back, rain spitting in his face as he headed toward Kinsey.

Kinsey lay in a crumpled heap at the base of a slash pine, spiky palm leaves fluttering all around her. The water was four or five inches deep, nearly covering her legs. Her short dark hair was plastered to her scalp, the mud they'd painted on their faces earlier washed away by the driving rain.

He didn't see any blood, but she wasn't moving, either.

He crouched next to her, balancing on one leg and using the tree trunk to hold himself up, and touched her shoulder. "Kinsey? You awake?"

With a groan, she rolled over. Her face hit the floodwater and she came up spluttering. "It hurts. It really hurts."

He helped her into a sitting position with his good hand. "Where?"

She looked down and fingered two holes in her tactical vest, both just south of her heart, about three inches apart. "That jerkwad shot me."

"Are you okay?"

She grimaced. "Bruised ribs. Maybe a broken one. But I'm alive and I didn't get eaten. I'm taking that as a win."

He didn't say anything, just focused on breathing, on staying conscious.

She eyed him. "You don't look so great either."

He rolled his injured shoulder and winced. It'd hurt like hell for a few days, but he didn't think there was any permanent damage. His leg, on the other hand, was a different matter. "I'm alive and I didn't get eaten."

She managed a pained grin. "What happened with jerkwad number two?"

He glanced through the thrashing foliage toward the water. The wind swirled and rippled the surface, but the roiling frenzy from only a few minutes ago had vanished.

"Trust me, it's better if you don't know. His spirit is on the way to Valhalla or Hades or whatever the hell they believe in, that's what matters."

Her eyes widened. "I won't even ask. What about our escape boat?"

"It's floating about twenty yards offshore. We'll have to swim for it."

Her face collapsed. She shook her head. "Oh no. No, no, no. Please don't make me."

He rose painfully to his feet, still balancing against the tree. The floodwater swirled almost to his mid-shins.

The wind was like a train, roaring down on them. The rain beat their heads. Leaves torn from their branches slapped at their arms and legs, twigs and small branches whirling past them.

The hurricane was coming.

He held out his hand to help her up. "I'll swim out and get it. I'll bring it as close as I can get to shore, okay? You'll just have to walk in a little bit."

"You've just earned your slot as my favorite person of all time, Logan Garcia. Tattoos and all." She sucked in her breath as she stood unsteadily. "But if Hawthorne heard that I waited on the shore like a scaredy-cat, I'd never hear the end of it. I'm afraid we're in this together."

Logan smiled for what felt like the first time in days. "Let's go find our people."

68
DAKOTA

When Dakota returned to Maddox, he was barely conscious. His skin was a sickly, sallow color. Blood was everywhere.

He looked up at her, eyes half-lidden, his mouth contorted in a grimace. "Please...please don't leave."

Gone was the rough, feral handsomeness. Gone was the sly smirk and cunning gaze. He was just a man in pain, scared to die alone.

Her gut clenched. She sank to her knees beside him. The cold metal of the hull pressed against her shins. The airboat rocked beneath her in the choppy water.

"Dakota, we need to go." Hawthorne gripped the propeller cage as another strong gust tore through the narrow channel, howling and moaning.

She felt the oncoming storm bearing down on them like a sinister force, an impenetrable wall of towering dark clouds, ferocious and relentless. The first fat droplets of rain spat from the pitch-black sky.

"Dakota—"

"Just a minute."

"The hurricane is less than six hours from landfall. We can't be out here when it hits."

She didn't take her eyes off Maddox. "I need a minute!"

Hawthorne didn't say anything more.

She withdrew her combat knife—the one Ezra had given her so long ago—and held it lengthwise across her thighs. Even dying, Maddox was unpredictable.

"Looks like you won after all," he said weakly.

She thought of the dead bodies strewn across the clearing—men, women, children. She thought of the burning compound, the screaming and running, the thunderous roar of gunfire, the blazing fire consuming everything in its path. "This isn't winning."

He shifted, his breath coming in sharp, shallow gasps. He fumbled at the straps of his tactical vest with bloody fingers. "I need this off."

She hesitated.

He managed a tight smile that looked more like a grimace. Blood smeared his teeth. "I won't try anything. I—I've always been a man of my word, haven't I?"

Cautiously, she helped him remove the heavy vest, pulling at the Velcro and helping him sit up enough to get his arms free. He sank back with a heavy sigh.

Water pelted her face. It was raining hard now, sheeting down and driven almost sideways. The wind clawed at her with cold frantic fingers. The airboats knocked against each other, their hulls scraping the mangrove roots on either side of the narrow channel.

They didn't have much time.

His gaze met hers. Even in enormous pain, his eyes were sharp, penetrating straight through to her core. "Thank you."

Her breath hitched in her throat.

His face was drawn, his eyes haunted. The radiation sickness had rendered him almost unrecognizable. His wet hair was plastered to his skull. Rivulets of rainwater ran down his cheeks like tears.

He looked at her with an emptiness that could never be filled.

"Tell me you loved me," he said, his voice cracking.

Her heart splintered inside her chest. Even now, after all this, in a terrible, inexplicable way, she didn't hate him. Even though she wanted to with every fiber of her being, she couldn't.

He had hurt her. Burned and scarred her. He'd hunted her through the radioactive ruins of Miami and nearly killed her. Because of him, Ezra was dead.

The memories were like weeping wounds. Maddox was the one who'd let her go the night she and Eden had fled. He was the one who'd offered her an escape from the harsh, stifling cruelties of the compound. More than an escape—he'd been her lifeline.

She saw him in her mind's eye as he used to be—the tough, troubled boy with the sly blue eyes and sarcastic smile. The only one who truly saw her. In a way, he'd saved her.

He was something different now. Miserable and wretched, but deep down, still that love-starved boy desperate for approval from the father who'd despised and abused him, a boy twisted by hate, fear, and self-loathing.

Sometimes, love and hate sprouted so close together they grew entangled. But eventually, one always choked the other.

They were both abused, but she'd found her way to something else, something better. The world had tried to break her, too. But she wouldn't let it. She'd escaped—he hadn't.

"I did," she said. "I did love you."

Maddox nodded. He let out a breath, like something had been released inside him. Something flashed in his eyes so briefly it might have been mistaken for a glimmer of light or a passing shadow. But she saw it.

He leaned his head back and closed his eyes. Watery blood pooled in the hull beneath his torso, his breaths shallow and uneven. He was fading fast.

She shivered. The lashing rain stung her cheeks. She was soaking wet, tendrils of hair plastered to her cheeks and forehead, her clothes drenched, the tactical vest sodden.

The sky was black as silt. The torrential rain fell in gusting sheets. Beneath the boat, the water seethed. Great gusts of wind thrashed the trees, the branches creaking and groaning like ghosts.

The hurricane was coming. It was already here.

"I want it to be you," he said. "It was always you."

An aching numbness settled over her. She felt a hundred things at once: anger, grief, loss, regret, pity.

She nodded, her head suddenly so, so heavy.

She picked up her knife and gripped the slick wet hilt with both hands, blade facing down. She leaned over him, placed the point over his chest, and drove the knife into his heart.

She stayed with him until he died.

It was a mercy.

69

DAKOTA

Dakota rubbed her tired eyes. It had been three days since the attack on the compound, since they'd ended the Prophet's bloody reign of terror. Three days since she'd watched Maddox Cage die.

General Pierce had flown them back to Miami that morning. They'd spent the last three days recovering at a functioning hospital in Tallahassee after Hawthorne had them airlifted out of the path of the hurricane.

Eden, Logan, Kinsey, and Hawthorne had received emergency medical care by the remaining skeleton crew. Hawthorne's bullet wound had done minimal damage. Kinsey was recovering from her cracked rib. Both Eden and Logan were in bad shape upon arrival.

Eden was treated for the symptoms of the radiation sickness, but she needed a bone marrow transplant and ongoing intensive care.

Logan was treated for shock, given a blood transfusion and plenty of fluids, along with a round of heavy-duty antibiotics to kill the nasty infection he'd gotten from the swamp water. His shoulder and the right side of his chest were bruised an ugly bluish purple. The bullet that tore through his calf missed the

292

bone, but the muscles and nerves were damaged. He might always walk with a permanent limp.

But he was alive. Eden was alive. For that, Dakota would be forever grateful.

Now she and Logan sat in two plush leather chairs opposite a massive mahogany desk. Mahogany bookcases lined the walls, each shelf bristling with thick book spines. The wall behind the desk displayed several dozen photos of Governor Blake shaking hands with various celebrities and billionaires.

"Welcome to Governor Blake's office." General Pierce leaned back in his seat behind the desk and motioned for them to sit. "It's rather pretentious, but we'll make do. Please, make yourselves comfortable."

"Thank you for meeting with us, General Pierce," Dakota said.

General Pierce tipped his chin at Dakota. "You showed great restraint in not throwing public enemy number one to the gators. Your country applauds you."

The scars on her back prickled. The only reason she hadn't killed the Prophet was because they needed him to reveal the truth to the world. That, and death was too easy a punishment for what he'd done to her, to Eden, to the millions of innocent people whose lives he'd snuffed out. "He deserves to suffer for the rest of his long, miserable life."

The general twisted an engraved silver letter opener in his huge hands. "I like her. Hawthorne, have I mentioned how much I like these two yet?"

The corners of Hawthorne's mouth twitched. He leaned against the wall next to Logan and scratched at the bandages wrapping his left arm and shoulder. Luckily, the bullet was a through and through and did minimal damage. "Many times, sir."

The general's expression turned grim. His mouth flattened as he pointed the letter opener at Dakota, then Logan. "You interfered with a highly sensitive and highly classified military operation. A civilian, Zane Collier, was killed in the line of fire. The casualties could have been much, much worse."

Logan straightened. "And if we hadn't, the refugee camp would be a radioactive wasteland, hundreds of thousands of innocent people would be dead, and we'd be on the verge of World War III. Sir."

There was a long, uncomfortable silence. General Pierce stared at them. Dakota and Logan stared right back, steady and unwavering.

Hawthorne just rolled his eyes. "He's trying to decide whether to arrest you or give you a medal."

The general closed the folder. "Well, I guess we're all lucky how things turned out, aren't we?"

Logan and Dakota exchanged looks.

"I wouldn't call it luck," Dakota said.

"You're right about that." General Pierce said.

"We don't care about medals," Logan said, "but some answers would be nice."

"Ask away. Anything that's not highly classified, I'll share with you. You've certainly earned it."

"It was really Russia that gave the Shepherds the nuclear material?" Logan asked. "That's how they got the bombs?"

"That's how they got everything," Hawthorne said darkly.

The general nodded. "The Kremlin sponsored whatever the Shepherds needed—high-tech communications equipment, weapons, boats, buildings. They'd sell off a Russian-owned condominium in New York or Miami; the profits transferred to bank accounts in Panama controlled by Cypress-based trusts. They gave the Shepherds the bombs almost ready-made. And smuggled in the nuclear physicist to do the rest. They bided their time. They were careful. It appears the first bomb came through Port Everglades four years ago. We're tracking the evidence trail for the others now."

"And the FBI really had no idea?" Dakota asked.

"The River Grass Compound was on a watch list, and a few

of the Shepherds are in the FBI database for posting anti-American sentiment long before they disappeared off the grid, but they weren't a priority. No chatter. No alarms, no warnings. They communicated via old-fashioned snail mail letters in code and an obscure game on the internet, also in code. These operators were clean."

"So is Iran completely innocent in all of this, then?" Logan asked.

"Iran lied," Hawthorne said. "But they lied to protect their nuclear power program and escape further sanctions. The Hezbollah terrorists either were paid to lie or desired credit for their own twisted reasons. We're still investigating."

The general nodded soberly. "Much as I wish the dirtbag was buried six feet under with a dozen rounds to his most sensitive body parts, that's just one of the reasons we need the 'Prophet' alive. For now."

"What's going to happen to the Prophet?" Dakota asked. "Or Norman Perry, or whatever his name is." It sounded bizarre to call him by his real name after the years of horror he'd inflicted as a holy harbinger of God's righteous wrath.

It diminished his power, somehow. Now he was just a psychopath with a stupid name.

"They'll keep him alive as long as he continues providing the United States—and the world—with valuable information. Which he is."

The day after the attack on the compound, Norman Perry's videotaped confessions hit the airwaves around the world. With his cooperation, the FBI had already captured his handler, who'd named names—powerful names in the Kremlin and upper echelon of the Russian oligarchy, all the way to the top.

In a matter of hours, Russia was outed. Iran was relieved of suspicion. The U.N. and nearly every developed nation on the planet denounced Russia's vicious acts of sponsored terrorism on a foreign country's citizens.

The news channels announced aid pouring into America to

the tune of ten times the amount donated in the previous month—in one day. Would it be enough to turn the tide?

Dakota had no idea what would happen now. World politics wasn't her area. She'd given everything she had, and then she'd given more.

She just wanted to go home.

"What about the women and children?" she asked. "What will happen to them?"

"The surviving Shepherds will be charged with domestic terrorism, treason, and various other crimes against the state. We'll throw the book at them. The women? That remains to be seen. Maybe they're victims. Maybe they're perpetrators."

Some of both. With a pang, Dakota thought of Sister Rosemarie. She had suffered, too. Maybe she'd made the wrong choices, but that didn't make her evil. In the end, she'd sacrificed everything to do the right thing, to save them.

She'd earned her redemption—at least in Dakota's eyes.

What about Maddox? He'd turned on the Prophet. He was the one who grabbed the detonator. They might all be incinerated ash right now if not for him.

Had he earned redemption, even after all the terrible things he'd done? She had no energy to waste any more thoughts on Maddox Cage. That was for God to decide, not her.

He was dead. He no longer mattered at all.

Dakota rubbed her temples, feeling incredibly tired. "And the children?"

"Will be considered victims under the law. Though not everyone sees it that way. As of now, thirteen women and twenty-one children under the age of eighteen remain in a detention center in Tallahassee."

She closed her eyes, a fresh wave of grief sweeping through her. The terrible images flashed in her mind—women and children screaming, bullets flying, fire everywhere, the black shapes of the helicopters wheeling in the sky like great metal dragons, unquenchable beasts belching death and destruction.

She clutched the arms of the chair until her knuckles whitened. "That's all that survived? Out of seventy-seven?"

General Pierce's eyes flashed. "Young lady, Norman Perry planned to use those women and children as human shields from the beginning. That was their sole purpose at that compound. He infested their impressionable minds for years with lies aimed at that very goal, training them to lay down like lambs to the slaughter when the time came.

"If the FBI or ATF ever got wind of his activities, he would use them as bargaining chips to protect himself in a stand-off. If the compound was ever attacked, he would do exactly what he did that night. Listen to me. You lay one hundred percent of the blame, guilt, and recrimination on that man's head, where it belongs. Not on yours, not on DHS or the U.S. Army, Hawthorne, or anyone else. Everyone who fought that night did so to save their country. And that's exactly what they did. That's what you did."

She thought of the women who had refused to come, so brainwashed they spurned their own salvation and that of their children. Sour acid burned the back of her throat. Anger boiled through her veins. Not anger—outrage.

There was so much brokenness in the world. Sometimes, it was overwhelming. General Pierce was right. Julio was right. You couldn't save everyone. But that didn't mean you did nothing.

Dakota had given her all, and then some. So had Eden, Logan and Julio, Hawthorne and Kelsey, and Haasi, Maki, and the Collier brothers.

They'd risked their lives to do everything they could. Ezra had given his life for it. So had Zane Collier. Park. And Sister Rosemarie.

In the end, it had made a difference.

That's what mattered. That was everything.

LOGAN

"I t's such a shame that Governor Blake couldn't be here to greet us," General Pierce said, "but he's being investigated by a grand jury at the moment."

Logan raised his eyebrows. "Is he a Russian collaborator, too?"

"Unfortunately, no. He's just a greedy, ambitious, power-hungry jerk."

Logan snorted. "So, a politician then?"

"I didn't say it." General Pierce grimaced. "He'll escape jail, but I doubt he'll finish his term. His reputation is far too sullied, what with his chief aide getting arrested for treason. Not to mention the intense criticism from both sides of the aisle regarding the forced detainments at Camp Disney. He'll slink away in shame and find some slimy rock somewhere to disappear beneath for a while, hopefully forever."

Logan stared at the photos on the wall, the governor's smug, self-satisfied grin repeated over and over in each picture. Maybe he wasn't guilty of treason, but he was still a slick, fat cat politician, always watching out for himself instead of the people.

"And Alfred T. What's his face?" he asked. "Please tell me he'll never see the light of day again."

The FBI had traced the Prophet's satphone calls to the governor's chief of staff, Alfred T. Forester. He'd acted as the Shepherds' inside man, keeping them apprised of the government's progress in the bomb investigations.

He'd also alerted them hours ahead of the raid. Eight soldiers had died who might otherwise still be alive, including those in the downed Blackhawk.

"Oh, he won't." General Pierce pushed the rolling chair back and stretched out his long legs. "That filthy rat turned for money, can you believe it? A couple million wired into an offshore bank account. That's all it took for him to betray his country and facilitate the death of hundreds of thousands of innocent people. Oh, he swears he tried to back out, but the Kremlin sent their goons as his babysitters to keep a constant threatening watch on him."

"If he was turned, chances are there are other double agents planted at the state and federal level and elsewhere," Hawthorne said in a low voice. "We will thoroughly investigate every possibility."

No one spoke for a long moment.

The general shuffled and reshuffled the papers on the desk. "Much as I hate to admit it, in some ways, that 'Prophet' is right. He took our weakness—the disillusioned and disaffected among us—and turned them against us.

"Make no mistake. We have two enemies here. The first is Russia and other foreign threats that would do us harm. But the second enemy is a cancer within us. Almost two hundred American citizens hated other Americans enough to justify murdering hundreds of thousands of people outright and dooming millions of others to hardship, suffering, and early deaths." He shook his head wearily. "We have to do better."

"We will," Hawthorne said.

Logan spread out his hands. "What about Miami?"

"It may be too late for Miami," the general said.

"For now." Hawthorne ran his hand over his head and rubbed his jaw. "Shay says we shouldn't give up. And we won't."

They'd flown over Miami by chopper that morning. From the windows, Logan glimpsed a nightmare. Businesses were ripped from their foundations, houses scalped and open to the sky, hollowed-out schools and apartments and gas stations all flooded. Brown water swirling with detritus swept the corridors between broken buildings and mounds of rubble.

Downed power lines twisted and writhed like great black snakes. The blackened carcasses of cars were turned upside down, street signs floating down water-logged streets. Everywhere, wood and steel lay in mangled piles, filmed in silty layers of mud.

He hoped there were no people left down there.

"And the United States?" Dakota asked.

"It will be a long time before safety and security returns to the U.S. Much of the country will be on their own for a year, maybe two. Maybe more. Without access to food, clean water, and proper sanitation, hundreds of thousands more will die."

The United States had a long, arduous journey ahead of her. The country would rebuild, but it would never be the same. The world was still broken and would be for a long time.

The searing anger was still there. The sorrow. The grief. The aching pit of loss and regret in the center of his chest.

Maybe you just had to move forward, walk away, let the scar tissue etched in your heart remind you of what was then, and what was now.

Logan had learned that the hard way. But he had learned.

He would never forget Tomás and Adelina, would never for one second abandon the weight of the memories he carried, the knowledge of the things he'd done.

The bruises on his body would heal. His leg might not. He might live with this constant, throbbing ache and limp for the rest of his life. So be it.

He had nearly died in that swamp, but he hadn't. He was

still here, still fighting for something better. Still working to tilt the scales.

As long as he was breathing, he had a chance. A way, a path forward.

General Pierce leaned forward, settling his forearms heavily on the desk. "I was serious before. I'm even more serious now. Both of you—join the Army. Join the National Guard. Ten weeks of boot camp and I can put you to work. We need soldiers like you."

"Thank you for the offer, sir," Logan said carefully. He glanced at Dakota, a crease between his brows. "But I have other plans."

She beamed at him, a slow sweet smile spreading across her face.

It filled him with something warm and bright and whole. He couldn't help but smile back.

He was alive. Dakota was here beside him. And that was something.

It was enough.

71

DAKOTA

D akota shielded her eyes and searched the sky.

A small black dot appeared to the north. It was still strange to see aircraft sailing above the clouds after all this time. It'd only been a matter of weeks since the world had irrevocably changed, and yet it somehow felt like forever.

Earlier that afternoon, a convoy of Humvees had escorted them to the Miami International Airport, formerly the Emergency Operations Center. Everywhere she looked, she saw the drowned wreckage of millions of lives.

The airport itself wasn't much better. It was deserted and eerily quiet. Their boots crunched over shattered glass from the huge windows. Most of the trucks and buses were long gone. The few that remained were crushed against each other or tipped on their sides.

Wet rotting trash and shredded palm fronds littered the tarmac. The trees still standing were shorn of their leaves and many of their branches, the palms stripped of their fronds.

The asphalt shimmered in the heat. It was as hot as Hades again, humid and sweltering. Typical South Florida. Fifty yards away, several Guardsmen leaned against two parked Humvees, keeping watch.

Logan was standing next to her, staring out at the long stretch of damaged planes with a furrowed brow. Julio was on her other side, arms crossed over his chest, humming off-tune to himself.

Hawthorne leaned against the hood of the unmarked white SUV he'd used to drive them here this afternoon. Two black duffle bags sat at his feet. His left arm was still bandaged and cradled in a sling.

Eden stayed in the air-conditioned car where she could rest and regain a bit of her strength. Dakota still wasn't sure what to do with her. She wanted desperately to take her back to Ezra's cabin, but Eden needed intense medical care for weeks, maybe months.

Remaining in that bathroom for two days had saved Eden's life, but the fallout's deadly gamma rays cut through the flimsy cinderblock walls like they were paper. Her white blood cells were failing her. She needed a bone marrow transplant.

If she received the transplant, she might live twenty or thirty years before cancer developed. If it developed at all.

Hawthorne had found several medical universities accepting radiation patients in a few Midwestern states. But there was still insurance, bills, housing, transportation—all the looming problems Dakota didn't have any idea how to deal with.

She would deal with them, though. She had no doubt. If she could help take down a sadistic terrorist cult, then surely, she could find a way to take care of her sister.

The black dot drew closer, slowly growing into the familiar shape of a military helicopter. The faint *whomp, whomp, whomp* of the rotors shattered the still, muggy air.

The helicopter was on its way back from Camp Disney, bringing Shay along with it. It would touch down at Miami Airport briefly to pick up Hawthorne and Julio.

Hawthorne had requested to return to Miami to oversee the massive reconstruction efforts. Shay volunteered with the Red

Cross and would remain with him while she worked with the displaced refugees outside the hot zone.

No matter how overwhelming the task before them, they were both determined to make a difference.

First, they were traveling to Tallahassee for a few days with General Pierce. On their way, they'd drop Julio off in Palm Beach to reunite with his wife and extended family. He and his family were planning to move in with some friends in a rural area of Central Florida, staying away from the cities until some semblance of law and order was restored.

Dakota cleared her throat and turned to Julio. Her chest tightened. Julio had earned a special place in her heart, and always would. She hadn't thought it would hurt this much. "I guess this is...I guess we should say our..."

She stuck out her hand, fighting to keep it together. Blubbering like a baby wasn't her M.O., and she sure as hell wasn't going to start now.

Julio sidestepped her hand and pulled her into a bearhug. His embrace was warm and comforting and full of affection. She didn't want to let go. Not now, not ever. She wrapped her arms around him and squeezed him back as hard as she could.

He coughed. "Don't crack my ribs, girl."

She buried her face in his shoulder. His now full beard scraped her cheek. He smelled like sweat and dish soap, but she didn't care.

Still hugging her, he lowered his voice. "It has been an honor to be your friend. My nieces will grow up hearing the story of the brave girl who saved my life, rescued her sister, and managed to save half the civilized world while she was at it."

She couldn't swallow over the lump in her throat, and she couldn't see through the blurry wetness in her eyes. "Now you're just being dramatic."

He laughed, a full deep laugh free of anxiety or worry. "When I open that mechanics shop I've always dreamed of—and I will, the de la Peñas land on their feet—you will *always* have a standing job offer, no matter what. And not for bussing tables, either."

Now she really was crying. Grief and joy and a fierce, bitter-sweet longing crashed over her in waves. She wanted him to reunite with his family more than anything. But it meant good-bye. Not forever, but for now. Even that felt like too long. "I couldn't have done any of this without you."

"Flattery will get you nowhere, girl."

She smiled into his soggy shirt. "Promise you'll come visit."

"I promise." They both knew the state of the world would prevent safe travel for quite a while—at least for the normal people who didn't have a chartered chopper on standby.

But there was hope. Justice had been served. The world could take a collective breath as the U.S. turned its eyes toward the long painful process of rebuilding.

That's what humanity did. The best of it, anyway. It rebuilt what was destroyed. It kept going in the face of devastation, grief, loss. It never gave up hope, even when it should.

The chopper lowered toward the ground. She pulled away from Julio, and everyone shielded their eyes as the rotor wash kicked up a cloud of dust. When it touched down, Julio hurried in, opened the door, and helped the first passenger out.

Shay bounded out of the chopper. Julio enveloped her in a giant hug. She was so much taller than he was, she had to bend to hug him back.

Over his shoulder, she waved excitedly to Dakota and Logan, her wide, bright smile so contagious it was impossible not to smile back.

Logan elbowed Dakota gently in the ribs. "You missed her, admit it."

She wiped at her eyes and flashed him a look. "Not as much as you did. You needed her to mend all your countless injuries."

He gave her a wry grin. "I sure did."

A slim Hispanic man climbed out of the chopper, followed

by a woman who held his hand as she stepped gingerly to the ground and tucked her long black hair back from her face.

Dakota's heart caught in her throat.

The SUV's passenger door flew open. Eden staggered out and half-ran, half-shuffled as fast as she could toward the couple, her arms flung wide.

"Who in the world is that?" Logan asked.

"Gabriella and Jorge Ross," Dakota said, her voice raw. "Eden's foster parents."

7 2
DAKOTA

Dakota watched their faces light up in pure joy as Eden ran into the open arms of her foster parents.

Gabriella dropped to her knees with a choked cry. She burst into tears as she clutched Eden to her chest and rocked her in her arms. "Baby, you're alive. You're alive. You have no idea how much I've missed you. I love you, honey. I love you so much."

Jorge knelt right there on the hot tarmac and enclosed the two of them in an exuberant embrace. His eyes glistened, his expression contorting in a mix of happiness, disbelief, and enormous relief.

Eden burrowed herself as deeply into their arms as she could, her shoulders quaking. Dakota couldn't see her sister's face. She didn't need to.

She saw the way they looked at her, the way Gabriella looked at her.

It felt like the ground was opening beneath her and she was falling, falling, with nowhere to land.

Julio and Shay hurried back toward where Dakota stood, frozen.

Shay hugged Dakota.

Dakota could barely hug her back. Her arms had gone numb.

"It's a miracle!" Julio's eyes were wet. He touched his cross, grinning. "In the midst of all of this chaos, they found each other again."

Dakota nodded dully.

Logan was watching her, a look of concern on his face. "Are you okay?"

She nodded again. She didn't trust herself enough to speak.

"You did this, didn't you?" Julio asked Shay.

Shay laughed. "Oh yes, I orchestrated the whole thing! I just —we kind of bumped into each other, you know? A thief jumped me, trying to steal my bag, and Gabriella was the only one who tried to help me. We started talking about her missing daughter...and I just had this feeling, you know? Like goosebumps all over? I just knew. I knew something special was happening."

Shay looked beyond Dakota, Logan, and Julio, her eyes lighting up as she caught sight of Hawthorne.

Hawthorne gave her his best big goofy grin. "Just how I feel, now that you mention it."

She flew into his arms. He cupped her elbows in his big hands, leaned down, and kissed her deeply. She wrapped her arms around his waist, avoiding his injured arm, and gave him an enthusiastic kiss in return.

They made a lovely pair, those two. Another beautiful thing rising from the ashes.

"You did good, Shay," Julio said. "You really did."

Shay broke away from the kiss and straightened her skewed glasses. She grinned at Dakota. "Anyone would've done the same thing."

Dakota knew differently. Shay was Shay, kind and gentle-hearted and generous. How many people would take the time to comfort one brokenhearted woman in a sea of brokenness and heartache? Not many. If not for Shay, Eden would never have seen her foster parents again.

The thought was simultaneously wonderful and terrible. Dakota felt her own heart crumbling into pieces. Here she was, surrounded by all this joy and happiness—and she was happy, she was—and yet, a hollow space was already spreading inside her chest.

The space where her sister belonged.

Logan moved closer. She felt the heat of him, his warmth and strength, steadying her. He slipped his arm around her waist.

"You're not okay," he murmured into her hair.

She leaned into him, letting him anchor her.

"You didn't tell me about them," she said to Hawthorne, because she couldn't answer Logan right now. If she did, she would fall apart right here on the tarmac.

Hawthorne shrugged, grinning. "I thought it'd be a fun surprise."

Eden and the Rosses were on their feet now, Eden nestled between them, Jorge with his arm around his wife's shoulder, squeezing them both close like he still couldn't believe this was real, that Eden was real.

Eden was gesturing rapidly, her fingers weaving so elegantly in the air, Jorge nodding and Gabriella smiling as she signed right back.

Eden signed something and gestured toward Dakota. As one, they turned and headed toward her. Dakota's lungs contracted. She wasn't ready for this.

Jorge put his other arm around Eden to hold her up and keep her steady. Her skin was sallow, dark smudges beneath her eyes, but not even the radiation sickness could dampen the happiness emanating from every fiber of her being.

Dakota stiffened.

"Dakota." Fresh tears leaked down Gabriella's cheeks,

streaking her makeup, but she didn't seem to care. "It's such a pleasure to see you again."

Dakota swallowed, her face burning. "Yeah, um—nice to see you, too. I'm...really glad you're alive."

She *was* glad they were alive. She didn't think she'd ever seen her sister so overjoyed.

"We heard what you did, how you saved her," Gabriella said in a husky voice. "We can never thank you enough. We owe you everything."

Dakota wasn't sure what to say to that. Before she could mumble something idiotic, Gabriella hugged her. Not a pleasant, polite side hug, but a deep strong hug full of warmth and compassion. The woman gathered her in her arms and squashed her so tight she couldn't breathe for a few seconds.

Once Gabriella released her, Dakota swiftly retreated to the safety of Logan. Breathing wasn't any easier. Her chest was still squeezing, squeezing, her heart a fist in her throat.

"Shay tells me you're headed to live with the in-laws in Idaho," Hawthorne said.

Jorge nodded. "Thank goodness Governor Blake finally saw reason and started releasing people from the camp who have somewhere to go. Gabriella's parents have a sprawling farmhouse on twenty acres outside of Sun Valley. A beautiful farm, well water, neighbors who watch out for each other. It's as good a place as any to ride out the storm."

Gabriella gazed at Eden like she'd never get enough of her. "You would really love it there, Eden. You'd have your own bedroom. My mother breeds and raises Great Pyrenees mountain dogs. She has a litter of puppies right now."

Eden glanced from the Rosses to Dakota and back again, confused.

Apart from the growl of the chopper's engine, the tarmac fell silent.

It hadn't hit Eden yet. She hadn't realized what this meant.

Not the way Dakota did the instant she recognized Gabriella's face.

"There's a good hospital there," Jorge said as much to Dakota as to Eden. He met her gaze, imploring, his eyes asking for far more than she wanted to give. "They have a bed for her. We've already checked. They're having great success with radiation patients using experimental stem cell treatments. She'll get the best care possible."

Dakota nodded, her head suddenly incredibly heavy. She wanted so many things, too many to name.

But it wasn't about what you wanted. Not when you loved someone.

"You can go." The words felt like they were being ripped right out of her throat. It was the hardest thing she'd ever said. "It's okay. I—I want you to go."

Eden's forehead creased uncertainly. Her lips quivered. She made a circle with the index and thumb of each hand, forming two "F's", her other fingers splayed and pointed straight up. She used each hand to trace a circle.

You're my family, she signed.

"So are they."

Eden smiled, but it was a tremulous smile, one on the verge of breaking. *Come with us*, she signed desperately. *Please.*

"We'd be thrilled to have you," Jorge said immediately, without even a flicker of hesitation.

"You're more than welcome," Gabriella echoed just as sincerely.

Dakota believed them. She really did. They were good people. She understood why Eden loved them.

For one heart-wrenching instant, she considered it. Imagined a life with food on the table at every meal and two loving parents to tuck her in at night, somewhere far away from the chaos, destruction, and death. But they weren't her parents. They were Eden's.

She understood why Eden was better off with them, but she wasn't. Eden would be happy, taken care of, loved dearly. She would be allowed to grow into whoever she wanted to be.

The Rosses would give Eden the family she needed and deserved. But that wasn't where Dakota belonged.

"Thank you, truly. But I need to stay here."

Eden's face collapsed.

Dakota wrapped her arms around her distraught sister and pulled her close. Felt her heart beating against her own. She rested her chin on the girl's blonde head and closed her eyes, breathing in the sweet, freshly washed scent of her, relishing every last moment.

"This is the right thing, the best thing for you." Dakota could hardly swallow around the lump in her throat. "I love you, but I also want you to go, okay? It's okay to want to go. It's okay."

Dakota met Gabriella's gaze over her sister's head.

Thank you, Gabriella mouthed.

"Take care of her," Dakota said.

"With all my heart," Gabriella said.

Eden pulled away. Her cheeks were wet, her eyes red-rimmed. She signed something that Dakota didn't understand.

"What if you forget me?" Gabriella translated for her.

"I'll never forget you." She flattened her hand and made a downward swipe, like a squiggly karate chop. She hadn't been great at learning American Sign Language, but she'd made sure to learn this one. It was important.

She did it again for emphasis. *Never, ever.*

Something changed in Eden's expression—a flash of understanding—and resolve. She nodded solemnly and repeated the signs back to Dakota. *Never, ever.*

Dakota cleared her throat and wiped her face with the back of her arm. Took a moment to pull herself together. She gripped her sister by the shoulders and looked steadily into her eyes. "I'm going to fix up Ezra's cabin. Someone needs to look after Haasi and those crazy Collier brothers."

She already had plans to finish fixing the solar power, restore the gardens, and repair the damage after the hurricane—and after that, develop trade with Haasi and the others. They'd need to create a security patrol with surrounding homesteads to protect the entire area.

It was time to think long-term, beyond survival. It was time to think *living*.

She squeezed Eden's shoulders. "When things settle down, I'll find a way to visit you. And you're always, always welcome here."

Eden smiled through her tears. She had accepted the new trajectory her life—all their lives—had just taken.

So did Dakota, no matter how hard it was.

Eden hugged everyone, giving Logan an extra hard squeeze, then made the rounds a second and third time, Jorge hovering close by to make sure she didn't fall. Hawthorne, Shay, and Julio hugged everyone, too.

There were tears, and laughter, and more tears.

"Time to get a move on," Hawthorne reminded them.

He stowed his bags in the back of the chopper. One by one, Hawthorne, Shay, the Rosses, and then Eden climbed inside.

Julio was last. He paused beside Dakota. "I'll pray for you every single day."

"I'll always take your prayers, Julio."

"I'm proud of you, you know. Ezra would be, too." He gave her a gentle smile, like he knew exactly how her heart was breaking and mending itself at the same time. "And not just for your courage on the battlefield, but for what you did just now."

She couldn't speak, but she knew he could see it in her eyes —everything his words meant to her.

She watched her friend climb inside and shut the door. Everything she loved was in the belly of that chopper. No. Not everything.

The rotors spun, kicking up grit and debris, forcing her to turn away and shield her eyes.

When she looked back, it was lifting up, up, up into the wide blue sky.

Logan took Dakota's hand. "Let's go home."

The End

AFTERWORD

Thank you so much for reading the *Nuclear Dawn* series! I hope you enjoyed reading it as much as I enjoyed writing it.

Thank you for coming along on this wild ride with me! In this survival thriller series, I wanted to explore the ramifications of nuclear terrorism, which I think is far more likely than a nuclear war. And I wanted to create memorable characters who find a way to survive in one of the most unlikely of places—the Everglades.

Researching and writing about the Everglades was a ton of fun. I can't tell you how much I enjoyed upending Logan and Kinsey in that swamp with all those hungry gators lurking just below the surface.

The thing with endings is that it can be hard to say goodbye. characters of Dakota, Logan, Eden, and even Maddox came alive for me on the page. Dakota and Logan are probably my two favorite characters I've written so far. They're both flawed but fierce in their determination to protect the people they love. I can only hope that I would rise to the occasion in a similar situation.

I freely admit that I shed a tear or two at the end when Dakota realizes she must let Eden go. A new beginning is also the end of something else, which can often be bittersweet in real life, too.

With this last book, I wanted to tie all the important threads together while also completing each character's arc and providing you, the reader, with a satisfying and rewarding ending.

I hope you loved this last book as much as I do. Thank you so much for following me on this journey.

If you have a minute, I'd love it if you would leave a review of your thoughts on Amazon and/or Goodreads. I read and cherish every review. They also help my books find new readers.

Thank you!

-Kyla

ACKNOWLEDGMENTS

Thank you as always to my awesome beta readers. Your thoughtful critiques and enthusiasm are invaluable. This book especially was difficult to write, but your support and encouragement meant everything to me

Thank you so much to Fred Oelrich, Mike Smalley, Wmh Cheryl, and to George Hall for his keen eye and battle expertise. Huge appreciation also to Michelle Browne, Jessica Burland, Sally Shupe, and Becca Cross.

To Michelle Browne for her skills as a great line editor. Thank you to Eliza Enriquez for her excellent proofreading skills. You both make my words shine.

And a special thank you to Jenny Avery for volunteering her time to give the manuscript that one last read-through and catch those pesky typos. Any remaining errors are mine.

To my husband, who takes care of the house, the kids, and the cooking when I'm under the gun with a writing deadline.

And to my loyal readers, whose support and encouragement mean everything to me. Thank you.

ABOUT THE AUTHOR

Kyla Stone is the *USA Today* Bestselling author of over 25 novels. With over two million copies sold worldwide, her books have been translated into several languages, and her *Edge of Collapse* series has been optioned by Sony Studios for television.

She lives in Michigan with her family and spends her days writing apocalyptic, survival, and psychological thrillers. Her favorite treats while writing include dark chocolate and coffee.

When she's not writing, she enjoys reading, hiking, playing board games, and traveling around the world. She loves adventures, including rappelling down waterfalls in Costa Rica, off-roading on the dunes of Lake Michigan in her blue Jeep, skydiving and parasailing in the Dominican Republic, and scuba diving in Roatan and Belize.

She loves to hear from her readers.

Email her at Kyla@KylaStone.com

ALSO BY KYLA STONE

www.ingramcontent.com/pod-product-compliance
Lightning Source LLC
Chambersburg PA
CBHW061635190726
48289CB00006B/1608